I Choose ^{TO}Love Bravely

A NOVEL

BRAVELY TRILOGY
BOOK ONE

NICOLE DWIGANS

Inked Paper Press
Beaverton, Oregon

Published 2018 by Inked Paper Press
Beaverton, OR 97008

ISBN: 978-1-7321386-0-5 (hardcover edition)
ISBN: 978-1-7321386-1-2 (paperback edition)
ISBN: 978-1-7321386-2-9 (ebook edition)

LCCN: 2018905119

01050919

Edited by Emily Mulica
Cover model photography by JW Photography & Covers
Cover model Emily L'Nae
Cover and interior design by Inked Paper Press

BOOKS BY NICOLE DWIGANS

BRAVELY TRILOGY
I Choose to Love Bravely
I Choose to Live Bravely
I Choose to Dream Bravely

Thank you for choosing this book.
It is for you that I write.

Love,
Nicole

For my husband, Sean.
My rock, believer, chef, teller of jokes, and *inspiration*.
Thank you for surviving.
xoxo

CHAPTER 1

*A*s I reach the top of the stairs to board the commuter jet a hummingbird zips past me, so close I hear the hum of its wings. It stops and hovers next to the pilot's window. Under the bright morning sun, its feathers glitter like a faceted emerald. I feel as though it's watching me.

"Good morning," I whisper to it, then step onto the plane.

The slow line of people comes to a complete stop as passengers shift and make room for each other. In the coveted front row is a man at ease in the extra space his sizable frame takes up. His fancy shoes catch my eye: wingtips made of brown leather with stitching the color of the deep ocean and laces that match. He looks up to me from the magazine in his hand.

"Nice shoes," I say with a smile.

The man looks at his shoes as if he has forgotten what he's wearing, but then a hint of a knowing smile tells me that he is completely aware of, not just the shoes, but something else entirely.

"Thank you," he says.

He is a handsome man, one I imagine I'd have been attracted to years ago.

As the line begins to move again, I check my ticket to confirm I'm in 2A. I ask the woman in the aisle seat, "May I join you?"

"Of course you may." She holds her newspaper flat against her chest, stands, and steps back. Her face is kind, and her smile welcoming.

I settle into my seat and turn my gaze to the window. Although I'm on a plane at least twice a week, I still love takeoff. As the wings lift us higher into the air, I feel my earthbound form defying the odds. I watch Seattle shrink and disappear behind us. Then my heavy eyelids close. Sleep is near when the woman next to me says, "You look smart," in a soft, grandmotherly voice.

It takes effort to lift my eyelids. "Why thank you."

She looks at me over the top of her rimless glasses with bright gray eyes, almost the same color as her hair. "Do you think you can help?" The newspaper in her hand is folded twice over isolating the daily crossword. Only two blank lines remain.

"I'm not great with crosswords, but I'll do my best."

"It's eleven letters."

"All right."

She lifts her chin to look through her bifocals. "Gold medalist that is more than a double threat. The fourth letter is an A."

Immediately I think she must be joking.

She taps her pen on the paper, and says, "I know. It's a tough one. I mean, it could be so many people. More than a double threat."

"May I see that?"

She holds it in front of me and points at the clue. "Here."

I read it and count the spaces. I'm not sure if I'm more flattered or embarrassed to see my name as the answer to a crossword.

The woman points to Mr. Wingtips, who is seated across the aisle and one row up. "He doesn't know it either. I'll give him credit, he got a couple, but we're both stuck on this one."

Mr. Wingtips adjusts so he can see me, then winks. I have a feeling he knows the answer now.

Quietly to the woman, I say, "It's Nyla Tripple. Double P."

She tosses her hand up, then slaps the newspaper back down on her thigh. "Of course! Even I should have known that one." She pokes Mr. Wingtip's shoulder playfully. "This pretty lady got the one we couldn't figure out, the one about the gold medalist. It's Nyla Tripple. How could you miss a sports question? You're a guy."

"Consider it an unfair advantage," I say.

She writes N and then asks, "Is it an I next?"

"It's a Y."

"And you said double P." As she fills in the rest of the letters, she asks, "What's the unfair advantage?"

"I'm a sports journalist."

She draws her head back and removes her glasses. "A sports journalist? A pretty lady like yourself?"

"Yes, ma'am."

"What kinds of sports?"

"All kinds, but most of my time is dedicated to reporting from the football sidelines on Thursday."

She taps my forearm—pat, pat-pat—a rhythm just like my mother used to do. "What's your name? I'll have to tell my husband. He's a sports nut, especially football."

"Nyla Tripple."

The woman laughs so loud that people turn to look at us.

"Oh my goodness, Tripple Threat Nyla. I knew you looked familiar. I just didn't place you right off, being out of context. Out of your signature running style and your hair down, you look quite different. It's longer than I thought." She takes a deep breath and with a more gentle tone continues, "I know all about you and your story."

Sometimes I feel like an animal living behind one-way glass where the world can look into my space, but I can't see into theirs. I never expected to be thrust into the limelight when I became a runner. In time I thought *my story* would fade, and people would forget about me, especially after I retired from competitive running. But they still care and hold onto my experiences, pieces of my life, as if they are their own. It doesn't bother me because, for the most part, people are inspired by it.

"You're bigger than I thought. I don't mean big, as in fat, but rather taller. That husband of yours, Lorenzo, he must have been tall I—" She shakes her head. "I'm sorry dear. I just can't seem to get anything out right this morning. I didn't get much sleep last night, but that is certainly not an excuse for being rude."

"There is no need for apologies. I am a big woman and happy for it. My Lorenzo measured in at six-eight. I loved that about him."

Even though Lorenzo has been gone four years, every time I refer to him in the past tense it feels like I've misspoken. This morning it feels even more strange because I left my picturesque home on Bainbridge only a few hours ago; the one I shared with Lorenzo and hadn't been back to since I moved. Really, I should sell it, but I can't.

The woman squeezes my hand. "I'm sorry about your husband." She pats my forearm again—pat, pat-pat—and with effort tries to change the subject, though her voice is a little rough like she's choked up. "Are you on your way home from a game?"

"No, this was a personal trip. The regular football season doesn't start for a couple more weeks."

She smiles sympathetically then returns her attention to her crossword.

Sometimes I wish I'd find a way to move on so that people wouldn't feel sorry for me, and my family wouldn't worry. But I don't think I can, or will. Ever. It isn't for lack of wanting, no, it's something else I can't quite figure out.

I lay my head back and close my eyes again. After a few minutes, I find a stretch of silence between my ears, but it doesn't last long because the captain announces that we have begun our descent.

We arrive in my hometown of Portland where it is a perfect summer day. I deboard down another set of stairs onto the tarmac. Some of the passengers from my flight gather around a spot marked baggage claim to retrieve their gate-checked bags from Seattle.

Mr. Wingtips is there, his eyes on me are a mixture of curiosity and something I can't place. He smiles and takes a step in my direction. "Nyla Tripple, I'm Gavin Boston." He has an air of unshakable confidence that reminds me of a quarterback.

I accept his extended hand, and say, "Like the city?"

"Exactly like the city." He pauses, then quickly continues, "I've known Samuel for years, Kevin too. I've heard a lot about you and wanted to take a moment to introduce myself."

Just as I begin to respond to him, the woman I sat next to on the plane rushes up.

"Nyla," she says, "I am sorry to interrupt. It dawned on me that if I tell my husband that I met you and didn't get your autograph, I will never hear the end of it. You should see his collection of footballs, basketballs, baseballs, even a few pairs of running shoes. Would you mind autographing this for me?" She holds out the crossword and a black felt tip marker.

"I'd be happy to."

"Right over it, except not on your name."

I sign it and hand it back to her. "I'm sorry, I didn't get your name."

"Debra." She shakes my hand enthusiastically, then turns to Gavin. "And you sir, thanks for all of your help with the crossword. What's your name?"

"Gavin."

She carefully puts the paper into her purse then pulls out a small camera, and asks, "Would it be okay? One photo with you? Wonderful. Gavin, would you mind taking a photo of us ladies?"

Gavin appears amused by this situation. "I'm happy to assist." He takes a few snaps and hands the camera back.

Deborah reviews the photos on the small viewfinder. "Perfect. Thank you, both." Then she hurries off.

Gavin asks, "Does that happen often?"

"No, not really."

"Incoming." Gavin reaches for my arm and gently guides me out of the way of a luggage cart. "May I get your bag?"

I tug at the strap of my oversized purse. "No, this is all I brought with me, but thank you for the offer."

"Would you wait a minute while I grab mine?"

"Sure."

The crowd of people moves toward the cart, some rather impatiently. An older woman with a tight perm reaches for her bag on the second shelf just above her shoulders. She has it halfway off when suddenly she looks like she might topple over. Gavin moves quickly between the people and takes the bag for her.

"Are you all right?" he asks setting it down.

She looks up at him surprised. "Yes."

"Are you sure?" He lifts the handle of the bag for her.

"Yes sir, thank you."

A curvy blond with a big smile lays her elegant hand on Gavin's arm. "Would you mind grabbing mine as well? It's right there."

She doesn't look like she needs help with her luggage any more than I do, but I remember how I used to flirt with Lorenzo like that. He always loved to do things for me, even when I was capable.

Gavin sets the bag down in front of her and pulls the handle up. She gives him an open invitation with her eyes, and says, "Thank you."

He smiles politely then turns back to the cart in search of his own bag. As far as I can tell, he doesn't notice the woman who looks back over her shoulder at him twice. She's a pretty woman. It's unfortunate he missed such an obvious opportunity. Although, I don't know a thing about this man, and it's highly likely he's married.

Gavin returns with a silver hard-sided carry-on. "I apologize that took so long. Thank you for waiting."

"Not a problem at all."

We resume our path to the terminal, and Gavin says, "No luggage on a later flight would make sense, but none on a morning flight . . ."

"You are observant. I own a house on Bainbridge Island."

"I hope it wasn't damaged in the storm?"

I hold my arms out a little wider than my body as if this is to indicate something, and say, "My house is on some property with lots of trees. It's a beautiful spot. Anyway, the tree closest to the house lifted right out of the ground. It broke a couple of windows and put a nice big hole in the roof."

He grimaces. "I'm sorry to hear that."

"It's okay, things happen. I don't live in the house so getting repairs done hasn't been a priority. I flew up yesterday to take care of things. I thought I'd make it up and back the same day."

"Dealing with damages like that always takes more time than you think."

Gavin lengthens his step and opens the door to the terminal for me.

"How is it you know Pop and Kevin?" I ask.

"Well, we sit on a couple of boards together, but we've been working together for years. I'm an architect and co-owner of a business. We mostly purchase older buildings and restore them. Then we either rent or sell them. We've done all our real estate transactions with Samuel."

My pop, Samuel, owns Tripple Properties, a multi-city commercial real estate company. Kevin, my brother, runs the Chicago office now. They are both well-regarded members of the Portland business community.

"You said that you mostly purchase older buildings . . .," I say because I feel there is more to this description.

With a pleased smile and an imaginative twinkle in his eye, Gavin says, "We're in the process of purchasing a property that would be our first ground-up project, which is very exciting for me as an architect."

"Something small like a little office building?" I say in jest.

He shakes his head and looks up at the ceiling almost like he actually sees it. "It will be about as big as they'll let me build in downtown Portland."

"What's the name of your company?"

"Boston Smith."

This name rings a bell, and with a sudden realization, I say, "Okay, all right, I'm putting the pieces together. Linda Smith is married to your business partner, correct?"

"You are correct, Trace Smith. Linda and I grew up together in Seattle. She'd mentioned reaching out to you about the gala."

"Yes, I'll be hosting it in just a few weeks. I haven't had the opportunity to meet her in person yet. Actually, I need to give her a call. I assume you'll be there as well?"

"Yes, I go every year."

We come to a major cross-section of the airport where traffic flows in several directions.

I stop and point up the stairs. "I parked in the short term since I only planned to be gone for the day."

"I'm in the long term."

I extend my hand to Gavin. "I'm glad you introduced yourself. It was nice to walk and chat with you. I'll tell Pop I met a very kind associate of his today."

"The pleasure has been all mine."

I walk up a couple of steps, then turn back, and holler, "Gavin!" I thought he would have been on his way, but he's still where I left him. He has that look in his eye again, curious and perhaps sure, but of what I don't know.

I walk back to him, and say, "This exciting purchase, is it scheduled to close before or after the gala?"

"If all goes as planned, the purchase should close before, but I'm sure you know how these things go sometimes."

"Yes, I do. That's why I want to wish you good luck for a smooth transaction, and an early congratulations, Mr. Boston."

"Thank you, Ms. Tripple. I look forward to seeing you at the gala."

As I walk back up the stairs, I'm hit with an unusual feeling. Almost like I should look back or check to make sure I haven't forgotten something. I'm positive, though, that I have all of my things. The feeling persists as I make my way across the sky bridge, get into my old SUV, and drive home. I wonder if it has something to do with Gavin Boston.

CHAPTER 2

$\mathcal{A}$t home I find my neighbor, Ms. Marshall, hard at work in what has become the conjoined space of our front yard. I don't know when or how the property lines were erased; it just happened with silent permission and acceptance.

"Whatcha up to?" I ask.

She points to a small bush in a pot on her walkway. "I found that plant on clearance at the nursery, and I knew we have the perfect spot for it."

I kneel down to inspect the plant, which looks one day away from qualifying as yard debris. It has a few lonely leaves left, of which only a couple are a healthy green. The tag says it's a daphne and the photo shows a bush with abundant foliage and delicate bunches of flowers.

"Have you seen one before?" Ms. Marshall asks.

"I'm not sure that I have."

"They smell divine. I've only seen ones with white flowers before. But that one there caught my eye because it has purple flowers, or will." She stabs her shovel into the hard ground. "Last year after all of the leaves dropped I realized we need more evergreens."

"And this is evergreen?"

"Yep."

"Do you think it will make it?"

Ms. Marshall makes an "eh" sound and drops her shovel on the ground. She disappears along the side of her house and returns with a hose. She turns the sprayer on and waters a bare patch of ground. "I figure if it doesn't make it, then the ten dollars the plant cost wouldn't be much of a loss, and if it survives and thrives, it will be well worth it."

She picks her shovel up again but doesn't make it two inches into the soil before it sounds like she strikes a rock. It's been a dry summer, more than a month since we've had even a trace of rain. I'm not sure how she'll dig a hole big enough to properly plant her clearance find and give it any chance of survival.

"This is going to take a while," I say.

"Nothing a little water and time can't fix. Water, let it soak in, dig, repeat."

"Sounds tedious."

"I'm in no hurry. Besides, you know I like to watch the people stroll past."

Even though Ms. Marshall is sturdy and full of energy, I feel guilty leaving her alone with the task.

"Would you like some help?"

She dramatically lifts the back of her hand to her forehead then lets it fall away. "No, you don't get to take the fun from the old woman. This is the only way I get to play in the dirt without getting funny looks."

"Could I at least bring you back some lunch after I get done with my run?"

"Now there's an offer I won't refuse."

"Usual from Rico's?"

"Would you add guacamole to it for me?"

"The usual plus guac, you got it."

Three years ago I moved back to Portland and purchased this buttercream yellow 1908 bungalow next door to Ms. Marshall. The front porch is lined with mature jasmine vines that bloom from spring to fall with tiny fragrant white flowers. When the wind blows just right, I can smell them from the driveway ten feet away. On warm days, like today, I leave the front door open and let the sweet scent fill the house. It's better than any candle.

I bought the house from a man who spent six months renovating it. Everything has been redone, some of it is more modern than the style of the house. There are, however, still charming touches that speak of the house's history. A large archway leads from the living room into a dining room that is open to a kitchen fit for a personal chef, yet rarely do I use it to make anything aside from cookies.

Upstairs I have two rooms. The largest is my bedroom, and the other is my office. The bathroom boasts the original claw-foot tub which is what really sold me on the house. I love to take long baths with bubbles mounded up to my chin on Saturday nights when I'm home.

In my bedroom, I shed the teal blue T-shirt dress I wore yesterday and had to put back on this morning. I pull out a pair of running shorts and a tank from a drawer and get dressed. Then I braid my hair as I walk back down the stairs. My running shoes are lined up next to the front door, ten pairs that I rotate through. I select a pink pair with my signature on them. I'll admit it's a little pretentious to wear my own line of shoes, but the truth is, they are the best.

I'm often asked if I still like to run, and the answer is yes. Not only is it a part of my DNA, it is my required daily happy pill.

My running has changed since I retired from competitive sprinting. I used to work out with one goal: to be the fastest in the world. Now I simply want to stay healthy and happy. I don't look that much different from when I competed. Maybe my muscles aren't as big or strong, but I could probably still hold my own with the best of them. Some days I wonder if I could be the best again.

I start my run at a relaxed pace. First I match my foot-falls to the rhythm of my music. Then I bring my attention to my lungs, steady full breaths that stretch and open them. When I get to the one-mile mark, my body settles into the run. Stress releases and trickles down my shoulders, through my legs, out my feet, and I leave it all behind on the pavement.

•••

An hour later I return home with lunch to find Ms. Marshall still hard at work. Strands of her long gray hair have escaped her ponytail. Mud is streaked across her cheek and splashed all over her clothes. Unfortunately, the hole doesn't look much deeper than when I left.

I hand her a burrito, and ask, "Are you sure I can't help you?"

She leans heavily on her shovel and flicks her wrist in dismissal.

"Could I at least offer you my shovel? It's ergonomic and has a good point. It might make the digging a little easier."

She takes the offered ice water and draws a big drink from the straw.

"That's another offer I'll take you up on."

I set my lunch down on the porch, then head to my backyard. I unlatch the gate and push it, but it catches on something. With a bit of leverage, I'm able to open it enough to squeeze through. It looks like an overgrown golden wheat field back here.

My crazy travel schedule has made it hard for me to take care of my backyard and house the way I would like. I have not had time to mow or figure out why the sprinkler system doesn't work. If I'm honest with myself, my lifestyle is best suited for condo ownership, but I can't do it. If anything I crave more space. My dream is to have a big house, that I don't have to clean, on a patch of land that takes no maintenance.

Back here is my tiny garage that was built to hold the buggies of the 1900s. Now I use it to store the few yard tools I have, but rarely have time to use.

I get the shovel, take it out front, and give it to Ms. Marshall. "You can keep it," I say. "In the rare event that I need it, I'll borrow it from you."

Ms. Marshall looks over my shoulder to the open gate. "What are you doing with that backyard?"

"I know, it's bad. The sprinkler system broke in June before I left. I haven't had time to trim the bushes or mow it. Someday soon, I'll clean it up."

"It's August. Get a man to mow it for you."

"I don't need a man to mow it for me. As soon as I have time, I'll do it."

She looks at me like she knows best. "I think you need a strapping young man to mow it for you."

"Young man?"

"Someone your age." She nods her chin to a passing man who smiles and waves. "Look at that fella."

His shirt is so tight I can see the outline of his pectorals.

"He'll be happy to mow it for you," she elbows me, "and you, too, I bet."

I shake my head at her. "No man needed for either task. I'll take care of it myself. All of it."

Ms. Marshall bites into her burrito again and tips her head toward another group of passing men.

I back away toward my house, awkward laughter escapes me. "Nope. I got it."

In my kitchen, I eat lunch while I read the sports section of the newspaper. Then I take a quick shower and blow-dry my hair, which takes a while because I have a ton of it. I swipe on a clear lip gloss, which is about all the makeup I ever wear unless I'm on camera. Today the only place I'll be going is to Pop's house for dinner with him, Kevin, and my sister-in-law, Mia. This means I get to put on comfy clothes and stay in them for the whole day. I put on a pair of loose black running shorts and a pink tank top and head into my office.

I sit at my old desk which is a relic from my high school days that has peeling laminate around the edges held on with tape. It barely survived the move from Bainbridge three years ago.

The large pine bookshelf behind me was put together last winter with Pop's help. On it is a stack of a dozen books I've picked up along the way, usually in airport bookstores, that I have yet to read. I promise myself that someday soon I'll make more time for leisurely pursuits, but that will probably be after the football season ends in February.

There are also three exquisite boxes made of rich mahogany and lined with black velvet. The largest one holds the eight gold medals I won in individual events.

The second, a little smaller, has three medals I won in team relays; one silver, and two gold. The third is about the size of an envelope and holds the two silver medals that Lorenzo won in shot put. I don't often look at them because it makes me want things I'll never again have.

Today I need to write an article about the new football season for the *American Sports Journal*, but before I do, I need to call Linda Smith about the upcoming gala. She picks up on the first ring. Her voice is full and vibrant. I picture her as a woman with a beaming smile and enough energy to carry a room. We decide to meet a week from today for drinks at her favorite restaurant, Mix. It's on NW 23rd, which is one of my favorite areas of town. I almost mention that I met her friend Gavin today, but hesitate and then don't. I'm not sure why. Funny thing though, the thought of him brings back the feeling that I forgot something at the airport.

CHAPTER 3

"*H*ey, NyNy, I'm almost done," my sister-in-law, Mia, says. The dining room table of my childhood home has become her temporary office: laptop, spiral notebook, sheets of paper scattered about. As a spice importer, she's a busy woman, but her work is portable.

"When are Pop and Kevin going to be home?" I ask.

She takes off her black-rimmed glasses that swallow her tiny face and pinches the bridge of her nose. "It's a double F."

My mother used to joke that it always seemed that a fire had to be put out on Fridays, one hour before quitting time. She came to affectionately refer to these as Friday fires, which over time shortened to double F.

"Kevin said it's a total mess, but they hope they'll be home by six. This always happens, he flies in for one meeting and ends up working a crazy day."

Unlike me, Kevin entered into our family business, Tripple Properties, straight out of college. He worked here in Portland under Pop for ten years, then he moved to Chicago to open a new office three years ago. Kevin comes home about once a month for meetings, and Mia, who is also from here, always comes with him.

Perplexed, Mia says, "Samuel told me groceries are getting delivered at four. Since when does he get groceries delivered?"

"He hasn't been back in a grocery store since mom passed. I was doing all of his shopping for him the first couple of months, but with my traveling, it didn't work well. He found a guy that owns a delivery company, and he does all of the shopping now."

"How did I not know this?"

"I don't think he'll ever grocery shop again unless he's in a dire situation."

Every Sunday, for as long as I can remember, Mom and Pop shopped together. It was the last thing they did together before she passed suddenly from an aneurysm seven months ago.

Mia reaches into her computer bag and pulls out a letter-sized manila envelope that she hands to me, and says, "These are for you. When I cleaned out for the move, I finally went through all of my photos and found a lot of doubles. I can't bring myself to destroy them because it makes me feel like I'm messing with the soul or something. I thought you'd like these. If you already have them, you can get rid of them."

"But you said it messes with the soul." I try not to laugh, but it escapes through my nose.

"Hey, then it's on your conscience and not mine."

A string wound around a paper disk clasps the envelope shut. I unwind it, then gently shake out a three-inch stack of photos into my hand. The one on top brings a smile to my face, but it also makes my heart ache. It's Lorenzo, a close up of his face with his brilliant sky-blue eyes so intense you'd think they were touched up.

The next one is the two of us when we first started dating. Lorenzo holds me tight as he presses a hard kiss on my cheek. My eyes are innocent, and even here I can see how much I loved him right from the beginning. Still, that has not faded.

I begin to put the photos back into the envelope, and say, "I'll look at the rest of them later."

"There's some good ones of you and your mom too."

"Really?" I pull them back out and shuffle through. "Thank you."

Mom was an rare beauty, thick black hair, catlike eyes. Everyone says I look like her, but I don't see it. No one could do my mother's beauty justice.

The doorbell rings and Mia jumps up like a jack-in-the-box. "I'll get it."

I should put these away, but I can't help but look at a few more of Lorenzo. The greatest source of love and joy in my life has also caused profound sorrow. The cost of love, I suppose.

"Hey, Nyla," Marco says as he sets down an armload of cloth sacks onto the counter.

Jarred from my trip down memory lane I put a smile on and look up. "Hey, Marco."

"How was the big trip? From what I saw, it looked like things went well."

"Everything went great."

His eyes bounce between Mia and me. "I've got a few more to bring in." He heads back toward the front door.

I indulge in a few more photos, then slide them back into the envelope and wind the string around the paper disk.

I look up and see the counters are filled with bags. I hadn't even noticed that Marco had brought the rest of the things in and left.

"That poor guy, he might be in love with you," Mia says.

"Marco?" I ask.

"Yes. Does he own the company?"

"Yeah. Marco's Delivery."

"Why is the owner of a company that big actually making deliveries? I see their trucks all over town."

"You know what it's like to own a business. You do whatever you need to. Plus, Pop is an investor in his business."

Pop is what people call an angel investor. He does his best to give small Portland businesses a chance of making it because he owes a lot of his success to people who helped him in the beginning, and now he wants to give back.

Mia rolls her eyes and sits back at her computer.

I laugh. "What? I am not interested in Marco."

"Trust me, I know he isn't your type. He's not tall enough or wide enough. But who are you interested in?"

I stand up from the table and begin to unload the groceries. "I am not interested in anyone."

"It has been a long time."

"I'm a little embarrassed to admit, but I think something in me died when Lorenzo did."

"Do you want to date again? I mean, it's been more than enough time."

I swallow the lump in my throat. Has it been enough time? That's what I keep wondering. It seems preposterous that anyone could come after Lorenzo.

"Recently I've thought it might be nice to have someone to do stuff with, aside from my girlfriends that I see occasionally. The problem is I don't feel anything toward anyone. No attraction, desire, or drive."

Something in me says this will never change. Do nuns feel this way? Maybe there are some of us that just aren't meant to have it, or in my case, to have it again.

"You're around hot single guys all day long. Guys that are clearly your type," Mia says.

"I really think I'm broken, sis. Irreparable."

"Have you tried?"

I put the produce away in the crisper and wonder if I should tell her about a recent situation which only serves to prove my point. But I can't.

Mia says, "I'm going to tell you about something, but do not mention it to Kevin."

With my index finger, I make an X over my heart.

"One night I was laying in bed completely stressed out about a container that was delayed. Kevin tried to put the moves on me, and I pushed him away and said not now. He rolled over without a word. Laying there, I realized it had been six months since we'd had sex. Six months! I hadn't wanted it, felt attraction or anything to him, or anyone for that matter. Then I read something that said sometimes you just have to schedule it."

"Like on a calendar?"

"Yes, an appointment."

"An appointment?"

"That was Kevin's response. He was livid that I suggested I needed to put my attraction to him on a calendar. At first, he refused to entertain it. Another month went by, and then we agreed to set a date."

The idea sounds peculiar, but I can't stop from asking, "Did it work?"

"Yes, it did for me because it gave me a block of time when I didn't have to think about anything else. It got the juices flowing, for lack of a better word, and soon we didn't need to schedule it anymore. Even now when it's been too long, we nudge each other with a calendar invite."

"I'm happy for you two. But how does this apply to me? Since I don't feel comfortable sending someone a calendar invite for sex. I don't even remember how to have sex."

Through giggles, Mia says, "Sure you do. What I'm saying is that maybe you have to make an effort to look through that lens again. Flirt and see what you might be able to bring back to life."

I shake my head unconvinced.

"I really cannot believe you. Nyla Tripple, the fantasy of so many men."

"I am not the fantasy of any man."

"You are oblivious, that's the problem. Completely. I see it all the time when we are out. And if you're ready . . ."

"No no, I'm not ready for anything serious. I'm never getting married or falling in love again. I'm just saying it would be nice to have someone to hold hands and go do things with."

Mia scrunches her face as she puts her computer away in its bag. "Things have changed since you last dated. It evolves past holding hands and into the sheets in a matter of hours. I've been listening to my friend Marci tell me about her dating life, and I get tired just listening to her."

"Well, maybe I'm just fine then."

"Just start looking around." She opens her eyes wide. "Notice the men and see how it goes. Do you ever hang out with guys that you work with or players?"

"Sure, but it's always professional."

Mia rolls her eyes.

I wasn't going to tell her, but now I feel like I need her to understand why this all feels impossible for me. "This weird thing happened. There's this nice guy named Blake that I've known for years. He's a reporter for the *American Sports Journal*. This week, after we watched practice, he asked me if I wanted to grab dinner."

"Nyla!"

I try to steady her excitement with my hands in a hushing motion. "I said sure, thinking absolutely nothing of it. Blake asked me to get dinner with him the next night, and I said yes, and then the third night—"

"Third night!" She claps her hands and scoots to the edge of her seat.

"Stop, please. Listen. He asked me as he's paying the bill—"

"He paid, every night?"

"We're on expense accounts when we travel, I didn't think anything of it when he said he'd get it. The third night he said, 'Could we maybe do something else now?'"

"Something else?" Mia winks.

"I asked him like what, and he said, 'Maybe we could go catch a movie, or go for a walk and talk about something other than sports.'"

"Is that all you talked about?"

"We are sports reporters, Mia. It's my entire life. What else do I talk about?"

"You and I never talk about sports."

"That's different."

"What did you say?"

"I had no idea we were on a date until that moment, and I felt stupid for not realizing it. I told him I was tired from the long week, and with my early flight, I needed to get to bed soon."

Mia's face falls. "Tell me you are kidding."

"I am not attracted to him."

"Have you heard from him since?"

Hesitantly, I say, "Blake sent me a message today to see when our schedules lined up again, or if we could make them, so he could take me out."

"Well, it sounds like you've got your calendar invite to experiment with."

I shake my head.

"You said he's nice," Mia says. "Is he your type at all?"

I shrug a maybe, and try to consider him. It all seems too risky. What if I don't feel anything for him? Worse than this, what if I do? Would that devalue how I still feel for Lorenzo?

"You have to at least try, or you'll end up an old wrinkled shrew, and things will close up down there."

I throw a wadded cloth bag at her. "Stop it."

"Hello!" Pop's voice booms from the front door.

Pop comes into the kitchen with Kevin close behind. They have on similar black suits. While Kevin isn't as big as Pop, they look nearly identical in the face: pale blue eyes and a broad nose. Kevin though, unlike Pop, still has a full head of light brown hair.

Pop's face lights with fatherly pride as he opens his arms, and says, "There she is, my Little Foot!"

He engulfs me in a hug that always makes me feel like the little girl I once was. There is no one else left in this world that makes me feel as safe as he does.

"I don't like you traveling overseas for so long," Pop says.

It's been eight weeks since I've seen Pop, which is far too long for both of us.

Kevin still hugs me like a big brother out to prove he's stronger. I think this is because until his junior year of high school, when he hit a growth spurt, I was taller and bigger than him. He has me beat now, but not by much.

"You two are earlier than planned," Mia says. "I haven't even started dinner yet."

"Let's just order in then," Pop says. He opens a drawer full of take-out menus. "Take your pick." He opens the fridge. "Oh good, Marco stopped by, and he brought my favorite beer. Who else?"

There is a unanimous "Yes" from us all.

"Chinese?" Mia holds up a menu. "Usual?"

"Yep," Kevin says.

Pop carries his beer into the living room and sits down in his favorite chair. He makes a sound of relief as he pulls his necktie loose.

On the couch across from him, I sit and curl my legs around me. "Did you get the double F resolved?"

"Not completely yet. Title issues on an important purchase scheduled to close in a couple of weeks." He groans, sips his beer, and says, "It's going to delay things, but it will work out just fine in the end. Thankfully, the client is a very patient man. You actually came up in my conversation with the client today, Little Foot."

"Me? Really?"

"He said you met at the airport this morning."

"Gavin Boston?"

"Yes."

"You were at the airport today?" Mia asks.

"I went up to Bainbridge yesterday and didn't get everything done that I needed to, so I had to stay the night."

"Really?" she asks curiously. "Oh, the storm. I forgot about that."

"What did you think?" Pop asks.

"Some of the houses are a mess still. Rick has been amazing though. He's gotten my property all cleaned up.

Today, he was installing the windows, and next week the contractor is coming to repair the roof."

Mia sits on the love seat next to Kevin, and asks, "Rick?"

"He is the handyman."

"Oh, that's right."

"I meant," Pop says, "what do you think of Gavin?"

Mia sits up straight, like a kitten that has spotted a bird.

"Um . . . What do you mean, what did I think? He seemed incredibly kind. And he had a great pair of wing-tips on."

"He is one snappy dresser," Kevin says. "He always rocks the vest sans jacket, no tie."

I have to think about that one. I'd not paid much mind to Gavin's attire, other than to note that he looked nice. Vaguely I recall the vest, I think it was blue, similar to the stitching in his shoes.

"He is a great guy, Nyla," Pop says. "A major player in the Portland business scene."

I know Pop's many facial expressions, the intonations in his voice, but right now I'm confused. Perhaps I've missed something. Did something in my conversation with Gavin not go well?

"Did he say I was rude?" I ask.

"No. Not at all. In fact, he said you were rather charming."

"Charming?" I'm not sure what I think about that. "All right, he was charming too. Good then."

Mia tips her chin down and looks at me with a suggestive eye. I shake my head no, and say, "Wow, I sure could use another beer."

•••

Later in the evening when I'm ready to leave Mia follows me out. We walk along the s-shaped pathway toward the street. Some things about my childhood home are exactly as they've always been: manicured lawn, three-foot azalea bushes, and walkways cleaner than the floors of my house. These are the things that Pop takes care of. Other things that kept the house alive are gone: annuals along the pathway, a front porch laden with pots of blooming flowers, and seasonal decorations. These were the things Mom did.

I wonder how long Pop will continue to live in this home. After Lorenzo passed, I lived in our Bainbridge Island home for a year before I finally admitted to myself I couldn't stay there. I'd hate to see my childhood home go, but I wouldn't blame him. The walls are alive with memories of Mom.

I open the door of my SUV and slip the envelope of photos Mia gave me into the door pocket, so they won't slide around or get wrinkled.

"Gavin?" Mia asks.

"No way." I shake my head.

"Is he handsome?"

"No," I say and instantly know it's not true.

"No, no, or no you don't know because you can't look at any guy and discern if he's handsome."

"I guess I can't accurately answer that. Can I?"

She grips my upper arms with her petite hands and looks up to me. "You gotta try, NyNy, or it will close up down there, and you'll become a cat lady."

"I'll never be a cat lady. I travel too much."

"Ugh, you're impossible sometimes!"

I get into my car and drive away as Mia throws me playful kisses into the air. Down the road is a car broken down with two men standing over the open hood. Perhaps I'm like a car, and something needs to be repaired. Or do I need to accept that pieces of me are destined for the wrecking yard? A swell of hope tells me I'm not ready to accept that. I'll heed Mia's advice and try to look with my eyes wide open. When I get home, I'll send Blake a message and see when we can find another time to have dinner. I'll do my best to look at him with fresh eyes and see if something in me can be jump-started.

CHAPTER 4

"*N*yla!" Ms. Marshall calls from her porch swing when I step out my front door. As I walk the path to her house she whistles at me loud enough that someone passing by joins her.

"Where are you off to with legs on display like that?" she asks.

"Ms. Marshall, don't tease me."

"Tease you! I'm congratulating you. Don't leave me in suspense. Are you going on a date?"

Ms. Marshall's surprise at my clothing is warranted. I rarely wear anything besides workout clothes or jeans and a T-shirt at home. When I'm on camera, I typically opt for ankle-length pants, flats, and a blouse. However, today after I finished my run I felt inspired to do something different and break out of my rut.

I dug into the deepest recesses of my overstuffed six-by-six closet and sifted through dresses, skirts, and strappy tops that I never think to wear. In the very back was a romper I'd purchased earlier this summer. Even though

I wasn't sure I'd be brave enough to wear it, I loved it so much I couldn't leave it behind.

The romper isn't revealing, but there's something about it. It's a silky fabric, pale pink with large palm leaves. I especially love the neckline and spaghetti straps that criss-cross in the back. Wearing it, I feel sexy. Something I haven't felt since Lorenzo passed. He always made me feel like a sexual woman. I've missed this feeling and him.

"No date," I say. "Sorry to disappoint. I'm meeting a woman from the foundation that I'm hosting the gala for. Remember, I told you about that?"

"Yep, yep. Where are you off to then?"

"Mix. Have you been there?"

"I don't go much beyond our neighborhood anymore."

"Well, if it's good I'll take you some time."

"You got yourself a deal there." She stands from her seat. "Hang on, I have something for you."

"Me?"

While Ms. Marshall goes into her house, I look at our yard. The daphne she planted last week has actually survived a whole seven days, and it even has a couple new buds on it. There are two more plants just like it still in pots near the porch. These ones look much healthier.

My phone dings with a text message, it's from Blake, "Good news, I'll be in Philly next week too. May I take you to dinner on Monday?"

I reply back to him, "I get in late Monday. How about Tuesday?"

My belly somersaults. There's a strong desire to say no, and not experiment with this part of myself. It feels strange to know Blake is attracted to me, while I only hope that I might, at some point, feel something for him. Is this fair, or kind?

His reply is immediate, "I'm looking forward to Tuesday. What do you think about the Cleveland trade?"

At least if all else fails, we have sports to talk about.

When Ms. Marshall's screen door squeaks open I stuff my phone into my purse.

"Where are these two going?" I ask of the plants.

"Five feet to either side of the one I planted."

"That will look nice."

She hands me a white box, taps the top. "Open it."

I set it down on the porch swing and use my thumbnail to cut the small piece of tape, then pull open the flaps.

"What's the occasion?"

"I saw it and thought of you."

Below several pieces of tissue paper I see a pink mound with a brass chain attached to it. I lift it carefully from the box. It's a ceramic fuchsia flower about the size of a softball. This flower has always reminded me of a ballerina skirt with two delicate legs ready to dance.

"It's beautiful," I say.

I notice now that the delicate little legs of the fuchsia flower are actually small tubes and realize this is a hummingbird feeder. My heart and lungs tighten.

"It's a hummingbird feeder," Ms. Marshall says. "It was the weirdest thing, I just felt like I had to get it for you. Do you even like hummingbirds?"

I run a finger along the legs of the flower that deliver sweet nectar. I'm not sure what to say or how to express that this means so much to me.

"I love them, they were always around my house in Bainbridge, but I hardly see them now."

I remember the emerald-headed one I saw last week as I was boarding the plane. It feels a little silly, but I hope in some way that it's all from Lorenzo.

"My husband loved hummingbirds," I say. "He had several feeders around the house and tended to them like a professional birdwatcher. For some reason, his favorites were always the little hummingbirds. Especially the ones with the emerald heads."

"Do you know how to make the sugar water to go in it?"

"Yes."

"Well, fill it up then, and you should start seeing them in no time."

I nod with excitement and return the feeder to the box. "Thank you, I'm going to go hang it now."

"Don't be late for your drinks."

"I won't. I planned extra time for shopping."

On my kitchen counter are two large jars. One holds flour and the other sugar that I scoop a cup from and pour into a pot. I add the water and set it on the stove.

The hair on my arms lift. Suddenly I don't feel alone. It seems crazy, but I whisper into the air, "Lorenzo?"

All I hear is the laughter of the kids that live behind my house playing on their trampoline. I'm both relieved and saddened by this.

The first time Lorenzo and I talked was on a sunny day like today, but it wasn't as warm.

•••

I'm with my relay team on the track at the University of Oregon. All three of them are seniors, but I'm a freshman. We've just completed an amazing, yet grueling, practice in preparation for our first meet next week. My chest heaves and sweat drips down my temples. Five male athletes walk over to us. I've seen them around practice, but I only know the one who is dating my teammate.

Everyone begins to chat, except for me. There is one, in particular, the tallest and hottest of them, who watches me with the hint of a smile. This both thrills and scares me.

I tap one of my teammates on the shoulder, and say, "I've got to get a cooldown done and head out." I slip away and find an easy pace.

Out of the corner of my eye, I see that guy running after me. He gives me an enormous million-dollar smile, and I can tell he wants to say something. I don't stop running, but I do slow down to give him a chance to catch up.

"Hey, where are you going?" he asks.

"Excuse me?"

Playfully, he says, "We were talking back there."

It takes him a lot of effort to keep up with me at my slow pace, but he doesn't give up, and finally makes it to my side.

"We were?"

He has big muscles that remind me of a line-backer, though I try not to notice.

"Yeah, we were."

"I wasn't talking, and I need to get my cooldown done and get going."

"Would you mind stopping for a second? I actually can't keep up with your cooldown."

He begins to slow.

"Sorry, I can't right now. Have a good day."

Before that day I'd never noticed him much. But after that, I begin to see him everywhere. I'm not sure if he's making an effort to be where I am, or if I'm now looking for him.

A few days later, after a particularly difficult practice, I hinge over and put my hands on my knees as I try to find my elusive breath. Sweat drips from my face onto the track. My running shorts and top are so soaked they feel like they've been glued to me.

Mr. Million-Dollar Smile walks up and sticks his hand just a foot below my face, heedless of my dripping sweat, and says, "Hello. I'm Lorenzo."

I look at his offered hand, and with what little energy I have left, I stand up straight.

"Our culture typically thinks that a refused handshake is a sign of insult," he says.

"Seriously? Why are you introducing yourself now?"

When I'm running on the track I'm confident, and I feel invincible, usually. But any other time I'm quite shy. Especially when it comes to guys I'm attracted to. This one seems so far out of my league, and so much older than me, I'm not sure why he's even talking to me.

"I can't keep up with you any other time," Lorenzo says.

I try not to smile at that, and then I try not to laugh.

"You do laugh!" he says.

"Stop it, of course I laugh." I shake his hand.

"Are you done for the day?"

"Maybe."

"Me too." He walks to the edge of the track, picks up my bag, and puts it on his shoulder.

"What are you doing?"

"I'm carrying your bag for you. You walk home after practice don't you?"

"Are you stalking me?"

"No. But I'm observant."

"I bet you know where I live, don't you?"

He looks as if he's been caught. "Yeah."

"You know my sweat towel and stinky running shoes are in that bag."

"I'm a guy. I'm immune to such things."

He stops right in front of me, and for the first time, we look into each other's eyes. His eyes are the color of a cloudless sky and just as vast. The current that pulses between us isn't something I've ever felt.

Immediately, I know I'm in trouble. I should run away from this guy. But already I know I won't.

•••

Lorenzo had been confident in an almost cocky way, but he had this childlike sureness about everything that made people love him.

That first day he walked me home I had a feeling about him, us, but I had no idea the adventure we had embarked on. I certainly didn't know our relationship would become the stuff of headlines or that the dreams we'd share would get cut short.

I stick my finger into the sugar water mixture and find it's cool now. I pour it into the new hummingbird feeder and carry it outside to my backyard. Around the sliding glass door is a pergola with an ancient wisteria trailing over it. There's an old hook in the corner that I hang the feeder from. Then I go back inside and sit at my dining room table, every bit of me hopeful that one little bird will visit me before I need to go.

It takes a lot of self-control not to clap with enthusiasm when the first hummingbird arrives. A minute later another comes, this one with an emerald head, like the one at the airport, the ones that Lorenzo loved.

I stand and gather my things to leave for NW 23rd.

Out front, Ms. Marshall pulls one of the new daphnes from its pot and sets it into a hole.

As I open my SUV door, I say, "Thank you so much for the bird feeder. I've already seen two hummingbirds."

With her hand over her brow to block the sun, she looks up to me. "Isn't it funny how stuff just works out sometimes. Things magically arrive, sometimes when you didn't realize you even needed them."

"It's true."

"You know, there are usually men where there are drinks."

I give her a firm look, and she holds her hands up in surrender.

"I'm just saying, Nyla, you never know what you might attract with those legs. Maybe, a man to mow?"

Ms. Marshall is incorrigible. But maybe, just maybe, she's right.

CHAPTER 5

*A*t Mix, I sit down in the last open seat at the bar next to Linda Smith.

"I'm so excited to finally be meeting you," she says. "Everyone at the foundation is thrilled and grateful you are hosting the gala."

"I'm very excited as well."

Linda's blond ponytail swings like a pendulum as she turns to unhook her white bag from the back of her seat. She pulls out a large blue planner and flips it open to a long list with my name on top.

"I've got just a few things," she says lightly, then raises her hand to get the bartender's attention. "I think we are ready to order now."

"Certainly," the bartender replies. He hands us menus printed on iridescent cream paper, similar to the walls that are aglow with the setting sun. "What can I get you lovely ladies tonight?"

Without a glance at the menu, Linda says, "It's overplayed, I know, but I still love a good cosmo. Please."

He winks at Linda, then turns to me. "And how about you?"

"This is quite a list. But I think I'll keep it simple tonight and go for my favorite, a manhattan."

The bartender raps the counter lightly, and says, "Cosmo and manhattan, coming up."

As he turns I notice a tiny rainbow on the bar, it looks like a hologram, then I see another on the wall, and they begin to multiply all over the room. My hands are covered in them. I look up to the three-tiered chandelier above us; it's so grand that it looks to have been plucked from a castle.

"Amazing isn't it," Linda says. "Sometimes the light bounces just right, and we get these." She cups her hands together as if she's scooping water from a lake, but instead, it's a handful of rainbows. "I love Mix. Something about it is magical."

I have to agree with Linda. There is something a little otherworldly about this place: rainbow spraying chandelier, glowing walls, and luxurious plum fabrics that cover not just the chairs and windows, but the waiters as well.

Linda points to the bag at my feet. "Looks like you got a little shopping done."

"The boutiques around here are amazing, and with the sun it's the perfect day for shopping."

The bartender delivers our drinks, Linda lifts hers, and says, "Nothing like topping off a good shopping trip with drinks. Cheers."

We tap our glasses then take a sip.

"Makes for a perfect afternoon," I say.

"Indeed." Linda consults the list in her planner. "You mentioned before that you aren't bringing a date. I wanted to see if you've changed your mind."

"No date."

"We'll be seated at the front table, closest to the stage entrance with the President and Vice President of the organization, and their spouses. Would you mind if Gavin sat next to you?"

I hesitate only because the mention of Gavin surprises me a little.

"Boston. I think you've met him?"

"Yes, I have. Gavin seems like a nice guy. That's fine with me if he doesn't mind."

"Fantastic. Gavin said he'd love to sit next to you as well. At set up Friday you two can work on a project together. That way you can get to know each other a little before the dinner. You still want to help with set up, correct?"

"Yes. I can be wherever you need me by noon."

"If you could come to the art museum at noon, that would be perfect. We should be done by four, five at the latest. But you're welcome to leave whenever you need to."

"I'll be happy to stay and help as long as you need. This really is an honor for me."

In fact, I owe a lot to the Starlight Hope Foundation that the gala is raising money for. That's why when Linda, who is the event planner, contacted me last June to ask if I'd host, I immediately said yes.

I take the last sip of my manhattan, and before I've even set it back on the napkin the bartender asks, "May I get you another?"

"Oh, n—"

"She'd love another," Linda says to the bartender, then with hopeful eyes she says to me, "You're not in a rush, are you?"

All of the items on Linda's long list have been checked off, so I'd assumed we're nearly done.

"No, not at all," I say. "I don't want to keep you though."

"I have just a few more things if that's all right?"

I look back to the bartender, and say, "I'll take another manhattan, please."

Linda closes her planner and slips it back into her bag.

I'm not sure what, but something draws my eyes past Linda, and they land directly on Gavin Boston. He moves through the crowded bar with the ease of a lion in prairie grass. Even if I wanted to, I don't think I could look away, his eyes magnetically hold mine.

Linda turns in her seat. "Oh good! I told Trace they should join us for drinks if he could pull Gavin away from work."

"Hello, Mr. Boston," I say. "It's wonderful to see you again."

Since I left the airport last week, I haven't been able to shake the feeling that I forgot something. Now, however, as Gavin shakes my hand, it disappears.

"The pleasure is all mine, Ms. Tripple."

He holds onto my hand a few beats longer than decorum would typically call for. This is the first time I get a good look at his eyes, vibrant green that reminds me of moss just after it rains.

I'd forgotten my manners until Linda clears her throat, and says, "This is my husband, Trace."

There is a reluctance in Gavin's fingers as our hands part, almost like he doesn't want to let me go.

"It's very nice to meet you," I say to Trace.

"Great to meet you as well. I'm glad this worked out."

Trace has jubilant round cheeks and a head that's as shiny as a waxed apple. He's in a proper suit, though no tie. He looks considerably older than Gavin, which means

I've either misplaced Gavin's age at being around my own or he has found the fountain of youth.

"Another manhattan for the lovely Nyla," the bartender says.

I didn't realize he knows who I am.

"And you two gentlemen, what can I get you?"

"I actually could use some food," Gavin says. "We worked through lunch."

"I'm sure we could find you a table in the restaurant if you'd like," the bartender says.

"Nyla?" Linda asks. "Do you have time for dinner?"

"Sure, I have nothing else planned tonight, and I'm pretty hungry myself."

We follow a hostess to a booth near the back of the restaurant next to a window.

"Aisle or window?" Gavin asks me.

"I prefer the window. I assume you're an aisle man."

"I am. What gave it away?"

"Those long legs."

I hang my shopping bag on a small hook at the end of the booth. The velvet fabric of the bench tickles the back of my legs as I slide in. When Gavin sits down, I realize there isn't enough room for us to sit like strangers without causing a cramp in my shoulder or looking like I'm trying to avoid him.

"This is a tight spot," Linda says.

Trace pulls her tight against his side. "Oh, it's not so bad."

Gavin moves his shoulder against mine, and says, "At least I'm left-handed. It will make eating a little easier. Do you have enough room though, seriously?"

I feel the heat of Gavin's body and the shape of his thigh through his soft wool trousers. My romper now feels far too short, and the fabric too thin. I cross my legs to compact the space I take up, but I kick Linda in the process.

"Sorry," I say to her and resettle my legs, then to Gavin I say, "This isn't a booth built for two people our size, is it?"

The corners of Gavin's mouth lift as his eyes slide over my face.

I shift again and find a comfortable spot. "But, I'm all right, as long as you don't mind."

Gavin looks down at our legs, and says, "I don't mind at all."

Settled in our seats, very much like two people well acquainted, I look across our table. Trace seems amused, and Linda appears satisfied. I see the easily assembled puzzle pieces of this convenient situation. However, there was something in Gavin's expression when he walked in that makes me believe I was as much of a surprise to him as he was to me. I bet Linda fancies herself a matchmaker. Do I mind? I'm not sure. Right now I'm just trying to keep my eyes wide open. That sounds easy, but it isn't.

"Gavin mentioned you two grew up together," I say to Linda.

"We lived across the street from each other in Queen Anne our whole lives. Well, you moved there when you were what, three? Yeah, basically our whole lives. Our mothers were close which meant we were always at one another's house."

"Are you from Queen Ann as well, Trace?"

"No, I'm from Michigan originally. Gavin and I were roommates at Columbia. Our sophomore year, Gavin told me I needed to go home with him and meet his neighbor. I went for Thanksgiving, and the rest is history."

He and Linda look at each other, the sparks that had flown all those years ago are still alive.

"A matchmaker?" I ask Gavin.

"That would be my first and only attempt."

"Are you both architects?"

"No," Trace says. "I didn't know what the heck I was doing in life, so I got a business degree."

"Trace runs the business half of the company," Gavin says. "All of the day-to-day, rentals, clients, and employees. I run the construction, remodel, and design."

"How many employees do you have?" I ask.

"Fifty-six, and us," Trace says. "We need to hire more people, especially with the project coming up." He gives Gavin a look as if he's reminding him, again.

"I know," Gavin says.

"Gavin works all the time and doesn't want to admit that he needs help so that perhaps he can have a life."

"Come on, Trace. I have a life."

"Yeah, it's called work," Linda says.

Gavin shakes his head at her.

"Hey, that's okay, work is my life too," I say. "I completely get it. Do you still like what you do?"

"Love it," Gavin says. "How about you, do you still like what you do?"

"They pay me to go watch football. One of these days they're going to figure out that I'd do it for free."

It would be easy in a situation like this, three close friends and one new person, to be the odd man out. But the comfort I feel amongst them is like being with old friends. The entire meal is easy, conversation flows freely, and laughter is abundant. I feel at ease next to Gavin in this small space we share. My usual need to stay on point in public, this constant awareness of everything, eases.

Our waiter returns to our table and looks over our empty dinner plates. "It looks like dinner was good."

"Very," Linda says.

"How about dessert then? Did we leave room for that?"

Trace pats his belly and shakes his head no, but Linda says, "That's my favorite part of any meal."

The waiter hands one menu to Linda and another to me. I turn it so that both Gavin and I can look at it.

The waiter says, "We have a special this evening as well. A summer berry pie with vanilla bean ice cream."

Linda says, "I already know what I'm getting. Crème brûlée."

"And you Miss?" the waiter asks me. "Or would you like some more time to think about it?"

"I know what I want as well. The summer berry pie, sans ice cream, please."

"None for me," Trace says. "I'll share some of my wife's."

"I'd just like a scoop of ice cream," Gavin says.

"Would you just like the pie with the ice cream?" the waiter asks.

Gavin looks a little lost with how to answer this. "Would you be able to put it on the side? She probably doesn't want me digging into her pie."

"On the side is no problem," the waiter says as he collects the menus.

Gavin tips his head toward me, and quietly says, "I apologize. That came out weird. I didn't mean—"

"There is little, if anything, that would ever offend me."

It's not long before a young man sets Linda's crème brûlée down in front of her and the summer berry pie in front of me. It's in a small cast iron pan, berry juices drip down the side, and topped with a large mound of vanilla bean ice cream.

Our waiter, on the heels of the young man that delivered our dessert, looks at mine with worry. "I'm so sorry.

I requested the ice cream on the side. I'll be happy to take it back and get you another." He reaches for it, then slows. "Or I could bring you another dish?"

Gavin and I look at each other, he says, "I'm fine with it like this, but it's up to you, Nyla."

"You know," I say, "this works just as well. We'll make it work. Thank you."

The pie has a delicate lattice top that I hesitate to destroy, but I can smell the sweet scent of berries with a hint of spice which I don't want to resist. With a gentle hand, I use my fork to scoop out a bite.

Gavin slices into the ice cream with his spoon, and asks, "Do you like ice cream?"

"I love ice cream, but I don't like warm and cold things together because it hurts my teeth. The berry pie just sounded good. Do you like pie?"

"Yes. I'm just full from dinner, but there is always room for ice cream."

"Can I ask you a random question, about your last name?"

Gavin stiffens but nods yes.

"Any relation to the Boston Custom Furniture Company?"

The tension in his body releases. "Yes. My aunt and uncle own it."

"I have some beautiful pieces from them. My dining room and bedroom sets, also my coffee table."

"Really? That's great. My uncle has taught me a lot about woodworking. It's a hobby of mine."

"Gavin was worried you were going to ask about his brother," Linda says.

"Thanks, Lin," Gavin says.

Even though I can sense his irritation with Linda my interest is perked. "Brother?"

"Jax," she says.

"Jax Boston is your brother?"

"Yes, he is."

"Are you close?"

"We grew up doing everything together. As adults, we have busy lives, but we are still close. We make as much time as we can to talk and get together."

Jax Boston hit the pop music scene at least ten years ago. I knew of him but hadn't been drawn to his music until one day when I heard a song that stopped me in my tracks.

"One of my all-time favorite songs is one of his, 'Mystery Girl.'"

Gavin looks down at his napkin on the table, gives me a quick sideways glance, then says, "My brother is a talented musician. I agree with you, 'Mystery Girl' is one of his best."

The waiter brings a folio containing our bill, and before he sets it on the table, Gavin takes it.

"Wait, can we split it?" I ask.

"No."

"I have cash, I'll—"

"Please." He rocks onto his right hip and pulls out his wallet. "I got it."

"I'd just let him pay," Linda says. "He likes to do things his way."

I think to protest further, or just take the initiative to leave cash on the table, but I don't. Gavin has an authoritative air about him. He seems like a guy content to be in the background of life, quietly observing, but all the while making the decisions and directions that quietly rule the world around us.

CHAPTER 6

*E*ven though I've been next to the window in Mix for the last three hours, I don't notice that the day has given way to the night until we walk outside. Tiny lights wrap the branches of trees that line the sidewalks; they look like stars within reach. A light breeze laps my skin with crisp evening air, and I realize I left my jacket in the back seat of my car.

Linda and Trace don't exactly run off, but they waste no time in bidding adieu. I can tell that Gavin, just like myself, knows exactly what Linda is up to.

Alone with Gavin, things feel different from when I met him last week. He was a stranger then, though an easy one to share company with. But tonight it's like I've known him for years. That's how comfortable I am as we stand below a mass of lights while he looks at me like I'm the only interesting site around.

"May I walk you to your car?" Gavin asks.

"That's very kind of you, but you don't need to. I'm just down the street in a parking lot behind a building."

"Um, that's a very unsettling description, Nyla. I'm not sure I could let you walk away from me down a dark street to a parking lot behind a building, alone, and not worry about you."

I shrug dismissively. "I walk down dark streets by myself all the time."

"Well, that was before you knew me."

"Where are you parked?"

"My truck is still at the office."

"Would you like a ride then?"

"I'd like that."

We walk alongside each other, silence between us. It feels like we have so much to say, though we don't know where to start. Is it silly to think I'm supposed to know this guy?

We pass bars where the sounds of people and music pour out. I consider something bold—to ask Gavin to stop and have another drink with me—but, I'm not brave enough.

We turn right at the corner then walk down the street a little farther. In the middle of a long brick building is a narrow opening which makes a small tunnel that leads to the parking lot. There are two dozen tight parking spots and only one working light that flickers like a candle ready to burn out.

I press the unlock button on my key fob, but nothing happens. I try a few more times as we get closer.

"That's weird," I say. "The remote isn't working. I hope my battery isn't dead."

My SUV still looks new, but it's ten years old, and it seems like it's one thing after the next with it. I keep saying I'll get a new one, but there hasn't been time to shop for it.

I slip the key into the driver side door just as Gavin says, "Nyla, don't get in."

Over the top of my SUV, I look at Gavin. In this low lighting, I can't see his face well, but I can tell that his frame is expanding like he has something to protect.

I look inside my car. Something catches the few rays of light from the failing street lamp. It looks like glitter has been tossed about. It seems pretty until I realize it's glass from a shattered window.

I've never had a car, or anything else, broken into. I'm not even sure what I'm supposed to do. I walk to the back of the SUV, stop next to Gavin, and ask, "Should I call the police?"

He moves closer to me and runs his hand along the back of my arm. His presence is comforting.

"Did you have anything valuable in the car that they would have taken?"

Several weeks ago I cleaned it out before I headed to France, to ensure nothing of value was in it while I was gone. Since then I've returned a few things to it.

"I threw a light sweater in the back seat, which I forgot about. There was a pair of running shoes in there too. That's all though."

"These smash and grabs in this area aren't uncommon, and unless you have significant value loss, police won't respond. They'll just have you fill out a report online."

"Really?"

"Yes. It would have been nice if they'd just broken the one window though."

"There's more than one?"

I hand my shopping bag to Gavin and walk down the passenger side. Both the front and back side windows have been smashed. Glass is everywhere: dash, seats, and floorboard where I spot the manila envelope that Mia gave me last week. I unlock the car and pull the door open.

"Be careful," Gavin says.

The envelope has been ripped open and tossed back in so carelessly the photos of my family are scattered all over. I do my best to shake each one clean and return them to the envelope. Once they're all collected, I stand back up. Gavin is right next to me, so close I can see every feature of his face.

He places his hand back on my arm. "Do you have gloves or something I can brush off the seat with?"

Rarely do I feel shaken in life, but when I do my composure is such that no one knows what's going on inside. I keep my breath slow and steady as I try to think through my next steps, but I feel bewildered. It smells like rain. I press the envelope to my chest and start to shake. I never shake.

Gavin takes the envelope and puts it into the shopping bag. Then he takes my hand and leads me to the back of my SUV. His touch calms my body.

"Do you mind if I look in the back to see what you've got that I could brush off the seats with?"

"I can do it."

I open the trunk and unhook the cover that stretches over the back to conceal valuables. It's just as I expect, empty. Gavin reaches past me, lifts up the false bottom where there are a spare tire and an old set of chains.

The skin of my index finger stings. I turn my hand toward the light to check it, but I can't see anything.

"Did you get glass in your hand?" He gently takes my finger and examines it.

"I don't know. It just stings."

"I can't see anything in this light. Do you have gloves or a first aid kit, maybe a few paper towels? Was there anything in the back here?"

"No and no."

"Let's do this. We'll walk back to my office and get my truck. I have everything to clean your car enough so that I can drive it home for you."

"Drive it home for me?"

"You can drive my truck."

"I can drive my car, that's fine."

"It wouldn't be gentlemanly of me to let you drive a car with two shattered windows. Especially when it's about to rain."

"You should know, Mr. Boston, I'm the kind of person who likes to do things on my own." I try to say it playfully, even though it's true.

Gavin reaches for my hand, and says, "For some reason that doesn't surprise me. You should know, I'm the kind of person who likes to help."

We leave the SUV and walk back through the narrow tunnel to the street.

"Gavin, I really can drive it home."

"If I don't get every single shard of glass off the seat your legs could get cut. Since I'm wearing pants, it would be safer for me to drive it. Unless you want to trade clothes."

I bump him with my shoulder. "You might look good in this romper."

His laugh is deep and silky. "There would be a sight for you."

Tonight I've already learned that I love Gavin's laugh and his smile. I wish I had some good jokes to keep it going.

"Do you park in a garage at home?" he asks.

"My old bungalow has a garage, but my SUV doesn't fit in it. I'll just duct tape plastic over it for the night."

"No duct tape."

We turn left onto a neighborhood street lined with enchanting old Victorian homes.

"We can take your car up to my house for the night," Gavin says. "I've got a garage with an open bay. Then tomorrow I'll pick you up and take you to get it fi—"

"You think I can find someone to fix it on a Saturday?"

"I would think so."

I shake my head. "Hang on. No, this is already more than I can ask of you. You don't need to dedicate the rest of your night or any of your Saturday to running me all over. I'll just drive it home and duct tape a bag over the window. It really won't be that out of place in my neighborhood. Then I'll take it in tomorrow. No inconvenience needed."

"Parking it at my house would be easier than taping it up. Safer too."

"Gav—"

"I insist."

Gavin squeezes my hand which makes me look at him. He seems a little unsure, or nervous perhaps. It pulls at my heartstrings.

"Besides, Nyla, I want to ask you out. Maybe I could take you on a date while it's getting fixed tomorrow?"

"A date?"

"We could drop it off and then go do something fun."

I'm trying to keep my eyes wide open.

"You're sure? Because I don't want you to feel roped into anything."

"I am sure I want to help you, and I am sure I want to take you out on a date."

I nod yes, but for some reason, can't actually say it. I'm nervous, unsure, and excited. I try to steal a glance at Gavin from the corner of my eye, but he catches me and gives me a look that flutters my belly. Is it wrong to be happy that my car got broken into?

Gavin and I take up the entire sidewalk with arms stretched out between us, hands joined. He pulls me closer and tucks our hands behind his back to let a group of people pass. Once they do, he lowers our hands, but he doesn't put the distance back between us. Neither do I.

We walk through the neighborhood of beautiful Victorian homes for several blocks before it gives way to an industrial area that is in the process of renewal. There are some open lots with chain-link fences, a few modern row homes, and a couple of old bars with people seated outside on wooden benches.

A full block away I see an illuminated Boston Smith Company sign. The building takes up an entire block and is four stories tall. It looks like an old factory that has been renovated into a modern structure.

In the parking lot, there is only one vehicle, a black full-sized pickup truck with dark tinted windows.

"You drive this thing around Portland?" I ask.

"Once you see where I live you'll understand why."

"Gavin, I'm not sure you want me driving this. Last time I drove a full-sized pickup I was eighteen and in the woods."

"We'll drive down nineteenth where there is less traffic, you'll be fine."

His trust is encouraging, but it doesn't make me any less nervous.

Gavin opens the driver side door, and says, "Hop in," then hands me the keys. He walks around the front of the truck and gets in. He grins, almost like he's proud of something as he buckles his seatbelt.

I start the truck. The engine is quiet, but I can feel the powerful hum which is so different from my small SUV.

"Ready?" I ask and put it in reverse. I grip the steering wheel, petrified to drive this thing, but I refuse to let it show.

On our way back to the parking lot where my car is I realize how far we walked, at least two miles. How is it that I thought we'd only gone a few blocks?

The two spots next to my SUV are open which makes parking this monstrosity easier. I get out and go around to the passenger side and stop next to Gavin.

He rubs my arms reassuringly. "You did great. You're a good driver."

"You're insane for trusting a woman you hardly know to drive your baby."

"I do love this truck, but I try not to worry too much about anything because it's all replaceable, aside from people. Right?"

"Right."

Gavin lifts up the bottom of the back seat under which is a large storage area that he has neatly organized. He grabs a pair of leather gloves, a small blanket, and a window scraper that has a brush on one side of it for snow. I think he's a guy that's prepared for just about anything.

Gavin takes off his vest, folds it neatly, and sets it on the seat. He removes square gold cuff links from his shirt, tosses them into the cup holder, and rolls up his sleeves.

"May I have your keys?" he asks.

When Gavin opens the driver side door a few pieces of glass fall onto the pavement. He squats down and gently sweeps the seat clean. Once he seems satisfied, he lays the blanket on it.

He returns the gloves and the scraper to the truck and shuts the doors. "That will do for now. Are you ready?"

I'm overwhelmed by his kindness. "Thank you so much, Gavin."

"You're very welcome."

I get back into his truck. The tan interior is perfectly clean, except for one small bright blue paper laying on the little tray between the seats. I don't mean to be nosy, but the letters are so large my brain absorbs the message before I realize I've read it, "6:00 at Mix. I promise it will be worth your time."

CHAPTER 7

Thankfully, Gavin makes it easy for me to follow him as he drives my SUV. We turn right onto Burnside and drive all the way up to the top of the hill where we turn left. A series of hairpin turns would have had me absolutely lost without Gavin leading the way. He slows, puts the left blinker on, and turns. The road sign reads Appleton Way with another below it that reads private road.

I follow Gavin and find that this is where the pavement ends and everything changes. There are no houses, only trees, along this narrow road. We drive for some time with only the illumination of the two vehicles' headlights until the tunnel of trees gives way to a clearing. Here there is ample landscape lighting, an enormous house, a four-bay garage, and another structure large enough, and nice enough, to be another house. A bay door of the garage opens, and Gavin pulls my SUV into it. I get out of the truck and take in the surroundings. Only the sounds of nature: rustle of leaves, low whistle of wind, rain patter.

The house is so grand it reminds me of Timberline Lodge, but with more windows. Inside a few lights are on which allows me to get a glimpse of the interior: a large open living room with a couple of different sitting areas, two hallways which lead in opposite directions run along the front of the house, and an office with floor to ceiling shelves that are filled with books.

Gavin shuts the garage and walks over to me. He holds his hand out to catch the rain. "Made it just in time, didn't we?"

"We did."

He lifts his chin at his truck. "You did a great job. I know this place can be a bit crazy to get to. Tired?"

"What?"

"You were yawning."

"Unfortunately I am tired. Busy week. It's a bit pathetic, but I'm usually in bed by now, except on Thursdays."

The word bed makes me think of Mia's comment about how holding hands nowadays leads to the sheets in a matter of hours. That is something I'm not ready for, at all.

"Do you want to drive to your house, or would you like me to?"

"You."

He opens the truck door for me and closes it after I get in.

As he pulls away from the house, I ask, "How long have you lived here?"

"Three years. I wasn't in the market for a new home, or at least I didn't think so when I found it. I was out for a drive and saw the for sale sign at the end of the road, and on a whim, turned down it.

"The house belonged to a couple that raised their family in it. After they passed, their kids weren't sure what to do with it. They held onto it for five years, didn't do anything to care for the property, then decided to sell it with a very

bold 'as is' disclosure. But I knew the moment I pulled up
to the house I wanted it, despite that it wasn't inhabitable."

"Not inhabitable?"

"The roof leaked, subfloors were rotted. It was a mess."

"Yikes."

"Up until last year I lived in a little trailer on the property while I worked on it. I'm glad that part is over. I still
have a lot of work to do, but the main stuff is complete."

"What made you undertake such a big project?"

He looks at me with that imaginative twinkle in his eyes,
the one I'd seen at the airport when he told me about his
future high rise.

"I knew I could bring it back to life, and I did not doubt
that it would be worth it."

"It looks pretty amazing."

"Tomorrow, I'll show you around the house and property.
It's a special place."

Gavin pulls into my driveway and puts the truck in park.
"May I walk you to your door?"

"Actually no need to. I'm going to say hi to my neighbor." I point to Ms. Marshall who is seated on her porch
swing, eyeing the truck curiously. "I can't tell you how
much I appreciate everything you've done for me tonight
and tomorrow."

"Thank you for letting me help you."

"Thank you for helping me."

I place my hand in Gavin's, our fingers thread together,
then he squeezes it affectionately. When I pull away, there
is hesitation from both of us. Although I'm tired, I'd also
like to spend more time with him, even though I'll see
him tomorrow.

I get out of the truck, shut the door, and walk around
the front of it toward Ms. Marshall's house.

The earthy smell of Mary Jane reaches me even before I step onto the porch. A thick trail of smoke swirls from Ms. Marshall's lips as she adjusts her purple sweater tighter around her thin frame.

"Legs is back," she says. "What did you find there? Secret service?"

I glance back at Gavin's truck as it turns off my street. "No. It's . . . a new friend."

She holds her joint out to me in a wordless offer.

"No, but thank you."

"Who, exactly, dropped you off?"

"Just a man."

She makes a "humph" sound, and says, "Just? He must be a gay man."

"Ms. Marshall. He definitely isn't gay."

She takes a drag from her joint and blows rings of smoke. "If he's a man, dropping off a princess like you with legs on display like that, and not following your hot little behind in, he is gay."

"Or a gentleman."

"Gay."

"Would it be bad if he were?"

"Please, I don't care. I choose to hit from both sides of the plate myself sometimes. It's you I should be wondering about."

"I've told you—" I inhale a cloud of Ms. Marshall's smoke, which sends me into a coughing fit. When at last it subsides I add, "I don't date."

She slaps my leg playfully. "If I had your looks, body, and age, I'd be out seducing the most eligible bachelor. He would be able to speak Spanish to me as we made love, he'd be able to dance, and most importantly he would be well situated."

"Rich?"

There's a naughty glint in Ms. Marshall's eye. "No dear. I don't care about money. I have more than I'll ever need. But I don't have—" She makes a crude gesture with her fingers.

I laugh, then sincerely say, "That man is the first I've felt any attraction to since my husband passed away. And until tonight I was almost certain I'd have to accept an unfeeling, celibate life. But now, perhaps I'm not as hopeless as I'd feared."

"I outlived three husbands." She holds up her hand and extends three fingers. "I loved them all."

"Did you feel guilty? Moving on? Or was it hard?"

"Yes, at first. But then I realized my husband wouldn't have wanted me to be alone the rest of my life. And I wouldn't have wanted that if he'd outlived me."

"What if I can't?"

There's a shift in Ms. Marshall in the space of silence that follows. Her rough edges seem to soften as she adjusts to look at me directly. "Do you remember how good it is?"

"How good?"

"You know."

"Sex?"

She moves her head side to side. "Not just that. Do you remember what it is to be loved?"

The words "I remember" slip almost silently from my lips.

Love, however, is not what I'm looking for because while I know how high it can take me, I now also know how far there is to fall. I've had my one great love, and in this I am satisfied. This doesn't mean I always want to be alone. A little creature comfort on a cold night would be nice, should I ever find myself brave enough for such a thing.

I wonder if my wounded heart, limited availability, and the fact that I'm still in love with Lorenzo—and always will be—will allow me to be enough for someone else.

I stand and wish Ms. Marshall a good evening. As I walk back down the stairs of her porch, I see Gavin's truck turn back onto my street then into my driveway.

Ms. Marshall hollers, "Secret service is back."

Gavin hops out of his truck with my shopping bag in his hand which has my photos inside.

"You forgot this," he says. "The photos seemed important, and after everything tonight I didn't want you to worry about them."

Ms. Marshall walks up next me, the smell of Mary Jane lingers as strongly as if she were still smoking. She has to lift her chin to look up at Gavin.

"This is Ms. Marshall, my neighbor."

She sticks her hand out and shakes his in a way I'd expect from a sergeant in the army.

"And this is Gavin, my friend."

"That's a nice truck there, young man."

He looks pleased by her compliment. "Thank you."

"Do you live around here?"

"Yes, about ten miles away, across the river."

"Are you employed?"

Gavin looks down at his shirt, wrinkled from when he'd cleaned my car. He tries to smooth it with one hand. "I am, ma'am. I'm an architect, and I own my own business."

My heart begins to beat a nervous rhythm. Gavin wouldn't get this kind of interrogation from my family. The thought of Pop makes my stomach twist. What would he think?

"Single?" Ms. Marshall asks.

With an uncomfortable laugh, I say, "All right."

In all the time I've known Ms. Marshall it has generally been conversations between us or with my family. Never someone new like this.

"Yes, for the time being." Gavin winks at me.

"I have a very important question," she says and shifts her weight to her left foot. "Do you mow lawns?"

"Do I . . ."

She holds her hands as if she's pushing a lawnmower. "You know, mow lawns."

"I don't have a lawn myself, but yes, I can mow a lawn."

Ms. Marshall elbows me, and I'm thankful for the darkness which I hope conceals how embarrassed I feel. To guide Gavin away I thread my arm around his, and he bends his elbow as if we've joined this way a thousand times.

"Goodnight, Ms. Marshall," I say.

She chuckles, "Goodnight you two," and heads back to her house.

"I appreciate you bringing this back," I say.

Gavin places his hand on top of mine nestled in his elbow. "Of course, I hadn't gone too far when I noticed it. That Ms. Marshall, she's a character. She apparently believes your lawn needs tending. I'm almost certain she is inferring something else, but if I'm off base, and it's simply . . ."

I press my forehead to his shoulder, and immediately I pull back surprised at my own comfort. "She's inferring. Just let it be. She has absolutely no filter which is usually funny, but clearly embarrassing in this situation."

We stop next to the door of his truck, and I begin to slide my hand from him, but he snugs it tighter to his body. Is it strange that I want to keep touching Gavin? Is it wrong to admit that even though I feel resistance inside of me I know he's capable of helping me fix something?

"I appreciate that she has no filter," Gavin says. "It's been a long time since anyone has called me young."

Age doesn't matter, but it doesn't mean that I'm not curious. At dinner, Trace made an offhanded comment about turning forty soon which means that Gavin has to be close to that as well, but I just can't believe it. Perhaps he's some whiz that went to college early.

"You look pretty young to me," I say.

"A week ago today I turned thirty-nine. I still think of that as young, but everyone makes such a big deal about nearing the big four-o."

"A week ago?"

"Yep. Getting to meet the great Nyla Tripple was my birthday present."

"Meeting me is not a birthday present. Why didn't you say anything?"

"I'd only met you, not sure how I'd work that into the conversation. Besides, I'm not into celebrating my birthday."

"Gavin, every year is a gift. Birthdays are a gift," I say, possibly too urgently. It breaks my heart when people don't want to celebrate their birthdays, or they loathe getting old, completely unaware of how some people don't get those chances. Life isn't an obligation, it's an opportunity.

"I am very appreciative." He glances at the ground. "Trust me, I'm grateful for each year I get. I just don't like big celebrations. I'm a quiet guy, keep to myself pretty well."

"Did you do anything to celebrate?"

"Linda, despite my asking her not to, brought a cake to the office."

"And?"

He laughs. "I don't want to tell you."

I shake his arm, and say, "Tell me, please."

"I ate a piece of cake and worked until midnight."

"That's it? You worked until midnight?"

"Linda wasn't kidding, I am a workaholic."

I'm sure Gavin has plenty of people in his life who want to help him, but something tells me he doesn't often let people do things for him. After all he's done for me tonight, and hearing that he glazed over his birthday, I want to do something for him.

"Why don't you come over earlier tomorrow and I'll make you a birthday breakfast? I have no idea what it will be, and since it's late it will have to be with whatever is in my fridge, but I'll come up with something."

"A birthday breakfast?"

"Yes, what time do you get up?"

"I'm a creature of habit. Up at seven, out the door at eight."

"On a Saturday, where are you going at eight?"

"Usually, the office."

"Do you need to work tomorrow?"

He pulls his full lower lip between his teeth like he's trying not to tell me something. It's incredibly sexy.

"Gavin, I really don't want to inconvenience you. I don't expect for you to change your plans just because my car was broken into. I'll work around your schedule. And if tomorrow doesn't work, I'll take you out for a belated birthday dinner another time, in between our crazy schedules. If you're interested, of course."

Gavin's hesitant eyes search mine, and he squeezes my hand tighter in his. I think if we'd allow any more contact than this he would kiss me right now.

"You won't hurt my feelings," I say. "Honestly. You can tell me what you're thinking, I won't be offended, and I won't judge."

His face relaxes as if he's given in. "I was just thinking, I'd skip out on work for you anytime, but I was worried that would sound too strong."

It is probably the ultimate compliment in Gavin's world, and I get it.

"You tell me the time that works best for you," I say.

"I'll be here by eight-thirty."

"That's perfect. Eight-thirty for a belated birthday breakfast. Should I invite Trace and Linda, or any others?"

"May I be selfish and wish for a party for two?"

"Wish granted."

CHAPTER 8

"*Y*es, I'll hold," I say to a man on the phone at the third glass repair company I've called this morning.

From the spout of a glass bowl, I pour batter onto a hot griddle to make pancakes that are the size of a CD.

The doorbell rings.

My throat tightens, and my skin flushes with warmth.

Last night everything with Gavin was easy, it evolved unplanned. I never felt nervous. Now though, I've had time to think, to worry, to realize I'm going out on my first date (well, one that I know is a date).

I press the phone between my ear and shoulder, wipe my hands on my red striped apron, and hurry to the door. I take a deep breath and open it to find a gorgeous man with a bouquet of lilies in his hand.

"Good morning," Gavin says.

His leaf-green button-down shirt, which complements his eyes, is casually untucked and the sleeves rolled up. Straight leg jeans, while relaxed, hug close to his thighs. He looks so different out of his work attire.

Just as I open my mouth to reply, the man on the line returns. "Yes, I'm still here," I say.

I step back to let Gavin in and try not to look as attracted to him as I feel, but I think I fail because he gives me a shy but appreciative face before he looks around my living room.

The man on the phone says, "Yes, I've got those windows here. If you can get the car here by nine, I'll get it done for you today."

"Ah, nine? Can we do ten-thirty?"

"Ten is the latest I can do for today. I'm trying to work you in between some other appointments."

"All right, I'll make that work. Thank you so much. See you at ten."

I hang up the phone, and say to Gavin, "Sorry about that. We'll have to be quick."

Gavin hands me the flowers. "I heard, I'll get you there by ten."

Without a thought, I reach up to hug him, and his arms wrap around me. He's warm, and something about him soothes me. I draw a slow breath in, Gavin's cologne, or perhaps aftershave, is light, but the scent is refreshing and natural, like standing on the edge of a flowing river.

Slowly I step back, but Gavin doesn't totally let me go.

"You are beautiful," Gavin says as if he's been wanting to tell me this for some time.

"Thank you. You're handsome."

He looks down at my row of running shoes, organized by color like a rainbow, and picks up the last pair.

"Is this your signature?"

"Maybe," I say embarrassed.

"Did they get made like this?"

"Yes."

"That is cool." He sets it back in the row. "Why so many?"

"Different types depending on my run, the weather, what color I'm feeling that day."

"I didn't realize it was so complicated. Something sure smells good."

It's the sweet scent of pancakes. Swiftly, I go into my kitchen, pull a spatula from the drawer and check them; golden brown. I flip all eight, then turn around to see Gavin looking out my sliding glass door to the wheat field in my backyard.

"Your grass does need to be mowed," he says matter-of-factly.

"Yes, it does. But what Ms. Marshall was implying is that I need a man to mow it, and not just that. She was going to say as much had I let her keep going. And just for the record, I can mow it myself."

He presses a curled index finger to his lips and tries not to laugh, but he can't stop a low rumble in his throat.

I try to hide a smile. "Are you laughing at me? I'm not lazy, I swear, I just lost control of it this summer. I was traveling a ton. I was going to do it today, but then the car got broken into, and you happened."

"I really would be happy to mow it for you when we get back this afternoon."

I grab his arm and pull him away from the sliding door toward my kitchen. "You've got a problem with wanting to fix things."

"It isn't that I want to fix things exactly, it's just," his smile on his face fades, "I want to make sure things are taken care of properly."

Gavin's words are sincere. There aren't many people in the world like him. It isn't just me. I know that.

Suspicious, I ask, "You're that worried about my lawn?"

"More like, the owner of the lawn."

"You're a kind man. Coffee?"

"Yes, please."

I grab two mugs from the cupboard and pour coffee from the French press.

"Luckily I made it to the store this morning because I had nothing in my fridge. I have half-and-half if you want any."

"I like my coffee black." He takes the offered cup from my hand. "Thank you. You went to the store this morning?"

A hefty splash of half-and-half turns my coffee the color of caramel. "It's just down the street. I stopped by after my run."

"You already ran this morning?"

"Running is my happy pill." I wink at him over the rim of my coffee mug as I take a sip. From my fridge, I grab two containers and hold them up. "Strawberries, blueberries, or both?"

"Both."

There is a look in his eyes that makes me stop and then it makes me want him. I keep my eyes wide open even though I feel an alarm that tells me to close them.

"Are you going to tell me what you're thinking?" Gavin asks in a tone that compels truth.

I realize I'm still holding the two containers of berries up in the air, probably looking as conflicted as I feel. Do I tell the truth? Lie? Omission?

"You asked me to tell you what I was thinking last night," he says.

I turn to the sink to wash the berries, but we both know, I'm sure, that it's an excuse not to look directly at him.

"And I did," he says, "even though it was scary, to be honest."

"I'm not ready to tell you."

"I'm a very patient man, Nyla."

I cut the strawberries, and try not to look at him so that I can finish breakfast. "How do you like your eggs?"

"Over medium. The hummingbirds sure do like that flower."

As the last egg slips from its shell into the pan, I glance up and see three birds around the feeder Ms. Marshall gave me. One has an emerald head.

"Have a seat at the table," I say. "Facing my embarrassing backyard."

I plate a stack of five pancakes, then stick a single gold candle into the center of them. I arrange the berries to look neat, but spontaneous at the same time. From the frying pan, I slip the eggs onto a separate plate.

Even though Gavin knows what I was making he looks surprised when I set the plates down in front of him. Then the corners of his eyes lower. For a moment I wonder if something about what I've done has made him sad, or perhaps nostalgic for a past time, but then they lift with that joyful glint, and he smiles with his lips pressed together.

"Pancakes!" I say. "It works, right?"

Gavin puts his hand on the curve of my waist and draws me closer to him with ease. I place my hand on his, feeling the warmth of him between parts of me, and look down at the side of his face. He has perfectly shaped ears with a freckle the size of a pen dot just in front of the crease of his earlobe.

"Nyla Tripple," he says in an exhale. "Aren't you going to sing?"

72 ∾ Nicole Dwigans

I light the candle, and say, "Ah, no. You will run for the hills if you hear these broken pipes."

One corner of his mouth lifts like a man that always gets his way.

"Close your eyes so you can't see me," I say.

"You close your eyes. I want to see you." Gavin tightens his hand on my waist enough to reassure me that it's just him.

I listen and lower my eyelids. My voice shakes, and I sound like an out of tune jazz bar singer that no one stays to hear. I finish and open my eyes to find Gavin's fixed on me with fascination.

"Go on," I say. "Make a wish."

He closes his eyes, leans forward, and blows out the candle. I grab my plates and sit across from him.

"You have a beautiful voice," Gavin says. "You just don't believe it, that's what makes it shake." He cuts the stack of pancakes, pours maple syrup on them, then takes a bite. "Oh, this is goooood. Sure beats the apple and coffee I normally grab on the way out of the door."

"I'm glad you like it. It's my favorite meal of the day, which could be because I'm normally starving after my morning run."

"Do you think my birthday wish will come true even though today isn't my actual birthday?"

That is something I've never thought about. Are wishes only valid on certain days, or can we simply light a candle any time we have a wish?

"I have a feeling it will," I say genuinely, although I have no idea why.

•••

We've been at a standstill on the freeway for the last twenty minutes.

Gavin taps his steering wheel with an impatient finger. "I'm sorry about this. I'll feel horrible if you can't get your car fixed today."

"This isn't your fault. It's fine. I'm sure I can pick it up tomorrow, no problem. I always worry when a road closes or gets completely stopped like this. At least if it's moving slowly, you know the people are all right, well, all right enough."

At last, the traffic begins to inch along. We pass by a mangled mess of three vehicles, several police cars, and a couple of tow trucks. Silently I say a prayer for the victims and their families. Once past the accident, it's smooth sailing.

When we pull onto Gavin's road, he says, "Unfortunately, there won't be time to show you around like we planned."

"Another time."

"Definitely."

We pull up to the house which seems fit for the king of Portland, if there was one.

Gavin puts the truck in park and unbuckles his seatbelt. "I'll drive your SUV to the glass shop."

I open my mouth to protest, but he stops me with a look that reminds me that Gavin gets what he wants.

It's nearly noon by the time we make it to the glass shop. A man with an unkempt beard and bright blue eyes says, "Afternoon," as we walk through the door.

"Hello," I say. "I believe we spoke earlier. I'm Nyla Tripple. I have the SUV with two shattered windows."

"Ah yes, we did," the man says. He shuffles through a stack of loose-leaf papers and then pulls one out with handwritten notes on it. He pecks at a keyboard with his index fingers. "There is a pen there," he points to a cup, "and here is the paperwork for you to fill out." He draws the back of his hand across his brow. "I'll be back in a sec."

I fill out the paperwork and then glance over my shoulder. Gavin is seated in the lobby with a magazine in hand. Next to him is a woman with a small boy on her lap that is staring at Gavin like he's a famous person.

Gavin looks up to me, much like that day on the plane, and tosses the magazine onto the table. He comes to stand next to me and leans onto the counter, so our eyes are level. Nothing is said, but so much passes between our eyes and our skin where we touch.

The man behind the counter returns with a baffled expression. "I really apologize, Ms. Tripple, when I spoke to you earlier the computer showed we had the glass for your car in stock, but we don't. Well, I have the glass for the front door, just not the rear. I'll order it, but it won't be here until Monday. I can have it ready for you Monday afternoon."

"Oh, it's okay, no worries. But I'll be gone this week. Could I pick it up Friday?"

"That should be fine to leave it here for the week."

"Or," Gavin says, "I can pick it up Monday and park it at my house. Then after we get done with the gala set up on Friday, you can get it."

"I think it's all right if I leave it here," I say to Gavin. "I don't want to inconvenience you even more."

He gives me that look that says let me take care of it. "You'll never be an inconvenience. Besides, I owe you a tour of the property since we ran late today. I'll make you dinner too."

I surrender. "How do I let Gavin pick up my car?" I ask the man.

The man slides my paperwork back to me and points to a line. "Just add his name here."

As I add Gavin's name, I say to him, "If you change your mind just let me know."

"I promise, I won't change my mind."

Our first date isn't even over, but I think I just agreed to a second one.

CHAPTER 9

"Canby?" I say to Gavin as we take the exit off of I-5. "What's in Canby?"

"Do you want me to tell you the surprise?"

"Do you want to tell me, or do you want me to wait?"

He glances over his shoulder, then merges the truck. Both of us are silent as we pass a golf course, a farm field, then take a left at the Aurora airport.

"You're in charge," Gavin says. "You tell me what you want."

He says this in such a way that I know he doesn't just mean this surprise.

"Are you always such an agreeable man?"

"No," he says flatly. "It's just you."

"All right, I do want to know where we're going."

"I thought a little wine tasting and a picnic would be a nice afternoon together."

"You packed a picnic?"

He points to the back seat where there is a soft-sided cooler. I'm not sure how I missed it.

"How does that sound?" he asks.

I say, "It sounds great."

I'm touched by his thoughtfulness. I feel taken care of, not something I've felt in a long time.

Gavin slows the truck and turns the left blinker on. We turn at a sign that reads Whiskey Hill Winery. To the right are rows of grapes, up ahead is a large building, and to the left a tasting room, open lawn, and a covered patio. Gavin parks the truck, then grabs the cooler from the back. We walk through an opening in a low fence. The tables that edge the lawn are all occupied. But then we spot a couple getting up, and Gavin sets the cooler down on it.

"Busy day," Gavin says. "It's great to see that."

As we walk toward the tasting room I notice it isn't just busy, it's packed. My feet slow.

"You all right?" Gavin asks.

My earlier life, particularly my marriage, was swept into the public eye quickly and everything changed. While now things aren't like that, I never feel completely free of possible leering eyes or judgment.

"I'm good," I say. "This is a gorgeous place."

Gavin opens the door and ushers me into the beautiful tasting room which has a polished but rustic feel. Behind the bar, a woman pours wine, and at the far end a man rings up a customer.

A woman slides down the bar to make a small space for us.

A voice booms, "My man! I'll be right with you two."

"No rush, Brad," Gavin says.

I ask the woman next to me, "How's the wine?"

"Superb, as always," she says. "We're members."

"Oh?"

"Wine club."

"This is only my second time wine tasting."

"Really?" both she and Gavin say at the same time.

I say, "First time was for a bachelorette party years and years ago. I don't remember much of it."

"In a limo?" the woman asks with a giggle. "Those are always trouble."

Brad walks over to us and sets two wine glasses down.

"Allow me to introduce you to Nyla," Gavin says. "Brad is a good friend and also the owner and winemaker of this exceptional establishment."

Brad rolls his eyes like a man who doesn't like praise and pulls a cork from a bottle. He pours us each half a glass, and says, "If you give me about ten minutes, I'll have some help in here, and we can go taste from the barrels."

As we walk back out to our table, I ask, "What are we doing?"

"Brad is treating us to a behind-the-scenes experience."

"More than just wine tasting? I don't know much about it." I inhale the scent from the glass and catch something that reminds me of peach and then take a sip. "With all my years of training, I didn't drink much. Since then I've stuck with a few reliables like manhattans, pinot, and occasionally a stout."

"Those are sizable drinks for someone who doesn't drink."

"I like the taste, just don't know much about it."

"Well, you'll learn a lot today then. Why did you stop training?"

"Why did I stop . . . It's complicated."

Gavin pulls a chair out for me at our table.

"That sometimes happens, complications." He takes a seat facing me, and continues, "But, I'm up for a complicated story."

"Ah, that complicated story will probably kill the mood," I say. Gavin waits with patient eyes. "The press slammed me for retiring when I did, at the height of my career when everyone thought I still had a few good years left in me. But it was hard to run with a broken heart after my—"

"Your husband."

"Yes, I just couldn't keep competing. I needed my runs to be for me, and not for the next race."

"Then you became . . .," Gavin says.

I'd never thought of it in that way, that after Lorenzo I became something else. Parts of me I had to let go of. Some just disappeared. Others, however, still cling to me and seem to serve no other purpose except to tie me back to the past.

"A sports journalist and sideline reporter. Fortunately, I'd made some good contacts when I was running. Specifically Perry Taklin, who is head of American Sports Television. He's my mentor and always has my back in the crazy world of sports journalism."

"Was it something you'd wanted to do before?"

"You really want to hear?"

"Of course!"

"Okay, where do I begin? Kevin and I grew up doing everything together. We'd watch sports for hours and then go shoot hoops or skate. I didn't know there was anything different about Kevin and me until he started to play football when he was ten, and I was told I couldn't. But Pop would let me play with Kev and his friends when they were in the backyard or at the park."

"That was cool of your dad. What did your mom think?"

"Did you ever meet my mom?"

With remorse, he says, "Yes."

"Mom wasn't fond of me playing sports with the guys, although she encouraged me to play with the girls. I wasn't the girly-girl daughter I think she expected. I mean, I know she loved me completely, it wasn't that. Just I was, am still, a bit of a tom-boy."

"She was a good woman," Gavin says.

I nod in agreement and then continue, "In high school, I was appointed sports reporter for our school newspaper. I did nothing to earn it, I think they just thought, hey, that girl Nyla likes sports, and she can write, let's have her do it. It was the first time I realized someday I could get paid to watch and talk about sports. I was sure it was my golden ticket."

"Wow," Gavin says.

"Ah, of course, the career came crashing down, just as it began, when I realized being a reporter entailed talking to people."

He looks at me like he thinks I'm kidding. "What?"

"Yeah, I hadn't factored that in. The biggest problem was having to talk with boys who were either very put off by me being female, or intrigued. Both scared me equally because I was shy. So, I resigned my brief post as sports editor and decided I'd better figure out how to make a living doing the one thing I felt exceptional at, which was running."

"I'd never pictured you as shy."

"I wasn't just shy, it was something else entirely."

"Why do you think that was?"

"I was just a high school kid, not sure of who I was. A girl who didn't fit the feminine ideal and loved sports. But, after the sports reporter position ended, I decided to figure out how to maximize my body. And I found the things that made me feel out of place in the world, also made me the best in the world. At least for a while."

Questions flicker through Gavin's eyes, and just as he opens his mouth, there's a clap from behind me. Brad rubs his hands together eagerly, and says, "Ready?"

We walk toward the back of the property along a dirt road that's lined by rows of grapevines which are heavy with fruit. Brad stops, picks a tightly packed bunch, and hands it to me.

"Try, they are delicious," Brad says. "This block is Pinot Noir."

I admire the jewel-like bundle, and ask, "Just eat them?"

"Yep."

I pull a grape off the bunch and hold it out to Gavin who grins at me as he takes one. Then we put the grapes into our mouths and his eyes open wide just as I bite down into mine. The tight skin explodes with a sweet, concentrated juice, unlike anything I've tasted.

"Oh, wow," Gavin says.

"These are amazing," I say.

Brad nods with pride and continues along the path at the end of which is a large building. He opens the door, and says, "This used to be the old barn, but now, it's where the grapes become wine."

Inside it smells earthy and kind of like wine, but not exactly. Along one side of the room, barrels are stacked three tall, five across, and two deep. In front of each stack are two barrels on their sides with large round corks that point up to the ceiling like belly buttons. On the far left of the room is a large stainless steel counter with an assortment of gadgets and scales.

Brad grabs a long glass tube that looks like a fancy turkey baster, then he gets three clean glasses and hands one to Gavin and me.

I point to the tube. "What is that?"

"This is a wine thief." Brad pulls a cork from one of the wine barrels on its side and sticks the wine thief into it. "It's just a cool name for wine retriever." He presses his thumb over the opening at the top of the tube, and when he lifts it out it's filled with a beautiful purple liquid.

"I'm embarrassed to tell you this, Brad, but I know nothing about wine, so you'll have to be patient with me if I ask a lot of questions."

"Are you kidding? That's what makes this fun. Don't hold back."

We sample wines in various stages of the winemaking process, compare years, and even learn about blending wines. I feel a little ridiculous for never before considering the work that goes into making a single bottle. I'd never thought about the fruit being affected by the weather patterns, the soil, or the art of harvesting it at just the right time. Although I don't absorb everything that Brad teaches me, I walk out of the barn knowing so much more than when I went in.

As we walk back to the lawn area, Brad says, "I know you have lunch to eat. You two have a seat, and I'll bring your pours out to you. And if you'd just prefer a glass of something let me know."

"Are you sure?" Gavin asks.

"Absolutely, relax and enjoy."

We sit back at our table. Gavin sets the cooler by his feet and unzips it. "I tried to find easy finger foods that would go with wine, and I ended up getting a smorgasbord." He lays out a large selection of items: nuts, cheeses, crackers, jellies, grapes, strawberries, chocolate. "I know you're a vegetarian, but I couldn't resist." He sets down some salami. "I hope you don't mind."

"It doesn't bother me at all."

Even though Gavin and I have talked all day, it seems like we could keep going forever. He's an enthralling story-teller and makes me smile so much my cheeks start to hurt.

"Something I haven't asked, and I can't believe I haven't talked about, do you like football?" I ask.

"I do. You'll probably laugh at me, but I've been doing a fantasy league for the last five years. We get together for a draft each year, mostly an excuse to drink beer and catch up."

"Did you play sports?"

"In high school, I was a third-string running back. I hope that doesn't disappoint you."

"Why would that disappoint me?"

"I just wasn't sure if you were more into jocks. I'm just a guy that likes to build and repair things."

It dawns on me that Gavin has no idea how unusual me being on a date is.

"If I were only into jocks I wouldn't be sitting here with you now, enjoying your company, drinking this wine, eating this unbelievable selection of food."

"You're sweet," he says.

"What was the last thing you made with your wood-working skills?"

"My bed. I just got it put together a couple weekends ago, new mattress and everything. It's the biggest piece I've ever made. I'll show you next week when you come up to the house." He looks surprised by his words, and quickly says, "I didn't mean anything by that, just a simple, you know that I'll show you what I made, but there isn't, I'm not implying anything."

"I'd like to see it."

I look away from Gavin for the first time and see we are the last ones left outside.

"I don't know how it got so late."

"Me neither."

Gavin packs up the remains of our lunch, puts the cooler on his shoulder, and grabs our wine glasses.

In the tasting room, it's just employees left cleaning up.

"Sorry to keep you, we lost track of time. Such a great place," Gavin says to Brad.

"You aren't keeping us, and glad you enjoyed it."

"Thank you so much," I say. "It was such a treat to tour the place, and I learned so much."

"My pleasure really." Brad leans on the bar, and says to me, "Would you mind taking a picture with Maggie?" He motions over his shoulder to a girl stacking wine glasses. "She was a runner in college, and I didn't know until today, but she apparently idolizes you."

"Of course."

Brad raps on the bar. "All right, Maggie, now is your chance."

It wasn't until after the first Games that I realized that what I did mattered to people, or that I might be a source of inspiration. Still, knowing this, it surprises me a little when someone wants a photo or my autograph. I oblige, always, and hope they see I'm just like them. Perhaps then they'll know that, like me, they can accomplish anything.

Gavin and I walk outside hand in hand. The scent of grapes and earth permeate not just the air, but us: clothes, skin, breath.

At the truck, I open the back door so that Gavin can load the cooler and wine he purchased. He closes it, then opens the front for me. I start to get in but stop, then turn back and look up at him.

"I didn't realize how badly I needed a day like this. The last few months have been nonstop for me. This has been utterly relaxing."

"It's my pleasure."

Before I realize the situation I've placed myself in, my hands are on Gavin's chest. He searches my face as I bring my body to his. I like the way the curve of his chest feels against mine, the slight give of his stomach. His hands slide around my waist. In my core, it feels like a flower unfurls. I let out a breath of relief; there are pieces of me that will be revived.

My vision changes, everything around us fades, and all I see is Gavin. I lift onto my toes, turn my lips up to his, and just an inch before our lips touch, a surge of fear pumps from my heart dispersing through my veins like ice water. I freeze. My feet return to the ground. For a moment I look at his lips, then I drop my head onto his chest.

"Gavin, I'm so sorry."

I'm not sure what Gavin knows about my past, or if I should explain to him that kissing him isn't just a kiss, not to me. It's so much more. This is harder than it should be.

He hugs me in a way that makes me feel safe. "It's all right, Nyla. There will never be any pressure from me." His cheek presses to the top of my head.

Sometimes I feel like an island isolated by an ocean of my experiences. Though I desperately want to reach across the vast waters, I am not able to. I wonder not just if I ever will, but if someone will be willing to wait for me.

CHAPTER 10

*W*hen I walk out onto the football field to begin my workday, I feel as if I've come home. I know the part I play in these events is small, but I love it, and I'm privileged to be a part of the production that brings the excitement of the game into people's homes.

"Nyla, you have lipstick on your teeth," Tate, my cameraman, says. He's a tall, wiry man with a long nose and angular features that make him look like he's always deep in contemplation.

I scrub my teeth with my tongue and lift my lips back. "Now?"

"Good to go."

People say the camera loves me, and if that's true, it has something to do with Tate who always tells me when I have lunch in my teeth, raccoon eyes, or my hair has gone awry. He's also vetoed a few outfits by telling me the camera will hate it. Over the years we've become good friends, and now we work on almost all of my projects together.

Tate adjusts the camera on his shoulder and looks out to the field. "First game of the season. It's exciting. Isn't it?

"Yep! Would you take a picture of me?" I ask Tate. He balances the camera on his shoulder like it's nothing and takes my photo with my phone. I send the promised picture of me standing on the fifty-yard line to Gavin.

We've talked each day that I've been here, long conversations as I lie in bed at the end of the night. I've never been one to chat on the phone, but it's different with him. I like to hear his voice, the lively way he tells me things that are going on or happened in life.

Tate tips his head at something behind me. I turn to see Blake walking across the field toward me. He's thin with muscles that stand out and blond hair that reminds me of a surfer.

"Good afternoon, Nyla," Blake says. "You look beautiful."

Tate says, "I'll meet you over there in a second to get set up." As he turns to leave I catch the subtle question in his eye. He's spent more time looking directly at me than anyone, and I'd imagine he knows more of my tiny body signs than I do.

On Tuesday Blake and I dined together, and like before we had a great time. But I realized, even with eyes wide open, I don't have any attraction to him. I was a little lost with how to handle the situation, so I told him dating wasn't really an option for me right now, but I'd like to be friends and hang out when we're in the same town. He was agreeable to this. But now by the way he's looking at me so sweetly, I don't think he was all that deterred.

"I got a call this morning," Blake says, "asking me to fill in for sideline reporting next week."

"Really! That's great!" I give him a high five.

"Yeah, thanks. Monday night, you gonna watch?"

"You bet," I say, although I won't tell him that I watch nearly every televised game.

My phone vibrates in my hand, and I look down to see Gavin's name. "I need to take this," I say to Blake. With a friendly wave I walk in Tate's direction and answer the phone.

"Thanks for the photo," Gavin says. "I'm on my way over to Trace's to watch the game and look forward to seeing you."

"I'm only on camera a few minutes."

"Best few minutes."

I turn and see Darren Dryer coming down the chute. He's a retired wide receiver that now anchors the pregame and postgame shows. We always connect before the game, go over some back and forth points, and pump each other up.

"I have to get going," I say to Gavin. "Darren just got here."

Darren gives me a bone-crushing hug, just like my brother, and with a lift of his chin says, "Who ya talking to?"

"My friend," I say. "You hang on."

He pokes me with his elbow, then gives Tate a high five. "Gavin?"

"I'm here."

"I have to go. May I call you tonight if it isn't too late?"

"Of course. Have fun, and thank you again."

I jump when I see Darren is right behind me.

"You got a silly grin on your face," he says.

"I do not."

"Was that a man?" He exaggerates the surprise in his voice, or perhaps it's genuine.

"Maybe."

"Nyla, Nyla. All right. When you're ready, I want to hear about him."

"Let's just talk about football."

It's almost time now, everything is ready. I'm on my mark. Tate looks at me through the lens of the camera. As the stadium fills, the hum of the crowd swells. It smells of beer and fried foods. This is the moment I look forward to each week.

Tate holds his hand up in the air and then points to me. I'm live.

The game has begun.

•••

When I head home on Fridays for the weekend, it's always been just a stopover in my week to prepare to leave again. It isn't something I especially look forward to. But this week I am really excited to be here.

Gavin's truck pulls into my driveway just as my taxi pulls up to the curb. He takes my bag from the driver and slips him a tip in the palm of his hand. As he reaches for me, he says, "That was a very long week."

Gavin still wears his work clothes: steel gray slacks and a vest two shades darker, with a navy shirt. From his truck, he grabs a small duffel bag.

"You do know I am gone all week, almost every week."

"Are you telling me I have to get used to it?" He grins. "You are absolutely beautiful."

He follows me into the house, up the stairs, and sets my suitcase next to my bed.

"Would it be all right if I change here?" Gavin asks.

"Of course, any room you'd like."

A devilish grin pulls at his lips, not something I've seen before. It sends a thrill through me.

Laughing I put my hand on his chest and gently push him back into the hall. "Any room except this one." Before I pull my hand back, I run it down the buttons of his shirt. He lets out a breath of desire.

I close the door, lean my head on it and catch my breath. Then I change into a pair of loose shorts and a shirt that reminds me of something from an eighties dance movie with a scoop neck that falls over my shoulder. I grab a pair of sneakers I don't use for running, carry them downstairs, and drop them next to the front door.

On my way into the kitchen, I notice my backyard no longer looks like a golden wheat field. I open the sliding door and step out onto the perfectly manicured lawn that now has a few faint patches of green. Even the bushes have been shaped up and look hopeful.

I spin to see Gavin leaned against the open door. He's changed into shorts and a T-shirt and looks ready for a game of basketball.

"Did you do this?" I ask.

"Maybe."

This had to have taken a very long time. In fact, it's doubtful Gavin could have done it in one evening. I'm overwhelmed by his kindness.

"Why? And you got my car?"

"Because I want to help you. And yes I picked up your car, it's at my house."

Gavin joins me on the trimmed grass and slips his arms around my waist. My hands trace the shape of his chest, up onto his shoulders, then I lift onto my toes. I've thought about this a lot over the last week, finding the momentum to move with the desires of my body instead of allowing my fears to freeze me. I give him a chaste kiss on his lips, feeling shy about it.

"Gavin?"

"Yes?" His breath brushes my lips, then he reaches for one more soft kiss that I give.

I want more.

"My body wants to stand here and keep kissing you, but we should get going so we aren't late."

"My body doesn't want to go help anymore. I just want to be here with you."

I try to pull him toward my house, but he's solid and unmovable. Our arms stretch out between us like a line that holds a boat to a dock. His fingers curl tighter around my hand, and I drift back into his arms. He kisses me with a desire that makes me feel like I'm filled with a million blooming flowers.

"Nyla. I really like you."

"I really like you too."

"I'm going to kiss you more tonight."

His heated look makes me want to be greedy with my desires, to forget my trepidations.

"I do need to get my car tonight, and you still owe me a tour of your house."

"Dinner too."

I feel the thump of Gavin's heart against my chest, and within a few moments, my own synchronizes with his.

•••

At the Portland Art Museum, Gavin and I set up the silent auction tables. As I reach across for one of the bid sheets, he reaches for a pen, and we bump into each other. Quickly I look around, we're alone. I steal a kiss.

With a smitten grin, he asks, "Does that mean I get to kiss you whenever I want?"

"Maybe."

He tests me immediately and kisses me once quickly, searches my eyes, then kisses me again, this time he lingers, and his hand floats up against my hip. I feel lightheaded when our lips part and catch Linda out of the corner of my eye coming toward us.

"Aren't you two efficient! Is that the last box?"

I pull out a model train engine and a certificate for a week-long train tour in Canada. Out of all the things, this one sounds like the most fun.

Gavin adds a bid sheet in front of it. "The last one," he says.

"We are all done then," she says. "Do you two want to grab some dinner?"

"I'm always up for getting food," I say.

When she walks away I turn to Gavin. "I'm sorry. I didn't want to be rude by not accepting her invitation."

"It's all right. I'll make you dinner another night. But tonight there will still be room for dessert."

I'm not sure exactly what I'm ready for, there is still a part of me that is saying to stop, but it isn't loud enough to prevent me from asking, "What is it that you're serving for dessert?"

He is silent, but his smile clearly says, *me*.

CHAPTER 11

*G*avin and I meet Linda and Trace at the famous Ramen Bowl House in Southeast Portland. We get the last open table next to the door. It's the perfect spot because we catch a cool breeze that comes in through the door.

After I place my order, I excuse myself to wash up.

I follow a sign that reads "washrooms this way" and push a door open into a long hallway the color of an eggplant. There are several other establishments in this long building, all of which share the restrooms at the end of the hall; it makes for a busy thoroughfare.

As I wash my hands at the glass sink, a stall door opens and is quickly followed by, "Nyla Tripple! Is that you?"

Pandora Person is a woman I remember for her formidable beauty and sharp tongue. Her bright blond hair no longer reaches her waist, now it's a blunt bob that comes to a sharp point at her chin. Not a strand out of place.

"My goodness, how many years has it been?" she asks.

I pull a paper towel from the dispenser and dry my hands while she washes hers.

"It has to be at least eight," I say.

Pandora was a longtime girlfriend of Lorenzo's good friend, Travis. The first time I met her was at my wedding. We saw them regularly for the five years they were together. When they finally broke up, both Lorenzo and I were relieved.

"That just can't be," she says dramatically. "Where does the time go? A whole lifetime too." She reaches out and pats my shoulder with an exaggerated pain in her face. "I was so sorry to hear about Lorenzo, such a rare man. Good through and through, you know. And you two were just too stinking perfect together. But you seem to be doing well."

"I am."

"You look unbelievable." She flutters her hand over me as if I'm on display. "You're one of those exotic beauties that gets more and more gorgeous by the years."

"Thank you."

"I see you on TV a lot. Quite a success you've built yourself into."

"Things have worked out well. How are you? Life treating you good?"

"Goodness, life has been a roller coaster. My husband got sick, too, with cancer. Lymphoma, I think."

She flips her wrist as if it doesn't really matter what he had. Her casualness in this information twists my stomach.

"Really? I'm so sorry."

I look at the rock on her finger that must be five carats. She shakes her head no, holds up her hand, and says, "This is my upgraded version."

"Excuse me?" I ask confused.

"It's my ex-husband that had cancer."

"Ah."

"We were still married when he got sick though, but then it fell apart."

"When he was sick?"

"Yeah." She laughs like a villain, one of the many things about her that never settled well with me.

Pandora and Travis had a nasty pattern. She'd belittle him with her sharp tongue, slicing him at the knees, and then just as quick she'd whisper something in his ear that made him pant. Her power was unsettling. What's more, Travis was a confident man, not someone that I thought would put up with such antics. At least he never married her. I pity the man she roped and tossed away.

"Besides," Pandora says, "it was nothing like you and your Lorenzo. About the only place my ex and I were compatible was in the bedroom." She touches my arm and leans closer. "We were amazing there." Her eyes flutter as if she recalls something that feels blissful. "Everywhere else was a mess. Here," she opens the bathroom door, "let's go out into the hall."

We go out to the purple hall, but really I am ready to be out of her presence. Before I excuse myself, I have to know, "What happened to your ex-husband?"

"What?"

"Did he make it?"

"Oh yeah, near death my ass. Fucker survived. Good for him, right?"

I wonder if she knows how sharp her tongue is. Is it an accident, or is it intentional?

"Yes, I'm glad he survived," I say.

It angers me that this woman who was gifted her husband's survival didn't even appreciate it. My heart aches for Lorenzo, for my loss. I would have done anything to save him, and I would have been grateful.

Pandora says, "I'm sorry to cut this short, but I need to get going. My husband is just grabbing the car. The upgraded husband, though he's not as good in bed as the first. But everything else is better. Fair trade?"

"I'm not sure."

"Which restaurant are you at?"

"Ramen House."

"I'll walk out that way then. I'm meeting him on the corner, so that's perfect."

I follow her into the restaurant. We weave our way through tables that are set so close together that I have to be careful not to bump anyone.

"Where is it you live now?" I ask.

"Nashville. I'm in the music industry, not as glamorous as it sounds. I'm just here for a quick visit, retirement party for my old boss. How about you?"

"Here, I moved back about three years ago."

The front door never looked so good, I am ready for her to leave, but the closer we get, the slower she walks. Pandora's entire body shifts into something that reminds me of a snake about to strike. As I trail behind, I put a little more distance between us. I am worried about whomever she has in her sight. She slithers between the last two tables and comes to a stop right at mine.

Gavin looks between Pandora and me, his face twists in confusion. She reaches her hand out for his arm, but he slides it away, and her hand touches the table.

Pandora's eyes slide over his face and body. With a hungry curl to her lips, she says, "Gavin, so good to see you. And Linda, dear you look nice. Trace, always good to see you too."

Through clenched teeth, Gavin says, "Pandora." The muscles in his neck define.

I recall thinking how self-controlled Gavin is, everything about him is always on point. I'd speculated that if he ever lost control, it would either be a beautiful thing or earth-shattering. Just now I swear I feel the earth begin to shake below my feet.

"You two know each other?" I say.

I am praying it's a business deal gone wrong, and not that they've dated.

Pandora touches my shoulder and holds her other hand out to Gavin as if he's a prized possession. "My ex-husband."

My throat jumps up and pulls at my tongue. I'm not sure if something is swelling or constricting, but it hurts all the same. I can hardly breathe.

Gavin stands, stretches his full height, and looks down at Pandora. She is a very short woman, bone thin, but she carries herself with an attitude that makes you remember her, even see her, as being six feet tall.

"Wait." Pandora points at Gavin and then me with a long fingernail the color of blood. "Are you two? Just friends, please tell me. Are you two? Noooo, you aren't, together? Are you?" She laughs that laugh again, it's evil laced with arsenic.

Gavin's anger is near fury: pink face, hard eyes, clenched jaw. He growls, "Pandora, you need to leave."

I wonder if perhaps I should duck or jump on him so that he won't explode.

"Wait, Gavin honey, I was going to congratulate you. Nyla, well she is clearly a little out of your . . . no, I won't say it. But you have to admit it, she is, right?" Pandora looks at me, her snakelike eyes sizing me up for a meal. "You are even more stunning now. I suppose it's a bonus for you right? Makes for a beautiful story to write about."

My brain has been picked up and shaken like a snow globe. I'm trying to get the information I know is in my head to come back together so I can comprehend what is happening.

"What is that?" I ask.

"Your husband dies, so you find one that survived. I can see headlines now for the next Games. At least it won't be all about you and Lorenzo now. The press will eat this up."

My spine shakes.

Linda stands from her chair. "You need to go," she says in an intense and authoritative tone.

A car honks a happy beat, and Pandora's vindictive eyes vanish into something of a satisfied snake. Her meal now consumed.

"My husband," she says.

She leans toward me, lifts on her toes, and kisses my cheek with a pressure that is meant to say, do not forget me.

"Next time I am in town, we should get together for dinner. We can talk about," her eyes flick up to Gavin and then back to me, "what it's like."

She slithers away from our table, and all I can hear are her last words which turn my stomach like a poisoned apple: *talk about what it's like.*

I want nothing in common with that woman.

As I look up to Gavin, I think about those great plays on the one-yard line, when it could win the game and change everything. But the ball, it was just intercepted.

Game over.

CHAPTER 12

My cheek stings where Pandora kissed me. I sink down into my chair next to Linda, and Gavin takes his chair across from me. I feel horrible, but I can't bring myself to look at him. His hands reach across the table, palms up to the sky, like a man asking for forgiveness or offering salvation. I keep my hands in my lap.

Pandora's voice runs on repeat in my head, as if she is still here next to me: *great in bed, fucker survived, the press will eat this up.*

Never again do I want people writing about me and someone I care about.

Deep breaths. I look around the room for our waiter, dinner needs to come now so I can leave. Or can I go right now? My ribs hurt. I feel close to throwing up. I don't want dinner.

"Um." Linda touches her own cheek and then mine. "She left lipstick on you."

I touch my face and feel the sticky residue which transfers to my fingers, the same blood red as her nails.

"You need to go wash it off," Linda says.

I press my hand to my cheek, trying to hide the evidence, and leave the table. My feet don't feel as if they make solid contact with the earth.

The bathroom is empty, but a hand dryer still blows, and a faucet has been left on. I rip one paper towel from the dispenser, fold it several times, then wet it and suds up a drop of soap.

The red wound, a perfect outline of Pandora's narrow lips, is a stubborn stain. When I first try to wash it away, it just smears. But I'm determined to rid myself of her mark. I scrub. My cheek becomes so red I'm not sure if it's the lipstick or if I've rubbed myself raw. I stop, hoping I haven't caused damage that will still be there tomorrow, and I toss the paper towel in the garbage.

Scattered pieces of information begin to settle in my brain, though I don't think I've absorbed it. It feels like I've read a book with information that I know is important, but it is so complicated I'd need to read it three times over before I could understand a word of it.

The thing that worries me the most right now is how afraid I feel. Fear and I are not good companions. I need to leave.

Pandora's voice rattles in my brain: *yours died, so you find one that survived.*

I haven't felt this shaken in a long time, but I refuse to be Pandora's victim, or anyone's for that matter.

I close my eyes and still my body. First, I steady my breath, even inhales and exhales. Harnessing the breath is how I can control my heart rate; I slow it. My mind becomes placid. When I open my eyes, I see clearly, as if I have high-definition vision. This is my race mode, where I am in control, and here I can sustain anything, including war. Dinner should be easy.

A woman pulls open the bathroom door. I see Gavin's handsome form reflected in the mirror, leaning against the wall with his head hanging in defeat. My ribs try to separate, sending shoots of pain around my lungs. Each breath is agony, but I have to, slow and steady, despite the pain, I must breathe.

I'm shocked by how much I care for someone so new in my life, especially after everything. I should have asked more questions. How did I not know that he'd had cancer or that he was married? I thought we avoided talk of the last five years because of me . . . but was it because of him?

If I stay in here long enough will he give up?

The door opens again, this time two women laughing come in. Their steps are unsteady, either from the height of their heels or something else. Gavin sees me, his head now lifted. He stands on solid legs, arms crossed over his chest, but there is strain in his eyes. I want to save him, but I can't. I've learned I'm not capable of saving anyone.

I catch the door and walk out to him. Gavin lowers his arms and reaches for me, but I instinctively pull back. He makes no attempt to hide the sting I've caused.

"Sorry," I say.

We walk silently down to the end of the hall next to the emergency exit.

"I was getting worried about you," Gavin says.

"That lipstick was hard to remove, but I'm fine."

"I take it you didn't know?"

"I didn't know any of it."

"Please know I wasn't trying to keep anything from you, and I apologize for the shock it caused. I'd assumed, that with as long as I've known Samuel and Kevin they would have said something about my cancer, and I hoped it didn't bother you. I didn't know how to bring it up, or if I should."

"To be honest, Gavin, I haven't told either of them that we've spent time together."

Gavin and I look at each other, a stretch of silence before, he says, "I asked Samuel, out of respect, if he was comfortable with me asking you out."

This race mode of mine, the one that keeps me even and my face steady, doesn't have room for conversation. It allows me to hear the bombs that might go off around me, but I also don't feel affected by them. It all gets absorbed into a capsule that someday I'll have to sort through. But right now, this mode is only about winning, although I'm not sure what my winning outcome might be.

"Does it matter?" Gavin asks.

"What?"

"The cancer." He settles his hands on his waist, hinges forward for just a moment and then stands tall again. "I hate talking about it, Nyla, because of the way people look at me when they find out, the pity that proceeds some great declaration of 'oh it must make you realize how valuable life is.' So I don't talk about it. But I will, with you, whatever you want to know."

My heart rate becomes irregular, and my race mode threatens to falter. The only thing I can say without losing control is, "I'm sorry."

"No, no sorries, I want to hear what you're thinking, Nyla. Say it." His eyes narrow. "I never would have pictured you at a lack of words."

It's been a long time since anyone has pushed me emotionally.

Gavin squares his shoulders to mine, takes a step closer, our bodies only a foot apart, and in a calm and almost too quiet voice, he says, "Say it."

"I don't think I can."

"You can."

I can't tell if he wants to yell at me or if he has tears that need to be free, but I can't handle either here.

"I don't want to."

"Why?"

"Because there is no way to share with you what I am thinking without sounding like a complete—" I try to search for a more polite word, but there isn't one. "Bitch."

"I wouldn't ever think that of you. I've thought a lot about how hard it must be for you, after what you went through, to be willing to consider dating me. Honestly, I just had no idea you weren't looking at me from a realistic perspective."

I look down the hall, becoming very conscious of the activity around us. "I don't want to talk about this here. Can we just go back in and have dinner?"

"May we finish this conversation at my house?"

"Your—" My car is in his garage. "Yes."

As I walk back to the table, I feel the slime trail Pandora has left on the floor, on me, and I see it on Gavin.

"Oh good it came off," Linda says. "How do you know her?"

To protect these new relationships I'd not mentioned pieces of me—wife, widow, a life altered by cancer. It's no use now. Past, present, future, it's all me.

"My husband, Lorenzo, had a close friend that she dated for a long time. I've spent a fair amount of time with her, but it's been eight years since I've seen her."

"She's a witch," Linda says and lays her hand on Gavin's. "I told you not to marry her. She's filled with mean bones, not a nice one in there."

"Yes, I remember. Mistakes made and rectified as far as I can through the divorce."

Trace, who's been so silent I almost forgot he was here, gives a firm pat on Gavin's shoulder. "We all make mistakes in life," he says to Gavin, though his eyes are on me.

As much as I want to reach out and touch Gavin, to reassure him that I care, I need to be realistic about what I'm capable of. Right now I can only act in a way that allows me to keep my composure, to show the face the world knows so well: cool, calm, collected.

As we walk out of the restaurant silence settles between Gavin and me, but what he doesn't let continue is the space between us. He reaches for my hand and laces his fingers into mine. I don't want to be rude by pulling away, but I also don't tighten my fingers any more than necessary to keep my hand from slipping from his.

"I don't want to cause you pain," Gavin says, "but really, I'm as healthy as a horse."

"Are horses healthy?"

"So they say."

In his truck, I turn up the music and drop my head back against the headrest with my eyes closed. I need to come out of race mode, which isn't easy. It's like wiggling out of a wet swimsuit a size too small. There aren't a lot of people I'd do this for, bare my feelings, but Gavin needs to see me. It's the only way he'll understand what I cannot, and will not, put myself through again.

•••

When we get to Gavin's house, he gets out quickly and runs around to open my door. We walk next to each other, but I stop when we are equal distance to the garage and the house.

"Will you come in?" he asks.

I shake my head and then quietly say, "No."

The hope in Gavin's face melts into something I'm sure few people have ever seen. I hadn't realized he, too, had been wearing a mask of composure. The strength he'd shown me in the hallway, then the air of calm that he sat with at the table and rode home in silence with is gone. Now, standing before me is a man in pain.

I want to comfort him. I want to hold him. I want to tell him it doesn't matter. But it does, all of it, so I keep my distance.

The summer air is still. Daylight is slipping.

"You are a great man. This has nothing to do with you, and everything to do with me. With my past."

He shakes his head. "Nyla."

"Watching Lorenzo die shredded me. I've stitched myself back together well enough for how I live my life now. But I am not healed in a way that allows me to be ready for someone as amazing as you."

"Because I had cancer?"

"I haven't dated anyone since him." I try to smile with reassurance. "You are the first man I have felt any attraction to, and it's a lot of attraction. It pains me, makes me feel guilty actually with how much I do like you. But now, this fear is flooding me. Knowing what I do now, the cancer and her. Gavin, she is not a nice person, and I didn't even know you'd been married."

"I didn't realize it would matter. The cancer I couldn't help, and you are going to hold it against me. And the ex-wife, she was a horrible mistake, one I can't change now. And none of this affects you at all, or who I am now today."

I shake my head. "Gavin. You and I, we can be—"

"Don't say it, please."

He takes a step forward. I take a step back.

"Seriously," I say, "nothing has happened. And I am a good friend. I'll never forget your birthday, I bake cookies, not at the holidays because I am working too much, but lots of other times. I'm usually up for a movie, always up for watching football, although I am not fun to watch football with because of this horrible compulsive play-by-play thing."

"You certainly aren't making a case for being just friends."

"Sometimes my cookies, they aren't so good. So I'm that friend that bakes shitty cookies and wants you to like them. I fall asleep during movies, and I probably snore. Football, did I mention I do this really annoying play-by-play thing? All great for being friends. The other thing is, I'm never home."

"I am a very patient man."

"I can tell. Can't you make this easy for me?"

"What exactly is this about? Is it just that you don't want to date me because of the cancer? Is it because I made an awful decision to marry her? What?"

"How long has it been since you had cancer?" The question flies out of my mouth, and I don't even know where it came from.

He searches the air quickly for an answer. "I was diagnosed four years ago, and cancer-free for three."

My body shudders. It is a ghostly overlay of Lorenzo's own battle, although, he never got a cancer-free date. This understanding drains the last of my energy and cements my resolve.

Gently I say, "I can't go through that again."

"What if I promised if I get sick again, even with the flu, because you know that's deadly sometimes, too, that I'll let you go."

"You'd ghost me?"

"I don't know what that means."

"It just means that . . . never mind, it doesn't matter. Why are we even having this conversation? No, this isn't an option for me. You're amazing, Gavin, and you deserve a woman who can put you first. I am not whole enough for what you need in your life."

"From where I am standing, you seem pretty whole to me."

Patient and persistent he is.

"I really don't want you to hate me, but I really cannot date you," I say.

"I have a solution."

"What?"

He hesitates as a shy but hopeful smile spreads on his face. "We could skip it all, and just get married."

My heart thumps so hard it feels like a defibrillator has been placed on my chest. I want to go back into race mode, for a million different reasons, I cannot do this.

Trying to keep it light, and not let the internal battle show, I say, "Wow. Then that would make the whole ghosting thing super inappropriate."

"I still don't know what ghosting is. Like, disappear?"

"Yes, it's when you're dating someone and it seems to be going okay, but then suddenly they just stop responding."

"That isn't ghosting, that's just poor manners."

For the first time in hours I laugh, and it feels good. I like everything about Gavin—his personality, his intelligence, his body. But what I've learned tonight carries so much more weight than all of the goodness in the world.

"I can't, Gavin. I am so sorry."

The tremble in his chin causes my bones to release tiny shards into my bloodstream inflicting pain in every part of my body. I know if I show him how he affects me it might make both of us cry. And then, I wouldn't be able to leave him.

"May I get my car? I need to get some rest before tomorrow."

"I don't want you to go."

"I can't do this. Tomorrow will require me to show up on point, to stand on a stage and talk with people happy and composed. I have to be 110% for these kinds of events. If I stay here and continue this conversation, I won't be able to do my job. Please."

We look into each other's eyes. A cold evening breeze presses my shirt tight against my body. I hear the scurrying of some small forest creature. Gavin refuses to look away, so I do, up to the rustling leaves of a tree above me where one breaks free.

"Please," I say.

Hesitantly Gavin walks to the garage, flips up the cover over a number pad, punches four digits in, and slams it shut.

"Your keys," his voice cracks, "are in the car." A tear slips down his cheek.

I keep a small distance between our bodies as I cup the side of his face and wipe a tear away with my thumb. "Thank you for everything you've done for me. It's far more than you realize. You're an extraordinary human."

It isn't easy to drive away, but I do without looking back. I don't allow a single thought to enter my head until I pull into my driveway. A steady stream floods in then. That's when I remember that Gavin is supposed to pick me up tomorrow.

On my front porch is a package. I slice the tape open with my key and find inside the running shoes I ordered to replace the stolen ones. I carry them to my SUV and open the back. There is a medium-sized cloth box. Inside is a note that reads, "Just a few things that you should always have in your car. Yours, Gavin."

There are two pairs of leather gloves (one pair is a woman's large, the other is a man's extra-large), an ice scraper with a brush on it, a roll of shop paper towels, jumper cables, duct tape, tire sealant, four bottles of water, and a box of granola bars.

Not sure exactly how to handle this, I decide to err on the side of kindness because I can't bear causing Gavin any more pain, even if I can't see it. I send him a text message, "Thank you for keeping me well prepared and safe with the things you put in my car. You're sweet."

Thoroughly wrung out from the day, I crawl into my bed and just as my body sinks down into sleep my phone buzzes. I'm not going to look at the message, but I can't stop myself.

Gavin replies, "I try. Just to be clear, I intend to be around should any of those things need to be used. It's just so we wouldn't need to walk to my truck again. I'll see you tomorrow at three."

CHAPTER 13

Several months ago I was out for a stroll and happened to pass a small vintage shop. In the window a dress made of ivory lace with a rose-colored silk underlay reminded me of elegance from the early 1920s. I had no use for it, but it called to me, so I went in to try it on. It fit like it was fashioned for me, even the length, which never happens. That beautiful dress has hung in a gray garment bag in the back of my closet since I purchased it, but tonight I'm going to wear it to the gala.

As I remove the dress from the bag, I feel it again, like it's always been mine. It makes me wonder about reincarnation, maybe it was mine in another lifetime? I slip it over my head. The weight of the lace and silk easily settle into place over my curves. It has an elegant open back with a zipper that starts just above the fullest part of my backside and ends at my waist. It's secured with three pearl buttons which take some effort to hook. A delicate tract of lace just below my shoulder blades also closes with three pearls, but I can only get one of these hooked, just enough to keep it on me for now. Everything else about the dress is simple: sleeveless with thin straps, modest neckline, a hem that floats just above the floor.

This afternoon my hair stylist worked my hair into an elaborate and full braid that wraps from one side of my head to the other, then cascades over my shoulder. I did my makeup very simple, almost like I'm not wearing anything. I'd planned to top it with red lipstick, but the moment I looked at the color a shiver ran through me, and I tossed it into the trash. It's a color I'll never wear again. The lip gloss I have will work just fine.

In this dress with my hair braided and pinned to perfection and the simplicity of my makeup I feel that my feminine beauty is a tool, much in the way a superhero has a special power.

As I carry my white heels down the stairs holding my dress up, so I don't trip on the hem, my doorbell rings. I've firmly decided that I will enjoy this evening with Gavin, as I would any friend, but I will not let it progress further. At the end of the night, once I have done my job well and can think again, I'll explain to him all of the reasons why he deserves more than I can give him.

I open the door to a man who possesses his own superpower: masculinity perfected. My attraction to him is something I don't understand. I hope I don't look as thrown off balance as I feel.

Gavin hands me a bouquet of red roses, at least two dozen, then openly sweeps my body, bottom to top, like I am a rare piece of artwork. "Nature perfected," he says.

I open my mouth, but nothing comes out. What is it

about Gavin Boston that's already thrown my mind into such a flutter? Did he just happen to arrive at the right time in my life, when I craved some connection? Or, is it him?

Gavin follows me into the kitchen where I get a vase from the sideboard and carry it to the sink. He leans back against the kitchen counter and watches me.

"Your silence is unnerving," he says.

Something about him feels different. I sense a determination. Luckily for both of us, I'm a rather determined woman as well.

"Thank you for the flowers." I set the roses in the vase and smell two buds. "They are lovely, though not as lovely as you are handsome."

I carry the flowers into the living room and set them on the table between the couch and chair, then I walk toward Gavin. The weight of my dress hugs the curves of my thighs as I move, Gavin looks at them, and his throat bobs.

"Would you mind?" I turn my back to him. "Buttoning me in?"

He says nothing. I feel nothing. I begin to turn around, but his hand splays over the deepest curve of my back stilling me. He fastens the top two buttons which snugs the bodice like a second skin.

Gavin's knuckles graze the muscles along the side of my spine as if we have nowhere we need to go. "That dress, your hair . . . you. Dear God, you are the most beautiful woman I have ever seen. I mean that, genuinely."

His voice is like a potion that begs my surrender. I want to tell him just how handsome he looks, that I've seen a lot of tuxes in my day, but the way he wears it is so different. It's tailored to perfection, not a wrinkle, and complementary to the size of him. I can't though because my only focus tonight is to ensure that the gala is a success.

I walk past him toward my front door and tap the ivory bow tie that matches my dress. "You can't talk to me like that. I won't be able to concentrate on anything else."

Gavin grins mischievously, and says, "Talk to you like what?"

He holds his hand out to help steady me as I slip my heels on, then I stand tall and find with this extra height we are almost eye level.

"You know what," I say.

"Yes, I do. But, I'd sure like to hear it from your lips."

I pick up my clutch and open the door for him. As he passes by, I choose to look at him as if there were no limits or pasts that will keep us apart. I know he has more secrets, he's a man filled with them; and me, I have a few of my own.

•••

We pull up to the Portland Art Museum and a valet moves toward my door, but Gavin says, "I got it, please," and hurries around. I appreciate his help because getting in and out of his truck in my dress isn't easy. He keeps hold of my hand as we walk into the museum where Linda meets us near the entrance.

"You two are unbelievably good looking, both individually and together," Linda says. "You even coordinated your dress and tie."

"That was a coincidence," Gavin says.

"Was it? Perhaps meant to be," Linda says.

Trace gives Gavin a friendly slap on the back, then they shake hands and half hug. I see the silent conversation between the two close men, one that concludes with a somewhat happy smile on Gavin's face.

Across the room is a large banner that reads, "The Starlight Hope Foundation. Helping cancer patients and families through challenging times." It isn't that I forgot, but it's a shaking reminder that I was a cancer patient's family, and Gavin was a cancer patient, though our experiences were separate. I hear Pandora's silky voice in my head: *yours dies, so you find one that survives.*

Linda loops her arm into mine. "You'll have to let her go for a little while," she says to Gavin.

"What if I don't want to?" he says.

Gently I draw my hand away from Gavin and follow Linda's lead to a man who says, "She has arrived." A lanyard that reads "press" hangs from his neck. He has two female assistants with him; one carries a bag on her shoulder and a camera in each hand while the other has lighting.

Linda says, "Nyla, this is Pablo. He's doing the photos for the foundation tonight."

"Nice to finally meet you. If you are ready, I'd like to get a couple of you ladies with your husbands first before we lose them to the bar."

"You can get one with her husband," I say.

Pablo looks beyond me, then I feel a hand on my waist.

"Your date then?" Pablo says.

"Date?" I say. "Nah, I just paid him to hang out with me and look good."

"Her date, at least," Gavin says with a heat in his voice that makes me look at his eyes.

There is need, desire, and a touch of desperation in his beautiful green orbs that reaches my soul and makes me want to soothe him. A flash goes off. I already know it would be best if no one ever sees that photo.

"Perfect," Pablo says. "Turn toward him, hand further around on her hip so it doesn't look like a creepy hand that can't commit."

"No creepy hands," I say.

Gavin pulls me tight to him, and in my ear, he whispers, "I only have hands that commit."

We walk down to the ballroom which is decorated in the gala theme, Wish Upon A Star. Light projectors shoot stars across the walls, all of the cloth in the room is midnight blue, and on stage is a quartet that fills the room with the magic of strings.

It has been a long time since I've entered a crowded room on the arm of a man, and Gavin is so exquisite I'm not sure if people are looking at him or me. I'd venture to say quite honestly it's him. So far not a single piece of artwork I've passed by in this museum is enough to keep my eyes from finding their way back to him.

A man with a head of pure white hair approaches us. "Fran," Gavin says and shakes his hand. "Allow me to introduce you to Nyla Tripple."

"An honor," Fran says with a head tilt. "I don't know why, Gavin, but I had thought you were a single man. Clearly no."

We both laugh, but neither denies. Fortunately, the conversation goes straight to Gavin's project. This is the first time I see him talk about his work with someone else. His excitement is enough to make anyone feel the same way he does about designing and constructing buildings. It makes me feel in awe of him.

Across the room, Pop waives at me which breaks my attention from Gavin.

"Gentlemen," I say, "if you'll excuse me."

Gavin holds my hand. "I'll go with you."

"No, no you two talk." I pat Gavin's arm. "I'm headed backstage in just a few minutes, but I want to say hi to Pop before everything gets going. It was wonderful to meet you, Fran."

"Little Foot!" Pop says. He picks up a glass from the bar, whiskey on the rocks, his go-to. "What a beautiful dress, you look adorable."

"I stopped going for adorable at ten, Pop."

"You'll always be adorable to me. To other eyes," he nods in Gavin's direction, "you appear to be something else entirely."

I glance back at Gavin who is watching me over Fran's shoulder. A drip of nausea passes through my belly as I think of yesterday when Gavin contemplated whether or not to tell me that Pop already knows something about us. I'd like to ask Pop about this, but I know now is not the right time. It will have to wait until tomorrow when he comes over for Sunday football.

"We arrived together," I say.

"Together, as in a date?"

"Perhaps as friends."

"Perhaps?" He chuckles. "He's a good man."

"Yes, Pop, he is."

Pop groans as he hands me a wine glass. "To ease the things you do not show, but still exist. Sometimes I think that a dozen shooting stars would not move you enough to show some real emotion."

"I show emotion."

"Not much aside from this. Just like your mother. Always cool and calm despite the storms in and around. I, however, can see a little deeper into your eyes than most."

When mother was alive, Pop made comparisons like this with a big smile, but since she passed these reminders seem to make him sad.

Linda joins us, and says, "Good evening, Mr. Tripple. May I steal your daughter?"

"You may. I think I'll go say hi to Gavin."

•••

Backstage I set my wine glass down on a small table. Drinking just before I walk out on stage is not a good idea for me. I peek between two curtains. From up here, the room looks massive and the crowd larger.

"There you are," Gavin says.

I pull the panels back together.

"How are you feeling?" he asks.

"Nervous."

The stage manager, Tad, walks up to us, and says, "Two minutes."

"I'm ready," I say to Tad, then to Gavin, "You should go get your seat."

"Do you think a hug would help?" Gavin asks.

"With what?"

"To make you feel less nervous."

"Do hugs help you feel less nervous?"

"It's been a long time since someone has hugged me when I'm nervous."

"Do you get nervous?"

"Sometimes."

I slip my arms around Gavin's ribs below his jacket, and he wraps his arms around me. I love the way the fabric of his suit feels on my back. My breath shutters involuntarily as I take a deep breath to steady myself. His scent soothes me; standing on the edge of a flowing river.

"Ready?" Tad says.

"Have fun," Gavin says.

My nerves are not gone, but I do feel more calm.

I step between the panels of the curtains I'd peeked through earlier and look out to the crowd. "Good evening!" I say into the microphone.

When I ran competitively, I'd be nervous right up until I set my feet into the starting blocks and pressed my hands onto the track, but then I felt light and focused on the only task at hand. I have a similar experience now as I look out into the sea of well-dressed women and men.

"I would like to welcome all of you beautiful humans to the Starlight Hope Foundation gala. My name is Nyla Tripple, and I am your grateful emcee for the night.

"Linda Smith, the spectacular woman who put this entire event together tonight, reached out to me a few months back and asked me to join you. It warmed my heart to be called upon for such an honor because not only do I genuinely believe in this foundation, I am also a direct beneficiary of it.

"When I was in college, just entering into the world's competitive running stage, I met a man named Lorenzo. He wooed me, then married me, making me the luck- iest woman in the world. Together we lived life to the max. We traveled, had tons of great adventures, and just when we thought life couldn't get any better, Lorenzo was diagnosed with leukemia.

"I was making an okay living as a runner, and he was doing well as a writer, but we had a crummy health insur- ance policy because you never think you'll need one when you're young. Three hurdles we faced. The first was that while we made a good living, it wasn't enough to cover the bills it takes to keep someone alive. Second, navigating the medical world is hard. Third, the emotional side is very challenging to deal with, even if most days are good."

I've never cried in public, but I feel my eyes welling, and to keep them from slipping I look up at the ceiling.

"The Starlight Hope Foundation helped us a lot. They taught us about the medical system, and I don't think I could have figured this out without them." I pat my hand over my heart. "And they provided counseling while Lorenzo was in treatment and for me after, because getting left behind is hard. It's because of you, all of you, that I was able to get the help I needed. Thank you. And it's because of you that the foundation can continue to help hundreds of people every single year."

After going over the evening's time line, I go back behind the curtain where Linda is waiting for me. She throws her arms around me. "I didn't know that."

"I didn't mean to make you cry, but I did want everyone to see someone they helped."

CHAPTER 14

After talking about Lorenzo and our marriage, it seems strange that I came here with another man. I remember why for most of the last four years I never wanted to date again; I'm still very much in love with my husband.

I exit the stage opposite of where my table is and proceed to the back of the room, giving myself as much time as possible before I have to face Gavin again.

People share their cancer journeys with me as if they are in the confessional and need absolution. I answer questions about Lorenzo, his battle, my loss. But it isn't all sad. There is a lot of joy as people proudly tell me their triumphant stories of survival and the years they have been cancer free.

A woman with tight brown curls and wise eyes stands and takes my hands in hers like we are great friends that have been on a journey together. "My husband died right at the same time as yours. I felt alone in my grief like no one could understand what it is to lose a soul mate. Then one night I was watching a program, and you said, 'The emptiness I feel is the vastness of the universe, something that can never be filled.' It was exactly how I felt and knowing I wasn't the only one made me not feel so alone. Thank you."

We share a silent moment, two widows looking into each other's eyes. I can see the struggle she'd endured, but I also see a spark.

"Thank you for sharing. It means a lot to me," I say.

A man reaches up from his seat at the table and rubs her back. I am happy to see she'd not allowed the emptiness to keep her.

This is why I've shared as much as I have because if I can help one person feel a little less alone, it is worth it, whatever it cost me.

After another round of announcements on stage, I return to the floor and walk to Gavin who is now alone at the table. He stands and pulls out the chair next to him where the place setting has not been touched.

"Sit and relax," Gavin says. "I'll be right back." He follows a waiter through the crowd.

Pop sits next to me and hands me a new glass of wine. "I wish I didn't know the pain of losing a spouse, but seeing your pain is worse than feeling my own."

"I'm all right, Pop."

Pop looks past me, I can tell by the look in his eyes Gavin is returning. He leans close. "Do you think it's easy to be the next one?" he says quietly, then he lifts his voice, "Oh good man, Gavin, I was just going to try to find her a plate myself." Pop leaves us alone at the table.

Neither of us talks as I eat quickly, though I can't help but think that like so many here Gavin, too, has a story of survival. While I'd like to ask him about it, he looks so happy right now that I don't want to bring it up.

I set down my fork. "I can't possibly eat another bite."

"Now you should have enough energy to dance," Gavin says.

"You've been misinformed. I do not dance."

"Don't dance? Someone so confident on their feet, you must."

"No, not me. I've stepped on too many toes to count. I prefer to save myself—and you, for that matter—the embarrassment."

"May I take my chances?"

I drain the last of my wine. "No."

Undeterred, Gavin stands, takes both of my hands, and guides me to my feet. I don't even realize how far he leads me until we are in the middle of the dance floor. Then we're moving together.

"You don't dance?" he says.

"We are dancing like seventh graders rocking back and forth. Sure I can do this."

"Are you saying my skills are elementary?"

"No, middle school. That's okay, that is what my—"

Gavin lifts one of my hands, puts my other on his shoulder, and sets his hand on my bare back. I know enough about dancing to understand that the pressure of the hand on my back is a cue for movement. Usually, however, my feet don't respond in time for anything to look graceful. But Gavin seems capable of moving me not just with the pressure of his hand, but in the other places our bodies touch—hips, thighs, chest.

"I will have you know," Gavin says. "I took ballroom dancing in college."

"Is that so?"

"It is, and I passed."

"Did you do that to meet girls?"

"No. I did it so that one day I could dazzle a beautiful woman."

"Did it work?"

"I don't know. Is it?"

The stoic man I've seen all night peels back the layers, and in his eyes, I see a man that is vulnerable. A desire to connect with him beyond my physical body flushes through me. These are feelings I never wanted again. I open my mouth to say something and find every word catches in an invisible filter.

"You're breaking my heart," Gavin says.

He draws me closer to his body, the space between absorbed by us. I let my head lower onto his shoulder, eyes turned toward his heart, so mine won't have to avoid his. I can't let him see how scared I am. I can't let anyone see.

Tonight will be harder than I anticipated.

•••

The moment I buckle myself into Gavin's truck I take my shoes off. We danced so much my feet hurt.

"Are you tired?" Gavin asks.

"You made me dance a lot. And I don't normally do that."

"At least five people told me they'd never seen you dance."

"That would be true. The last time I danced was . . ."

"Your wedding. Samuel told me."

There is a duel inside of me, half wants him desperately, and the other half knows that the end of the evening will be the end of something that almost started.

Gavin reaches across and sets his hand on my thigh, turns his hand up and opens it for mine. I indulge in the pleasure of our fingers as they slide into place between one another because this will be the last I get.

At my house, Gavin follows me to my front door, and he accepts my unspoken invitation to come in. He runs his hand down my arm as he passes by me into the house.

I look at the clock on the wall of my living room. It's nearly midnight, the time when it seems fairy tales burst into the truth of the situation.

"Would you like a cup of tea?" I ask.

"I would appreciate that."

"Caffeine-free or do you need a little something to help with the drive home?"

"No caffeine for me after six or I don't sleep."

I turn on the electric tea kettle in the kitchen and get out two mugs. Back in the living room I find Gavin, face serious, hands in his pockets, and gaze fixed on the window which is dark.

"Do you mind if I change?" I ask.

At the end of the night, the dress that made one feel like a million bucks suddenly feels heavy, the bra that lifted the breasts with confidence feels too tight, and the elegant hair is now too structured.

"You are incredibly beautiful," he says.

I turn my back to him. "Would you unbutton me?"

It wasn't right, but I do need the help, and selfishly I want to feel his touch one last time on my back.

Gavin does not hesitate. He unfastens the three buttons at the top of the zipper, slides his knuckles up my back, and unbuttons the three at the top. I press the bodice of the dress to my chest and walk up the stairs without looking back, but I feel the warmth of his eyes on me.

My breath doesn't return until I close the door to my bedroom. I slide off my dress and bra, then lay them on an old chair in the corner, something I picked up at a flea market. I wash the makeup from my face and unbraid my hair. After I throw on an oversized cream T-shirt and a pair of cotton shorts, I look nothing like the woman who'd danced only an hour ago. I am, once again, me. With this transformation, the magic of the night fades into the reality of my past, present, and what needs to be done for the future.

In the living room, Gavin has shed as much of the formal wear as he can. His jacket and bow tie are laid neatly on the arm of the couch, and the top three buttons of his shirt are undone. By the front door, next to my running shoes, are his shiny black Oxfords. The bright green socks with ivory dots on his feet make me smile.

"Are you comfortable?" I ask.

"Yes."

I make two cups of chamomile tea and carry them back into the living room where I collapse onto the couch and stretch my legs out to the coffee table. Gavin looks between the sofa and the chair where he'd laid his stuff. He seems like he might ask me something, but instead, he sits next to me so close we touch. He looks at my feet and then up to me.

"Do you want to talk now?" I ask.

"Aren't you tired?"

"Yes, but I told you I'd talk tonight after the gala, and I think we should."

"Is it a different conversation from what started at my house yesterday?"

I shake my head no.

"Then I don't want to talk about it. I'd rather sit here in silence drinking tea in our close proximity because you don't seem to reject me as long as we don't talk about it. In fact, I think you rather like me."

"That's avoidance."

"I've been accused of worse. Do you blame me though?"

I set my mug down on the table and adjust on the couch so that I can look at him, then pull my knees into my chest and wrap my arms around them, but this makes me feel closed off, so I adjust again, sitting cross-legged. My knees are on his thigh, and I consider backing up, but I don't.

"Comfortable?" he asks.

"I enjoy spending time with you, Gavin, and I'd really like to be friends."

He sips his tea. "Are you suggesting friends that actually spend time together or friends that just say hi when they pass by each other in life?"

"I guess that is up to you."

He looks at me with abandon, like he would never hide anything from me. "It isn't. Because if it were up to me, we would be continuing on the trajectory we were on yesterday until 'she' happened. Frankly, the way everything felt tonight was perfect like it didn't even happen yesterday. If you're changing things, then it's up to you to tell me what you want. And, if you really just want to be friends you can't look at me like that."

"Like what?" I say, even though I have a good idea. Everything about my physical form reacts to him without my permission. When we dance it feels like I'm programmed to follow his lead. My hand reaches for his when he's near. Our eyes, no matter if I'm in his arms or across the room, find each other. How do I change this when it's all done without thought?

"Do you really want me to tell you what I see? Just to be clear, I love when you look at me like that, but everything in my body wants you when you do. And if we are friends, and that's all you want, we have to keep some lines here."

Not sure how to look at him any other way I lower my gaze to the mug in his broad hands. There's one long scar across the back of his left hand that must be old because it's the color of his skin.

Gavin says, "May I ask again though, why? Is it the cancer? Her?"

"Both."

"Both . . . I don't get it."

I wasn't going to ask him, but it just flies from my mouth, "Why did you marry her? I just don't understand how a man as kind and wonderful as you ended up with her. She is not a good person, and you are."

Gavin lets out a frustrated breath. "Nyla, does it matter?"

"I guess not."

He taps the side of his mug, drinks the rest of the tea, and says, "I'd been seeing her on and off, and by that I mean not much context to the relationship, if you know what I mean."

My stomach rolls. I wouldn't have thought Gavin was this kind of guy.

"I got her pregnant. I didn't want to have a baby born into a broken home or a nonexistent one, so I married her quickly before we told anyone about the baby. It was stupid because everyone knew there was an elephant in the room. We lost the baby when she was seven months along."

I place my hand over the scar on his. "I'm so sorry."

While our experiences are different, I do understand his pain.

"It was hard, but I feel it worked out as it was supposed to. She didn't want the baby, said it regularly. Nothing about us worked anywhere outside of the—" He looks up at me surprised by what he was about to say.

Pandora's similar declaration mingles with his in my head. The attraction I feel disappears like a snuffed out flame. I withdraw my hand from his and reach for my mug on the table.

"I got sick two months later. When it looked like I wasn't going to make it, she said it was too much for her and left. We never loved each other."

"That must have been hard, to go through all of that with someone you didn't love."

"Someone I didn't trust, but it was my fault. I should never have gotten involved with her."

I slide my feet back out to the coffee table and recline on the couch looking up at the ceiling.

"I'd never been in a casual relationship like that before, and I'll never do it again. She is the biggest mistake of my life, and it set off the worst couple of years in my life."

We're both quiet. I let my eyes close and try to absorb what he's said.

"Are you going to say anything?" Gavin asks.

"I'm tired."

"That isn't fair. Tell me what you're thinking."

"I'm glad you survived, Gavin."

"Who's avoiding now? Look, if you don't want to see me anymore because I'm a jerk, you think I'm not a good guy tell me. But it isn't fair to not give me a chance because I had cancer or because I tried to do the right thing a long time before I met you."

"It's more complicated than that. Can you possibly look at it from where I'm coming from?"

"I have, and I know I probably don't look that appealing to you. But you should see the way you look at me. I know you want what I do."

"To have sex?" I ask with a laugh.

"It's more than that . . . far more."

I stand and pace. "Gavin, I am not kidding. Stitched I might be, but I have not healed all the way and knowing this, all of this, makes me feel like being with you will pull my stitches too tight. I don't want to break. I won't risk it. I will not go through something like what I went through with Lorenzo again. And I do not want to have anything in common with Pandora."

Gavin presses his hands to his knees and stands. He grabs his tux jacket like a used napkin. "Perhaps I'm pathetic, but I'll take whatever you are willing to give me. Even if that is just friends. But I'm frustrated right now, and I need to go."

Why do I care so much for him? Why do I want to be the one that sticks around and ensures that no one ever hurts him again or that if he's going through tough times that he's not alone? I cross my arms over my chest. I want to cry. I want to hold Gavin. But I won't.

I follow him out the front door and stop on the porch.

He walks down the stairs, stops at the bottom, and turns back to me. "Thank you for being my date tonight. In spite of this," his hands lift in frustration and then fall like lead, "I really enjoyed the time with you. And even though you don't think you can dance, you are a great dancer. You shouldn't doubt your abilities, in anything."

"I'm sorry."

"I suppose we all have to decide if the risks are worth the reward." His chest lifts with a deep breath, and as it rushes from him, he says, "I'm sorry that I'm not. Goodnight, Nyla."

CHAPTER 15

My eyes open to a new day, and the first thing I feel is the smothering of guilt. It isn't just the things that I said at the end of the night. It was the whole night. I knew what I would say at the end, and yet I allowed myself to lead Gavin on, to give him hope. After everything he did for me last week, how gentle and caring he has been, my actions have not shown the kindness he deserves. There is a sense of desperation to keep him in my life, to be his friend. Gavin is all I think about as I run, and get ready for the day. I want to do something to atone for my actions.

"Morning, Little Foot," Pop hollers from the front door. He joins me in the kitchen and sets down a grocery sack on the counter next to the fridge. "What are you making?"

"Cookies. For Gavin, and us of course."

"Gavin eh? What kind?"

"Peanut butter."

"Good thing I brought extra chips and dip. What time will he be here?"

"Who?"

"Gavin."

"I didn't invite him over for football. I'm just going to drop these off at his house later, or by his office tomorrow."

"That's surprising. I thought for sure after how happy you were dancing together last night he'd at least get invited to Sunday football." Pop opens a drawer and pulls out a bottle opener. On Sunday, it's never too early for a beer. "What did you do?"

I grin guiltily at Pop. "What do you mean, what did I do?"

"You both seemed wrapped up in each other last night. But now you didn't even invite him to watch football, and you're baking him apology cookies."

I roll tablespoons of dough between my hands and arrange them on the cookie sheet.

"They aren't apology cookies."

"Little Foot?" he says like a parent.

"Pop, why didn't you tell me?"

"Tell you what?"

"That he had cancer?"

He shrugs like it isn't a big deal. "Well, I didn't know for sure what was, or is, going on between you two. Besides, it doesn't matter that he had cancer. Does it?"

"Of course it does."

"Why?" Pop sits onto a barstool on the other side of the counter and plucks a dough ball from the cookie sheet. "He's a guy that had cancer. Had."

I think about mentioning his ex, that I know her, but I decide not to.

"You know his wife left him when he was sick?" Pop says. "What kind of woman does that? I met her twice, and I haven't a clue what he saw in her, aside from her looks."

I've thought about her looks too. She's a drop-dead gorgeous blond bombshell. She and I look nothing alike, and I'd like to think I'm kinder than her, although I'm not sure if I am right now.

"Ugh, Pop. Come on."

"Why does it matter?"

"It just does," I snap. "I'll be Gavin's friend, but that is it. That is why I am baking him cookies. These are sorry I can only be your friend cookies."

He narrows his eyes at me. "What are you talking about?"

"I can't explain it. I just can't."

Pop commands, "Try."

"You know how hard it is to get left behind—"

"I hate when you say that. Lorenzo did not leave you. His death wasn't about you. Your mother dying wasn't about me. Was it?"

"No."

Pop rarely gets emotional, but his voice shakes, and he presses his hands flat on the counter. "Life expires, Nyla. Someday you will too."

"Don't say that."

"It's true. You should be thankful you got warning it was about to end. Your mother was just ripped away, fine one day and gone the next. You got time to say that you loved Lorenzo, that he was your world. Can't you just be thankful for that?"

My lips yank into a frown. "I am thankful. But I can't go through it again. I can't lose again. I'm not strong enough."

"If someone had asked you before you married Lorenzo if you'd be strong enough to survive his passing what would you have said?"

"No."

"If you'd known Lorenzo would die before you, so young, would you have decided not to marry him?"

"No! But that doesn't mean I want to put myself in a situation where I'll have to repeat a loss. And I know it's not a guarantee, but the risk is higher with Gavin, and I will not do it again. I want to die first next time."

My own words, which shock me, make Pop's face soften with empathy.

"Sweet Little Foot, are you going to rule out any guy that's had a health problem? Because as you get older, that is going to limit your pool drastically. And he is such a good person, and you both obviously like each other."

"Why do you want me to date him so badly?"

"I want to see you happy."

"I am just fine."

"Your mother's passing has made me think about my mortality. I think every parent wants to know their kids are well cared for and loved before they are gone. That's all I want. Look you don't have to marry Gavin Boston, but he looks like a man that wants to spend time with you, and you're lying to yourself about what you want as well. Spend time with him. Don't worry about if he gets cancer. You don't even know if you want to keep him long enough to find out. Maybe, I don't know, spending time with him will open you up to meeting the right person."

"What if I end up wanting to keep him? How do you know if it's worth the risk?"

"If I could have one more day with your mother, but that's it, I'd take it. Despite the pain of losing her all over again, I'd take the joy and love we had for a day in exchange for a thousand painful ones. When it's right, it's worth it. Silence your fear long enough to hear your answer."

Pop leaves me alone in the kitchen. I flatten the dough balls with the bottom of a glass. Then I use a fork to create a criss-cross pattern in the top and sprinkle them with sugar. After putting the cookies in the oven, I go into the living room. I push the coffee table out of the way and sit on the floor with a notepad and a pen so that I can make notes of the games we watch.

"Call him," Pop says. "Either you do, or I will."

"You need to stay out of it," I say with a grumble.

"You need a push I think. Remember, Pop knows best."

I'm not sure about anything with Gavin, but as I quiet the fears of the possible ways things can go awry, I realize that maybe Pop is right. What if I only have a year left on this earth? Would I choose to spend some of it with Gavin? Besides, if all I'm looking for is a little creature comfort, what does any of this matter? There's no harm in being kind, welcoming even.

I send Gavin a text message, "Watching Sunday football today. Would you like to join us? (Pop a.k.a. Samuel is here.) You're welcome anytime."

Gavin's reply is almost immediate, "I'd love to. Be there soon. Thank you."

After the first game finishes, I go back into the kitchen and transfer the cooled cookies to a rack and roll more dough balls. I hear the front door open, then the deep voices of Gavin and Pop talking, although I can't understand what they say.

Gavin comes into the kitchen, and the second I look up, the attraction I feel for him is even stronger. I think he feels it too.

"The house smells amazing," Gavin says. "Please tell me I smell peanut butter cookies."

"You do."

"You know, they are my favorite."

"I didn't, but duly noted. And that's good because they're for you."

"For me?" He sets down two cloth grocery sacks.

"They say the quickest way to a man's heart is through his belly." It flies out of my mouth. It wasn't even something I'd thought before.

He smiles and stands behind me, sets his hands on my hips, his lips next to my ear. "Are you trying to get to my heart?"

"I might be trying to get to other things."

"You're teasing me," he says, although he doesn't sound like he really minds.

I lean back into his chest and close my eyes. I quiet my fears. My intuition tells me he is worth the risk.

"May I have one?" he asks.

"Baked or unbaked?"

"The one in your hand."

I turn in his arms, he opens his mouth, and I feed it to him. My fingers brush his lips and those pieces of me I know he's capable of bringing back to life flicker.

"I'm sorry about last night," I say. "It's just a lot to process."

"I hadn't given up, I was just going to give you a little space to think things through and come to your senses."

"Oh yeah? Come to my senses?"

"You know how you're looking at me?"

"Yes, I am well aware, but I need to take things slow to make sure we actually like each other."

"We like each other, but like I said last night, you're in charge 100 percent. I'm just thrilled to be here. I was dreading the idea of having to wait to see you."

From the living room, Pop hollers, "What game now, Nyla?"

"AST."

"What channel is that?"

"I'll go help him," Gavin says.

He starts to walk away, but then he turns back. Without any preamble, he kisses my lips then backs away, looking at me until he gets to the door of the dining room and disappears into the living room.

I put the last two pans of cookies into the oven and then begin to do the dishes. A few minutes later Gavin returns to the kitchen with his phone against his ear.

"I haven't checked my emails," he says. "I don't know if she did, I'll ask her. Nyla, did you check your email this morning?" I shake my head. "No, she didn't either. That's an awkward conversation for me to have with her, but I guess I will."

"Awkward?" I ask when he gets off the phone.

"Do you have a computer handy?"

I point to the sideboard in the dining room. I'd brought it down with me earlier intending to get through emails, but I haven't had a chance to look at them.

"Linda sent photos from last night that the foundation wants to put on the website and release for some press stuff. She'd like you to look at them first."

"What's awkward about that?"

I pull off my apron and sit at the dining room table where I open my computer. Gavin stands behind me for a moment before he sits down next to me.

"They're asking how you'd like them to refer to our relationship. Linda told them to print friend, but the photographer made some crack that we sure don't look like friends."

I tap the mouse pad, type in my password, and open my email box. Then I reach behind me, grab my phone, and bring up my Instagram account. I've become diligent about posting something daily per the advice of my mentor, Perry. He believes that it's important to keep in touch with fans, both of the network and myself. Last night I didn't post anything because it was so busy, and I was preoccupied with other thoughts. I was, however, tagged in several hundred photos.

I feel sick.

Many of the photos I've been tagged in are from people who picked up other people's posts and added their own comments. Some of them are kind: "Looks like love, how can you not love this woman." "Lucky man, whoever he is." Others sting: "Goodbye Lorenzo." "Looks like Tripple Threat has another one." "Quarterback? At least she found another big one."

I'd thought about this at the winery, but the concern never passed my thoughts last night. What do I want out in the world? Do I even possess the power to shape what others see? Is this a chance I even want to take?

Gavin brushes a few hairs from my forehead, smoothing them back. He looks over my face with a soft gaze and relaxed expression. "What's wrong?"

I wiggle my phone, and say, "I didn't think people would care all that much. I mean, I'm old news in a lot of ways. It's probably just because I worked the Games this summer. I'm really sorry, Gavin. Maybe we should have talked about this beforehand. I just want my life, my personal life, to be mine."

Gavin pulls my forehead to his lips. "I'm not worried about anything except getting a smile back on your face."

That makes me smile a little.

I open my email and find the one that Linda sent this morning. It contains several photos of me: on stage, hugging people, walking through the crowd, holding a glass of wine laughing, talking to a couple with Gavin's arm wrapped around me, Gavin and me dancing, me curled into his chest with my eyes closed.

"Goodness . . .," I say.

My throat goes dry, and the heat of embarrassment flushes my skin. After these photos were taken, I said what I had last night. No wonder he was frustrated.

"You are rather photogenic, Gavin. I'm sorry about all of this."

In Gavin's face is a yearning. If we were alone in the house right now I think he would be very bold, but instead, confidently, he says, "I'm not."

The oven buzzer goes off.

I stand and hand my phone to Gavin. "Do you have an Instagram account?"

"Yes," he says. "I don't post as much as you do though."

"I'm kind of required to. Do you follow me?"

"I feel weird telling you that I've followed your account for a long time."

"Will you look up your account there and follow you through me?"

"You only follow a hundred people? Do these comments bother you?"

"Honestly, I'm still trying to figure out what I think."

Gavin's phone rings. "Hey, Lin. Yes, we just looked at them. Already? I'll tell her. Thanks for the heads up. If it's just on the foundation website can't they update it? All right." Gavin hangs up his phone. "Someone went ahead and posted what they wanted. Linda profusely apologized, she said the publicity stuff is out of her control, but if we need things revised to let her know, and she'll do her best."

Right now if you put my name into a search engine, the images that come up are of myself, or Lorenzo and me, but this changes things.

Gavin gets up and stands close to me as I pull the oven mitts from my hands.

"I was referenced as your boyfriend," Gavin says.

"Well, I can post something on my own account in my words that will hopefully clear things up a little. Or I can call a PR lady I know and see about getting things retracted, or corrected if it gets picked up. But it probably won't. I'm not hot news right now, just a blip of an antidote."

"I don't need anything cleared up. I understand where we are at."

I curl into Gavin's chest, and say, "I'll post a photo of us and say something cute so that it keeps things from going sideways. Can I tag you, or say your name?"

"I'd be honored. May I post something?"

"I think that would be a good idea."

It feels like Earth's plates have shifted, and the island I am has collided with the mainland. Now, I have no idea how to traverse this landscape.

CHAPTER 16

$\mathcal{I}$t's halfway through the first quarter of the next game before Gavin and I join Pop in the living room. Gavin takes a seat on the couch and watches me curiously as I sit on the floor and lean back against the couch. I pat his jean-clad leg, and say, "It's football time!"

"She doesn't usually do anything aside from football on the weekends," Pop says. "Missing all the games yesterday has her withdrawing like an addict."

"It's my job to know everything about the games and players," I say.

"Life is all about football," Pop says to Gavin like I'm not in the room. "August through mid-February, and even in between."

I narrow my eyes at Pop and then look up to Gavin, who says, "I like football."

Unexpectedly, my doorbell rings. I hop up, open the door, and am met with a yell of "Surprise" in unison from Kevin and Mia.

"Yes, it is!" I pull them inside. "What are you doing here?"

"I have a meeting this week," Kevin says, "and since we don't get to see you much this time of year, we decided to come out early and watch a little football with you."

Gavin stands, Mia's eyes bounce between him and me, then she smiles like she knows exactly what is going on.

"Gavin," Kevin says, "good to see you. I don't think that you've ever met my wife, Mia. This is Gavin Boston. We've been working together for years."

"Nice to meet you," Mia says.

I run into the kitchen to get a plate of cookies and return to the living room. Pop is back in the chair, which is where he always sits when he's here, Mia is next to Kevin on the couch with a magazine in her hand, and Gavin is on the floor, right next to where I'd been.

I give everyone a cookie then sit down next to Gavin and put the plate on his lap. His smile is bright enough to cheer up the world. He takes my hand in one of his and picks up a cookie with the other.

"Happy?" I say so only he can hear.

"You have no idea how happy I feel around you."

I had wondered if having Pop and Kevin around Gavin would feel businesslike, but it doesn't. Perhaps it's football, which has a way of drawing people together. Gavin is fun to watch the game with. He's sharp on the plays, knows who the players are, and yells at the TV as much as Pop, Kevin, and I do.

After the game, Pop checks his watch, and says, "I put an order in for lunch platters from Rico's down the street. You boys want to go for a walk and help me carry things back?"

Pop and Gavin walk out the door, while Kevin lags slightly and gives Mia a playful warning look before he closes the door.

"What was that look for?" I ask.

Her cheeks round with a suppressed smile that threatens to split her face.

"You're going to make me wait?"

Mia shakes her head yes.

"What if I guess it?"

She moves her shoulders as if she's considering my proposal.

"You're multiplying cells," I say.

It's almost too easy to guess. They're building the new house in Chicago because they "need" more space and a backyard. Plus they've always wanted kids "someday." More than these things, though, she has that motherly glow.

"It sounds so scientific when you put it like that," Mia says.

"How far along are you?"

"Eight weeks. I didn't realize when we were here last time that I was pregnant. We wanted to tell you and Dad in person. That's part of the reason we came out today."

"Pop is going to be so excited."

Pop is generally a happy guy, but since Mom passed there has been an underlying sadness. I haven't been sure how to help him, but I think this news might be the thing.

"Enough about baby news," Mia says. "I want to know what is going on with you and Gavin."

"It's nothing. Or, it's something that's so new that I'm not sure what to think yet."

"It's more than just something. The energy between you two makes me feel lovestruck, and Gavin's Instagram post sure had me swooning."

"Oh no, not lovestruck, that's not it at all. An attraction, that's for sure, though."

Curious about his post I pick up my phone. There is a photo of me, although it's not what I expected. The curve of my shoulder, a small bit of my lace dress, and my fingers lifting into the air as if to say hello or goodbye. The caption reads, "The moment, The touch, The word, That changes everything. Thank you Nyla Tripple for allowing me to accompany you to the gala."

The last time I was interested in anyone, there wasn't social media. This is a new part of the experience.

With a dreamy sigh, Mia says, "It feels like a piece of art, the photo, and nine words that weigh so much. Sure turns me on. What's more is he usually posts pictures of buildings and architecture."

She puts her finger on my screen and scrolls back through the photos as if to prove it. There are a couple of pictures of him in front of beautiful buildings, but none of anyone else.

"In the same way as he captured you, everything in his photos feels intimate, artful. He has an eye for beauty. Well clearly, he picked you. What's it like?"

"What?"

"Him, you know . . . sex."

"I'm a long way from having sex."

"What's a long way? We talked about this. You know that doesn't work so well when you're older."

"I'm not older."

"You are too. I don't think people that start dating in their thirties prolong, you know."

"It will be prolonged for me. Us."

Gavin and I like each other, but what exactly this means for us I don't know yet. As much as I don't want to think about it, or let Gavin's past affect us, it does. I'm still not sure how I feel about dating a survivor. Plus, after hearing about his casual relationship with Pandora, how it changed his life, and not for the better, I know that I do not want to be his next casual or his next pain.

It isn't just his experiences, though. It is mine too. After Gavin told me about the miscarriage last night, and the pain it brought, I remembered my own. A few months after Lorenzo and I were married I got pregnant, a complete surprise. I was training hard for the Games and didn't want to tell anyone. At ten weeks I miscarried. It was hard on Lorenzo because he was ready to be a father. The loss saddled me with guilt for training so hard and putting the Games ahead of our family. But I was grateful to have an unshakable relationship with my husband, one that saw us through the loss. We never told anyone.

I continued to train hard, year after year, and pushed off starting a family because of my career, even though Lorenzo was ready. He was endlessly patient with me. Too patient, in fact, I realized at the end.

The guys can be heard laughing from down the block. They push open the door, and it's strange, yet right, to see Gavin with Pop and Kevin.

Gavin catches my hand and holds me back while everyone goes into the kitchen. "Hi." He grins, then kisses me once, twice, three times. I really do want him.

In the kitchen, the guys set the bags on the island and Gavin proceeds to unload them.

Pop says, "Who wants a beer?"

I immediately look at Mia, and my brother says, "You are horrible at keeping secrets, Mia."

She hugs Kevin, and says, "I'm so sorry, she guessed."

This effectively softens his face. It's been amazing to watch the way my brother's gaze on his wife has shifted over the years: young college students nearly innocent, passionate lovers, mature adults, now as parents to be. Love doesn't have just one look, it evolves and changes with life.

Pop turns back from the fridge, no one has answered him.

"I'll have one," I say.

He looks at everyone with a puzzled expression. "Did I miss something?"

Gavin winks at me, and says, "I'll take a beer, too, please."

"Mia?" Pop asks. "Kevin?"

"I'm good," Mia says.

"Yes, please," Kevin says.

Pop hands everyone but Mia a beer. "What's going on? What did I miss?"

Kevin pats Mia's flat stomach. "You're going to be a grandpa."

"I'm going to be a grandpa?" A smile lights his face. He opens his arms and pulls Mia and Kevin to him. He waves a hand for me to join, then looks over to Gavin. "You, too, family hug."

"Let's toast," Pop says. "To the joy of a new life."

I say a silent prayer, *may this life be brought into the world healthy*.

•••

It's after nine o'clock when Mia, Kevin, and Pop leave. With their exit, I realize how tired I am. I haven't stopped for the last seven days between work and the gala. Plus, there was everything with Gavin.

"I need to pack and get to bed soon," I say.

"Is that a gentle kicking me out the door too?"

"Not at all. If watching me pack sounds exciting, you're welcome to hang out until I need to get to sleep. At ten."

"Ten!"

"I have an early flight and a busy week."

"I'm kidding."

Gavin follows me up the stairs and into my bedroom. "Cute sheets," he says.

I yank my purple bedspread over my sheets, blue with white clouds and rainbows. These girly sheets were something I indulged in when I found myself a single female without a thought of anyone ever seeing them.

Gavin picks up the dress I wore last night from the back of the chair and sits down. I reach to take it from him, but he pats it on his knee. "It's fine right here." His hand runs over the delicate lace as if it's something rare. "The feel of it reminds me of dancing with you last night."

I grab my bright pink suitcase from the closet, set it on its side at the foot of the bed, and open it. Everything I use daily is in here so that all I have to pack are my clothes. My main consideration when I travel is the weather, which as we get further into fall and winter can vary. This week I am off to Arizona, which means shorts, tanks, and something light for sideline reporting. I am also doing three player interviews this week, so I need to pack a professional outfit. I lay out three options and then tap my chin. Unable to decide, I look up to Gavin.

"Wanna help?" I ask. "I need something for interviews. You choose among these."

Gavin gets up from the chair and looks at the options on the bed. "One?" He runs his fingers along a royal blue pencil skirt that I've paired with a white sleeveless button-down shirt. "Do I get to see you model them?"

"You can see them on TV if you catch the interviews."

With his hand still on the blue skirt, he says, "Definitely this one."

Fifteen minutes later I'm packed.

"That was quick," Gavin says.

"I hate to toot my own horn, but I am an expert packer. You do realize how much I am gone, right?"

"I have an idea. Do you have an idea how much I work?"

"Yes, I do."

"Our schedules will work just fine together."

Gavin pulls his phone from his pocket and starts some music. It takes a moment before I recognize it; a strings-only version of "Mystery Girl."

He draws me to him with an enchanting air, and says, "Will you dance with me?"

"Now I can't use the excuse that I can't dance."

"And I don't even have a single toe injury."

"Maybe you can teach me more about dancing another time. But, right now it's almost ten, and I have to get to bed."

Gavin has a fuller bottom lip that rounds to a natural pout, but now he sticks it out a little more, and his eyes pull down in a sweet plea. "Just one dance, please?"

I hook my hand over his, set my other hand on the curve of his shoulder. Gavin's hand settles on the small of my back, and with gentle pressure, he ensures we can't get any closer. In the intimacy of my bedroom, the way we move no longer feels like a dance, but a prelude to something that comes later.

My body wants to betray my earlier declaration of waiting. But I won't, I can't, for two reasons. One, emotionally I'm not ready. Two, I don't want to get pregnant, and I will not leave this prevention up to a single layer of protection, something I don't even have right now.

But, I will dance with him.

I slide my hand from his and trace the curve of his arms and explore the texture of him all the way up his neck. My fingers slide into his hair, thick and soft. He leans his head into my hands, his chin lifts to expose his neck, and slowly his lips part. "Nyla," he says as his eyes close. I kiss his neck, lift onto my toes, and kiss his full bottom lip. He tastes of spring water and peanut butter cookies. Gavin's arms wrap me possessively, the muscles in his torso tighten as if he's holding back. He cups my cheek and returns my kiss, then draws my lip between his like a lollipop.

"You taste like candy," he whispers. "And your touch is enough to set a forest ablaze."

I begin to lead him back to the sheets I'd bought just for me, a selfish desire consuming me. The back of my legs hit the mattress, my eyes open, and seized with the realization that I am not ready to finish what I've started, I say, "I have to stop."

His eyes open slowly.

"I'm so sorry, Gavin. I'm not ready . . . for that, not just yet."

Gavin's heated gaze slides over my face and down my neck. He lowers his lips next to my ear, and says, "I understand." He nuzzles the side of my head. "There is never any pressure."

"I like kissing you, though."

"I like kissing you, too, and dancing with you, and touching you, and talking to you. I like you."

There is something urgent in the way the universe has brought us together, but there is also this expansion of time that makes me feel like I have known him forever. "I like you too."

This shared honesty, while both being very turned on, makes me feel like I should be ready.

His embrace shifts from that of desire and urgency to something that makes me feel protected. "I will wait as long as you need."

His kindness, his care, makes me feel guilty for not being ready for someone like him. Maybe it would have been better to have met him a year from now. Would I be ready then?

"I'm happy kissing you and touching you just like this," Gavin says. "More than happy."

"I might want to keep you, for a little while," I say.

There is something new in his eyes, a new glint perhaps, as he says, "I might want to keep you forever."

"Forever is a long time." I kiss him again, and the embers between us set a fire. "You have to go," I say into his lips.

"I'll dream of you," he says.

I press my hips into his, the feel of him makes my words breathy. "I bet you'll do more than dream of me."

"Nyla Tripple," he grumbles like the beginning of an earthquake capable of reorganizing the landscape.

I could easily forget myself: fears, doubts, limits. Gavin is changing everything.

How long should I wait? Can I wait? Will we wait? And what exactly are we waiting for?

CHAPTER 17

*A*s I unlock my rental car in the parking lot of the Arizona training facility the holler of my name makes me look up. Perry Tacklin jogs over to me, then pulls a square cloth from his khaki pants and wipes his brow.

"I sure hope you're wearing sunblock, kid," he says.

"I don't burn." I tug on the baseball cap that shields my face.

"Not like us Irish boys."

Perry is not a boy anymore, but he refers to everyone, including himself, as boy or girl, and to those he affectionately cares for as kid.

He pats his pockets and pulls out sunglasses. "Five minutes in the Arizona sun and I can feel myself cooking."

"What does bring you out to scorch in Arizona?"

Earlier I saw Perry talking with the head coach, and I was curious as to what brought him out here. Occasionally I see him at games, but I don't think I've ever seen him at a practice.

"I figured it's time that we catch up," he says.

"You came out here just to catch up?"

He smiles like there might be more. "Mostly. By the way, great job on the Games. How was it for you?"

"It was surreal. Weird to be there and not have thoughts of preparing for a race. Lots of fun though."

"Very good."

Perry has a full head of white hair that shines in the sun, and though he may not look like a man that was once an elite athlete in his day, he is still strong as an ox.

"So, what is it that you really want to see me about?" I ask.

"I'm hoping you have time to meet with me today."

"There is always time to meet with you."

He looks at his watch. "Do you have dinner plans?" I shake my head no. "Great, how's the restaurant at your hotel?"

"I haven't eaten there yet, but I hear it's supposed to be good. Would six work for you?"

"Six works great. I have a flight to catch at ten. Promised my wife I'd only be gone for the day. See you then, kid."

He begins to walk away when I say, "Perry, you can't leave me in suspense. What did you fly out here to meet about, without so much as a warning?"

He turns back, and with an indifferent look, he says, "I heard a rumor."

"A rumor?"

"That you're in talks with State Sport."

I am not sure if this is a statement or a question, but he waits for my response.

State Sport has exploded in the last decade as the second all-sports channel. For a long time, AST didn't believe that another all-sports channel would make it, but in the last five years, they've gained traction. I've heard rumors that it's making AST scramble to adjust.

"Is it true, kid? Did they get to you before me?"

"Interesting . . . I haven't heard anything from them."

"Good. Should they call between now and six o'clock, would you do me a favor and not answer your phone?"

"You have my word."

•••

Back in my hotel room, I take a quick shower. My phone rings as I turn off the water. A zip of excitement runs through me. Even though I don't have any interest in going to State Sport, it's flattering to think that my work is noticed and that AST doesn't want to let me go.

The majority of my loyalty at AST lies with Perry. We met when he was a sports journalist years ago, and I'd just begun my running career. In one of my interviews, he asked if I had any aspirations for the day I retired. I told him I'd love to do what he does, but with a focus on football. Time passed and Perry climbed the ladder. The day my retirement hit the news he called and offered me a job.

For the first two years, my schedule was insane: I wrote, conducted interviews, and flew all over filling in for absent reporters as needed. Then I was offered a permanent spot as a sideline reporter with the Thursday night crew. Now, it isn't any less hectic, but it's nice to have a regular travel schedule.

I get to the phone just as it goes to voicemail; it was Gavin. We've been talking every day, usually twice. I return his call with a flutter in my belly that is soothed to a pleasing low vibration when he answers the phone. Already, he has a distinctive way he says my name like it's something special that deserves time to be said.

"I'm walking to a dinner meeting and was thinking of you," Gavin says. "I wanted to hear your voice."

"I, too, am getting ready for a dinner meeting. What is yours for?"

"Closing dinner with Samuel, Trace, and Linda."

"You closed! Congratulations, Gavin!"

"I'm pretty excited myself."

I hear the smile in his voice, and I can almost see him walking down the street in his vest and fancy wingtip shoes at a slower pace, talking into his phone.

"I get back late Friday, but can I take you out Saturday to celebrate?"

"I'm already looking forward to it. What is your meeting for?"

"Do you remember Perry Tacklin that I told you about?"

"Yes, I do, head of AST and your mentor."

"He wants to meet because he heard a rumor that State Sport is going to make some sort of offer to me. But I think he might have misinformation because I haven't heard anything."

"Securing his talent," Gavin says proudly. "You are amazing you know."

I slip my shoes on and leave the hotel room.

"I am about to get on the elevator. I'll need to get going."

"I miss you. I still want to hear your voice tonight, but I just felt like I had to hear it now too."

"I'd like to be able to say goodnight as well. I'll talk to you soon."

Perry is notoriously early and tonight is no exception. He's already sitting at a table with an untouched bread basket in front of him, and what I know is tonic water in his hand, because he never drinks before he flies.

"I haven't heard anything," I say to his questioning eyes as I sit down. The waiter delivers a glass of pinot to me that Perry must have ordered. Anytime I see wine now, I think of Gavin and our day together. "Are you sure you don't have misinformation?"

"My intel is always right. You know, I hope, that I've always done the best I can for you. Once State does call, this might send things into a back and forth on money and such. And it can take time. First, I want to tell you I'll match whatever they offer plus ten percent."

"Have you been getting me at a bargain?" I ask sarcastically.

"Not at all, actually," Perry says.

I hadn't thought so, but the fact that he was so frank in his offer made me wonder.

"We can't afford to lose you," he says. "Aside from money, what is your ideal situation?"

"Ideal situation? I'd like to anchor the desk."

"Pre and postgame? Still football?"

"Yes, exactly."

Perry takes a drink of his tonic water, then says, "I don't have an open space at the moment. We could look at adding you to a team, but there will also be some shifts coming up shortly, but I can't talk about them yet."

"Really?"

"It will probably be next season, though. Is that something you're willing to wait on?"

"But you aren't guaranteed, and you seem to think State Sport has a similar offer."

"I don't know the details of their offer, but I am sure it will be enticing. Here though, we have a behind-the-scenes series that your name keeps getting brought up for. There is also a quiz show and several other projects in the works. You're a talent we want to leverage. You might say we want to make you a franchise player. You test well across all age demographics, male and female. Better than any other on-screen personality we have. We can't afford to lose you."

"Perry, you might have gotten wrong information."

"No, I'm sure."

"Okay, if I hear from them I'll call you."

He looks at me appreciatively. "Thank you. I heard another bit of news, from my wife. You have a boyfriend. The missus showed me a picture of you two."

"The press got carried away with that one. His name is Gavin. It's very new."

"I can see he makes you smile though. I'm happy for you. I hope he's a good man."

"He is a very good man."

"He doesn't look familiar. Not an athlete?"

"Architect, businessman."

"Good for you. Hopefully, he likes football or at least you reporting football."

"He is a big fan of both."

"See you really do test well across all demographics."

Even though nothing has happened yet, I can feel something is about to shift in my career. Isn't it funny how things can be steady and even for so long and suddenly everything begins to change?

•••

On Saturday mornings I have my "me" appointments. Always a sports massage and then anything else I need: facial, pedicure, manicure, wax. Usually, I'm able to relax and forget about everything. But today, all I can think about right now is Gavin.

He asked me to head up to his house as soon as I'm done. He'll show me his property, then I'm taking him out to celebrate the purchase of the land for his new building.

At the beginning of Appleton Way, where the pavement ends, is a mailbox. It's wrapped in old vines that look like they're holding it up, or maybe they look like they're going to swallow it into the ground. Along the sides of the road, evergreen and deciduous trees form a tunnel. A few leaves have shifted into shades of gold. I'd forgotten yesterday was the first day of fall.

I've just gotten out of my car when Gavin comes around the side of the house with a large saw in his hand that he carries as if it weighs nothing. He's clad in carpenter jeans with a tape measure hanging off one of the loops and a red flannel that's rolled up to his elbows. There is a light layer of sawdust on his clothes, even the top of his hat. It's the first time I've seen him in a cap and with stubble along his jaw.

He looks very excited to see me. "Hello, beautiful. I was hoping I'd finish before you got here."

I follow him into the large building next to the garage that looks nice enough from the outside to be a house. Inside is a well-organized workshop.

Pop was never a handy kind of guy. We didn't have any tools around our house aside from what fit in a tool-box. Lorenzo had a few, for basic home repairs. Gavin, however, has an entire building filled with tools I've never seen. Some hang on the wall while others sit on tables. There's a few that appear to be their own unit entirely, massive and intimidating.

Gavin sets the saw on a table and wipes his hands on the knees of his pants. "If I weren't a total mess right now, I'd be kissing you."

"You don't look like a mess. In fact, I'd say you look rugged and handsome."

With a crooked smile, he says, "Rugged and handsome? I'm thrilled that's what you see. I see a gorgeous woman who's glowing."

I wink. "I had a good massage and facial."

Gavin leads me to the house where he opens the front door. I step into a place that has a sense of wonder. The ceilings are high with huge wooden beams. A stone fireplace is almost as tall as me.

"Please look around and make yourself at home," Gavin says. "I'm gonna get cleaned up, so I don't have to resist kissing you any longer." He starts down the hall then turns back. "Do you want anything to drink?"

"No, I'm good right now. Thank you."

"The kitchen is just through there." He points to a large set of open double doors. "Feel free to help yourself to anything if you change your mind. I'll give you a proper tour when I get done."

I might expect to feel a little uncomfortable being left alone in a new house like this, but I don't. In fact, I feel at home.

The floors have a matte clear coat on them that's smooth, but it's sealed in old nicks and wear patterns as if securing history. The entire back wall of the house is made of large panels of glass. I open the back door with an ornate round handle, which looks like it might be original, and step out onto a deck bright with new life. Out here it smells like fresh cut wood. It's from this expansive deck that I see the property is set on the side of the hill and stretched out below me is Portland. The Willamette River snakes through the middle of the city; tiny boats draw white hairlines in the blue water. Microscopic cars seem to move at a snail's pace over bridges that unite the two sides of the city, proving that even a landmass that is divided can also be joined.

I have no idea how long I've stood here being wooed by this landscape, but it must have been a while because Gavin's hands slide around my waist and draw me back to his warm body. He kisses my cheek, and his smooth jaw rubs against mine.

"This view is like moving artwork," I say.

"I thought it couldn't get any better until I saw you standing on the deck as part of the view."

"You're sweet."

I turn in his arms to face him and reach up to run my hands through his hair. It's still damp, and without product it stands on end at least two inches high.

Gavin pats his hair. "It has a mind of its own. I thought I could give you a tour while it dries. Actually, that isn't true. I just couldn't wait any longer to kiss you."

"You really shouldn't wait any longer."

I'd fantasized many times about Gavin's lips this past week, but my memories and imagination don't compare to the reality. I draw his full lower lip between mine gently. He moans. What other fantastic sounds might he make?

I open my eyes to find Gavin's face soft with pleasure, eyes closed.

"This tour?" I say.

His eyes open halfway. "Yes, the tour."

The home isn't just impressive, it is inspiring. Gavin has taken great care to preserve and restore everything, even if not in perfect condition, which only makes the house feel more welcoming. Where things were not salvageable, like the kitchen cabinets, he made selections which bridged the current day styles to the early 1900s, when the house was born.

In the center of the house are all of the common areas: kitchen, dining room, and a large open living room with two separate sitting areas. Two hallways jet off from the living room along the front of the house. The south wing, as Gavin jokes, has four bedrooms, all of which sit empty.

"The entire house has been restored to a blank slate," Gavin says. "Now I need to figure out what to do with all of it. At a minimum, I need to make a proper guest room out of this one."

There are also two bathrooms down here, both of them larger and far nicer than my own at home. There's also an office, the one I saw from outside that first night I was here. While it has furniture in it, a desk and chair, and full bookshelves, it doesn't feel like it gets used.

"You don't work from home at all?" I ask.

"I've thought about it, but there really isn't a good reason to. For the most part, the only time I am here is when I'm working on the house or sleeping."

I point to a guitar case in the corner. "It isn't just your brother that plays?"

"I'm not that good."

"I don't think you do anything that you aren't good at, so I have to assume you are at least decent. Will you play for me?"

"Someday."

The north wing isn't far, but it feels private. The only door is at the end of the hall. It leads to Gavin's room where it feels like of an expansive, cozy slice of the galaxy. The walls are painted a luminous color that I think is black, though it seems a touch lighter than that. The wall that Gavin's bed sits against has a different texture. I run my fingers over it.

"That wall," Gavin says, "is made from wood I salvaged from the workshop. I painted it the same color, but I liked the texture."

"It's very unique."

"Unique as in . . ."

"I love it. Is this the bed you made?"

"Yes, it is. It's also salvaged wood, from the house."

It's made from old boards that are angled to form a V and finished with a lacquer that has made it perfectly smooth. On top of the bed are pure white sheets and a fluffy comforter.

There are two bedside tables with brass lamps mounted on the wall above them. On the opposite side of the room is a single club chair. Next to it is a small round table with an open book on it.

"You might like this," he says tipping his head toward a door. "My contractor insisted I needed this closet. If he weren't a personal friend, I would have said I got duped."

The closet is nearly as large as my bedroom. Pure white walls, two built-in dressers, lighting that is as bright as being outside. His clothes take up less than half the closet and are organized by type and color.

"My contractor also insisted I needed this." He leads me out of the closet and through another door into the bathroom. It's gorgeous, but by far the most unusual feature is the shower. One wall is made entirely of glass that peeks through into a space that looks like a cavern. An uneven stone forms the ceiling and walls, and what appears to be the same stone, only smooth, creates the floor. I can't tell where the water comes from, but I see the place where it gets turned on.

"I think your contractor was planning to move in with you because he built you a north wing for two."

"He claims it's for resale value."

"Well, if you ever are looking to sell it, please let me know. I'd be more than happy to take this slice of heaven."

"I'll keep that in mind."

This is the most unique and beautiful house I've ever seen. While this has a lot to do with the bones of the structure, it has even more to do with Gavin's diligent work, his ability to see a vision, and the love with which he brought it back to life.

CHAPTER 18

*T*oday I arrive home from a long week, and in my mail are three bills, all pertaining to the Bainbridge house. Every month I pay these, but today for the first time I wonder why I keep doing this. What am I trying to hold on to? Or what am I anchoring myself to?

I take the bills up to my office and pay them. From the window, I see smoke lift from Ms. Marshall's porch. It's been too long since I've been able to visit with her. As the fall days get colder, she's out less, and I've been gone even more.

I walk over to her house and find her hands are busy with knitting needles working yarn the color of a summer sunset. She pauses and pats the spot next to her.

"What are you making?" I ask.

"I never know for sure. It might be a square for a blanket, or it might be a washcloth."

The wooden knitting needles make no sound as her hands move. I remember my grandmother knitting, but her metal needles made a rhythmic tapping sound.

"I've seen a lot of that black truck in your driveway," Ms. Marshall says. She pokes my arm with her free needle as she turns the row. "And he appears to have kept that lawn mowed back there for you."

Gavin has been woven into the fabric of my life, the beat of my days, for the last two months. When I travel during the week, we talk on the phone. He calls when he wakes up, usually as I head out for my morning run, and at night I phone him as I lie down for bed. Fridays I fly home for the weekend, and I spend nearly every waking hour of it with Gavin. I can't stop smiling when I'm around him, and he makes me laugh more than I have in years.

I have been careful, though, never to let us linger at either of our houses for too long because Gavin Boston is a challenging man to resist. While he's remained the ultimate gentleman, there is no denying we both crave more.

"He's a good guy." I'm so tired of using that analogy for him as if he is just enough to get by on. "Actually, he's amazing."

"But?"

"I'm kind of at a sticky point."

"How so?"

"I feel tied to Lorenzo and before it used to feel good like I still have a connection to him even after . . . but now it's keeping me from being able to move on. I feel guilty."

"Gavin isn't getting to mow everything, is that what you mean?"

"You are always so perceptive."

"You know, I married Old Jester when he was thirty-two. We called him old because he walked with a cane. He'd been in a bicycle accident when he was a kid. Don't worry, it didn't restrict his ability in the way that mattered most."

"Oh."

"He was hit by a car. We lived on a little road just after a bend. Our mailbox was on the other side of the road. People were always speeding, and I was always telling him to be careful or else, one day . . ."

"I'm sorry."

"I married Sam just three years after. We called him Sam even though his given name was Samuel, like your dad. He had the sexiest blue eyes. When Jester died, I was sure I would never look at another man. I think I felt a little like you have with your loss. But the way Sam looked at me made my toes curl, and I couldn't resist him. We had a baby that we named Mary. She and Sam died on the way to get ice cream."

Ms. Marshall looks at me as she lowers her knitting needles. "I don't eat ice cream anymore."

"I imagine not."

She picks up her knitting again and continues, "It was losing Mary that almost killed me. I missed Sam, but losing a child, there is nothing that compares to that pain. She was just eight. My heart was so injured I was sure I'd never love anyone again."

"I met Old Tom, and I called him that because he was old. Eighty-two when we married, but he was as young as I was, maybe more so. Sex is good, even when you're old. You may get wrinkly, things might sag, but it doesn't matter. Your eyes adjust, and your expectations of everything accounts for the years of experience that gave you that body. He died when he was ninety. Just old age, I guess."

Feeling she has more to say, although I don't know what, I stay quiet.

"You don't make room for someone new by forgetting. Instead, you have to find a way to make your heart bigger.

You're lucky to have had the experience of loving and being loved so well. Think of how fortunate the next one is that you're willing to love." She bumps me with her shoulder. "And I have to imagine that you had a good physical relationship with Lorenzo."

"Very."

She nods. "Don't let your body or your heart go to waste. Especially when you have someone you'd like to share it with."

"Do you think you will date again?"

"I play around now and then, but I don't expect to be on this earth much longer, so I don't plan to get attached."

She looks at me with question. "There's something else. What's wrong with him that's got you scared?"

I'll never understand how she can sense my thoughts.

"He had cancer."

Even though I don't spend a lot of time thinking about it, I have to admit it worries me.

"Ah, a survivor," Ms. Marshall says.

"Yes."

"How long?"

"Approaching four years. That's the part of it that worries me. What if I break past these barriers, we keep dating, and I find myself caring even more for him. And what if . . ."

"He will die, we all will. Take comfort in that so it doesn't prevent you from living."

Gavin's truck pulls into my driveway. He gets out, still dressed in his work clothes, and waves at me.

"Go get him, Nyla, and don't hold back."

Gavin is always excited to see me at the end of the week. He wraps one arm around my waist, cups my face with his other hand, searches my eyes as if he wants to make sure I'm real, and then he reminds me with his lips why I look forward to seeing him all week.

"I need to change before we go," I say looking down at my sweatpants and shirt. While it is a stylish set, they are still sweats.

"I rather like these."

He follows me up to my bedroom where he sits in the antique chair that has unofficially become his. Each week he watches me pack from there. I've wondered if he'll ever venture over and lie on my cloud-covered sheets, but I don't think he will.

I pick out clothes for dinner: a tight pair of jeans, a sexy lace thong that won't show, and an oversized knit sweater. I gather them in a stack, and say, "I'll be right back."

"You can change in here," Gavin says with a deep and inviting voice.

I've never changed in front of him. If he's in my room, I sneak off to the bathroom. But I've wondered lately if I need him to be more assertive, to help me push past these barriers.

"Are you going to leave the room then?" I tease.

"No. Are you going to tell me what you're thinking?"

"It would be inappropriate."

The sexy grin spreads across his lips. "Maybe we shouldn't let anything be inappropriate for us. Maybe we should start erasing some lines in our relationship."

"Are you trying to get me to have sex with you, Mr. Boston?"

He smiles and settles back in the chair as if he intends to stay right there. "I'm ready when you are, but I won't rush you."

"If I change here, you'll stay in your seat there?"

"Is that a requirement?"

"Yes."

"All right . . . I'll sit right here and . . . watch."

"No, you can't watch, but you can stay in the room."

"Nyla, your eyes speak more than your lips sometimes."

At times I appreciate that my expression says the things I can't, but other times I hate it. Not since Lorenzo has anyone seen me as clearly as Gavin does.

At the end of the bed I set my stack of clothes, then turn my back to Gavin. I try not to let the nervous, yet excited energy that floods me take over. I pull the sweatshirt over my head, look over my shoulder, and throw it his way.

"Nyla, if you toss anything else at me, I'll come out of this chair."

"Threat?"

"Fair warning."

I keep my back to him and put the knit sweater on. It's very roomy and comes down to where my hip and thigh meet. As I slide my sweatpants and panties down my legs, I am careful how I bend so that he won't actually get to see anything. But when I slip the thong on, I let the hem of the sweater come with my hands and give him a view I'm sure he appreciates. Then my jeans, I slide them on slowly, wiggle a little to get into them, and then fasten them.

I grab a pair of socks from my dresser. I'm unsure about looking at him. I'm worried I'll see a need that will make me surrender, or worse, nothing. In an unusual surge of insecurity I wonder, will I be enough?

I turn, trying to look like what I just did was completely normal for us.

He's gripping my sweater like a lifeline; his lips pulled between his teeth. "I wasn't expecting that," he says hoarsely. "You do know I am a man right?"

"Yes."

"Then please be understanding that I need to sit here for a few minutes."

"Do you want me to leave the room?"

"No."

"What do you want me to do then?"

"I'm not sure I should say exactly what I want right now."

"Didn't you just say nothing should be inappropriate between us?"

"I was ready the night I met you, Nyla."

"I'm nervous about it."

"Me too."

"I don't know that I'm ready for that, but I can help you out."

"Oh, um, honestly I don't think I have enough self-control for that right now. I'd be better to quit talking about this and take a minute."

"You have more self-control than anyone I have ever met, perfectly composed at all times."

A small smile bounces in the corner of his mouth. "There is a place I lose control."

•••

We walk down my street to Hawthorne and turn right toward Fork and Spoon restaurant. On the way, we pass by Little Pea, a children's boutique.

"Would you mind if I stop in here real quick?" I say. "Kev and Mia found out they are having a girl and I want to send them an outfit."

He looks up at the sign and then through the windows. "A girl?"

I'd miscarried before anyone knew and before I'd purchased a single thing. But Gavin's child was lost at seven months, and I assume his experience was very different from mine. They'd probably bought clothes and maybe even decorated a baby's room.

"You don't have to go in. I can meet you someplace in fifteen minutes."

He opens the door for me. "I'm happy to go in with you."

The little brass bell that hangs from a rope rings as it bounces against the door. The shop is bright, and even though it's small, it's full. Toward the back is a couple, the woman quite pregnant, and a worker ringing them up.

"Hello. I'll be with you in a few minutes."

Gavin looks around the store and stuffs his hands into his trouser pockets.

"You really don't have to be in here," I say.

"I look that bad?"

"You look like I just told you I'm pregnant."

His eyes bounce away from me to toys on a shelf. "I'd be baffled if you told me that right now."

If Gavin had any lingering desire, I'm sure it's gone now.

I leave him at the front of the store and head toward the back where the clothes are. I've never purchased baby clothes. The few showers I've been to I'd opted to go in on a bigger gift like a stroller or crib. In fact, I don't think I've ever been in a store like this. I find a cute tiny dress. It amazes me that humans are ever this small. After I check the price tag, I can't decide if I'm horrified or impressed that it costs more than some of my clothes.

The clerk wishes the couple leaving best of luck, then she walks my way. "Do you need any help?"

Her name tag is shaped like a puppy with her name, Poppy, written on a bone.

"No, thank you. I'm just looking."

"If you have any questions please let me know."

I find another dress. It's blue with a pink dinosaur on it. It reminds me of Kevin because his childhood room was decorated with green tyrannosaurus. There is a basket of tights next to the dresses. I check the size of the dress; it's six months. I'm not sure that tights are needed for a baby that young so I forgo looking at them.

"These are amazing," Poppy says.

I look over my shoulder at Gavin who once again seems like himself, relaxed and confident. Whatever had shaken him appears to have resolved. He unzips a bag and rolls out what appears to be a portable changing station.

"Are these diaper bags for guys?" he asks.

"Yes, guys deserve to carry cool bags with your kids too," Poppy says.

He looks up at me. "That's cool, right? What do you think?"

"It's awesome."

"When are you two due?" Poppy asks.

I look down at my belly, and though I don't look pregnant, I can see how she is mistaken. My sweater is very baggy, enough to hide a bump if there were one to hide. And Gavin looks genuinely interested in the bag, not like he is shopping for someone else.

"Nothing in this oven," I say. "We are shopping for my brother and sister-in-law."

"I am so sorry! I normally never assume. You don't even look pregnant. I was sure you were shopping—"

"No, really, it's all right," I say.

"You know, why don't we get this," I hold up the dress, "and that bag for Kevin. Guys do deserve a cool bag."

"You can leave that one there," Poppy says to Gavin. "I have one still in the box. Do you want them wrapped?"

"I would appreciate that," I say.

I follow Poppy to the counter and hand her my credit card. Gavin kisses the back of my head and sets his hand on my waist. I wonder what he's thinking.

"Do you have kids?" Poppy asks as she wraps the purchases.

"No, we don't," I say and immediately feel discomfort at the word we in that response.

Gavin insists on carrying the bag. As soon as the door closes behind us, he says, "You don't look pregnant."

"I know I don't. It was an honest mistake." Sensing we need a change in subject, I say, "I'd like to go on a hike tomorrow. Would you be interested in going with me?"

"I'm interested in anything, so long as you are there."

I don't think what happened in the boutique was that big of a deal, but it seems to have been for Gavin. His touch earlier was sexual, and his smile meant to turn me on. Now the way he clings to my waist feels desperate, as if he thinks I might slip away from him, and his lips are pressed flat like he's about to tell me a secret.

CHAPTER 19

The next day Gavin and I drive to a trailhead in Forest Park. It's supposed to be the warmest part of the day, yet as I get out of the truck, the air bites me like a thousand razor-sharp teeth. I zip my jacket and button the wide collar, then pull my knit cap low to protect my ears. The only part of my body that shows is the space around my eyes and nose, although I'm still shivering.

In stark contrast to myself, Gavin's jacket is open to a beautiful wool sweater, a similar moss green to his eyes. No hat, no gloves, and I doubt he has on thermal underwear like I do.

He tries not to laugh at me when he asks, "Warm enough?"

"If it weren't for clothing technology, I don't think I'd leave my house in the winter. We have to start moving."

"It isn't even winter yet. What do you do when it actually gets cold?"

"I wear more layers."

I've hiked this trail many times, even in the winter. Unfortunately, it is a mess from all of the rain last week.

Rocks and logs have shifted and washed away. There are muddy patches which I do my best to avoid, but at some spots it's impossible. It feels like we're on an obstacle course.

As I skirt a wide patch of mud, I say, "It looks like brownie batter."

"I bet it doesn't taste like it," Gavin says.

I laugh and look back over my shoulder at him which causes me to lose my balance. My feet stumble and land right in the mud, but Gavin catches my wrist which saves me from landing on my ass.

"Are you okay?" he asks.

With a gentle pull on my arms Gavin tries to help me step out, but my boots are captives of the mud.

"I'm stuck," I say as my laugh turns into a giggle fit which makes Gavin laugh too.

"Try twisting your foot," he says.

I'm laughing so hard I can't do anything else. I take a couple of quick breaths, hold my laugh, then twist and roll my foot. There's a loud sucking sound, and then it's free. With Gavin's arms for balance, I step my foot outside of the mud and using him for leverage I twist the other free.

Gavin pulls me to his chest and squeezes me tight. "I love to hear you laugh."

"Thanks, I love to hear you laugh too."

Mud covers my boots, the hem of my pants, even a few rogue splashes have reached my waist. But I am undaunted. Actually, that was kind of fun.

We continue along the trail which narrows as we move up the hillside.

From behind me, Gavin says, "I reviewed the contract you forwarded from AST this morning."

The day after Perry and I met in Arizona, nearly two months ago, State Sport contacted me with a proposal that blew me away. A prime-time sports show at a studio that they would set up in Portland for me, and when I saw the pay I was sure they'd made a typo.

The weekend after I received the offer Gavin and I were out to dinner when he said to me, "I don't think I've ever seen you so quiet. Do you want to talk about it?"

I shook my head no, and said, "Sorry, I didn't mean to be rude. I'm good though."

Gavin reached across the table, took my hand, and nodded a bit of encouragement.

I'd been used to doing everything on my own for so long that it felt strange at first to talk about the future and my fears with Gavin. But he listened attentively and talked everything through with me. I'd always known Gavin was a trustworthy man, but that night I realized I trust him with everything.

We reach the crest of the trail where it opens up wide enough for us to walk alongside each other.

"I think everything we talked about is in that last contract," I say.

Gavin grabs my gloved hand and shakes it a congratulatory way. "It's more money than you asked for."

Ice cold rain hits my cheek. I pull the hood of my jacket up and take a few quick steps to a spot where the trees are thickest, stop, and turn to Gavin. He has a proud smile on his face.

"That was a surprise. AST does want me as badly as you said. Do you think it's good to sign?"

"Do *you* think it's good to sign?" he asks.

"It is."

"I am really proud of you, Nyla."

"Thank you for believing in me. I couldn't have done it without you."

"You were the one at the negotiation table, without an agent. I'm very impressed with you. Your focus and determination are awe-inspiring."

"With you cheering me on, it was easy."

Gavin unzips my coat so that my lips are free. "It has nothing to do with me. It's who you are."

He kisses my iced lips until they warm, making the rest of my limbs quite jealous.

I could stay here forever, but my rainproof jacket has managed to let rain reach my skin.

"I'm soaked," I say into Gavin's lips.

"Me too."

We make our way back to the trailhead, careful not to slip or land in the mud again. Once we get in the truck I look at the state of myself.

"I'm a mess." My teeth chatter. "And I'm cold."

"We need to get you warmed up. And it's getting close to dinner time. What sounds good?"

"Grilled cheese and tomato soup."

"That does sound good. What do you think about going back to my house? You can get warm next to the fireplace while I make you dinner."

"You want to cook for me?"

"Something you don't know about me yet is that I'm a good cook."

"You aren't just trying to lure me back to your house, are you?"

"Lure? You make me sound like a calculating man after one thing." He sets his jaw seriously. "You know better than that. I'm a gentleman."

I look out the window, and under my breath, I say, "Maybe I don't want you to be so gentle."

"I heard that," Gavin says.

I think I'm ready for what comes next, but I need him to help nudge me past my fears. Is this wrong to ask of him? Or maybe all it will take is the smile he's giving me.

•••

Gavin opens the door to his house and sweeps a wide arm for me.

I manage to stomp off most of the mud outside of the door, but my shoes are far from clean. "Maybe I should take these off out here," I say.

"No, it's all right, just take them off inside where it's warm."

On the stone entryway, I carefully untie the shoelaces and remove my boots without making a mess. I roll the hem of my pants up to mid-calf and stand.

Gavin walks across the living room and turns on the fireplace, which I'd thought was wood burning. He holds his hands out to the instant heat, tips his head, and says, "Come here, where it's warm."

I feel his gaze on me as I look at the fire.

"I'm going to get you a glass of wine and start dinner," he says.

The night presses in on the curtain-less windows like a midnight blue blanket. The city below is a tapestry of bright orbs, as if the stars hidden by the clouds above have been laid out below us. Some lights move at a snail's pace, although I know they are cars moving fast. I suppose speed and distance are relative to view.

Gavin kisses my cheek and hands me a glass of wine. "Zinfandel. It should pair wonderfully with your fancy grilled cheese and tomato soup."

"It's so beautiful here," I say unable to hide the wonder from my voice.

Ignoring the bright orbs outside, Gavin says, "It really is."

All I see now is him. Like a lion, he is large, strong, and graceful in everything he does.

I follow him into the kitchen and lean back against the counter to watch him cook. I never feel as comfortable in the kitchen as he looks. On the counter ingredients are lined up, as simple as they might be, in a neat and orderly fashion. He chops onions, quick uniform slices. I try to be discrete as I wipe my watering eyes with the back of my sleeve.

"What's wrong?" Gavin asks.

"Onions. They don't bother your eyes?"

He pulls a paper towel from the roll and hands it to me. "I wear contacts. But if I'm wearing my glasses when I cut them they do."

"Really?"

Is it strange that I didn't know this about him?

"My eyes aren't horrible, but I've worn them forever."

"Are they colored?"

"No, they're clear."

"I love your eyes."

"I love your beautiful brown eyes."

I blush under his gaze, something I never do, and I look away. "Are you sure I can't help?"

"You standing right there looking at me like that with those beautiful eyes is more help than you know."

"How did you learn to cook?"

"You can't give me too much credit, you asked for grilled cheese."

"And soup."

"My mother taught me to cook. She said it was so I never went hungry or expected a woman to cook for me."

"I like her already."

"You will love my mother. From the time I was little, she had my brother and me in the kitchen cooking with her."

"You've been hiding this talent from me."

Gavin smirks and shakes his head.

"What is that look for?" I ask.

Gavin shakes his head as if refusing to answer, and presses his lips together. Often it seems that he only speaks once he has it all figured out. Sometimes I'd like him just let it all go, uncensored.

"You have to tell me what you're thinking," I say. "Weren't you the one who said last night we have to start erasing some lines in our relationship? I think that applies to censoring your thoughts as you do."

"Does it? Does that mean you're going to share more of what you're feeling too?"

"I share them."

Gavin picks up the pan and walks to the counter, perpendicular to the stove where the blender is. He scrapes the onions into it and then adds a can of tomatoes along with several other ingredients.

"Getting you to slow down isn't easy," he says. "You move fast. I wasn't sure you'd be interested in quiet nights like this with me. But you seem happy."

"To be completely honest, I've been nervous about being alone with you for too long when there is no football to distract me."

He keeps his eyes focused on the task, and asks, "Do I make you nervous?"

"No, I make myself nervous."

Gavin flips the switch on the blender. The heat in his eyes as he looks over my face makes every thought in my head go mute.

He turns off the blender and opens the lid, steam rises. He pulls a spoon from the drawer and dips it into the soup, then holds it out for me to taste.

Warm, creamy, sweetness from the caramelized onions. "It is perfect, exactly what I am craving."

At the dining room table we sit across from each other. We are both hungry as evidenced by the quiet stretches that sprinkle our conversation. Up here in this house, in Gavin's company, I feel like I can forget the demands of the world below.

"I am happy," I say, thinking of his earlier comment that I'd not been kind enough to affirm. "Happy here, a quiet night with you. I could get used to this." I wink at him and stand to collect our plates.

He places his hand on mine. "I'll get it."

"This is a requirement."

"What is?"

"Fifty-fifty, in everything. You cooked, I'll clean."

I carry the dishes into the kitchen and turn on the water.

Gavin stands behind me and lowers his lips to the side of my neck. The soft kisses feel heavenly.

"It's hard to concentrate on what I'm doing with you doing that," I say in a rushed exhale.

I feel his smile on my neck.

"Would you like to watch a movie?" he asks.

I look down at my mud-splattered pants. "I am filthy, not really curl-up-on-your-very-nice-cream-couch and watch-a-movie kind of attire."

"I have answers for everything."

"I bet you do."

"I have plenty of clothes and a very nice shower. The coolest shower I've ever been in. No one but me has ever used it. I'd love a second opinion."

"Gavin, you don't need to go to any trouble."

"Will you stay?"

I feel a shift, both of us opening sides of us we've been shielding.

"Yes." I know what I've just committed to, and I'm ready. "What movie are you thinking?"

He lifts a shoulder. "Whatever you want."

I dry my hands and wrap my arms around his ribs, kiss his jaw. He slides his hands down the outside of my legs.

"Your pants are freezing," Gavin says.

"So are yours."

He takes me into the bathroom and gives me a tutorial on how to work the slightly complicated system of knobs.

Closing the door, he says, "I'll wait out here until you get everything going."

"Wouldn't it be easier for me to use the guest shower?"

"Trust me. It's worth it."

I undress, fold my clothes into a stack on the floor, then go back into the shower. The first knob releases a large circle of rain from the ceiling, the second sends water from the walls that converges in the center of the cavern-like space, and the third adjusts the temperature. The last two Gavin said don't need to be changed, so I leave them alone. I step into the water, and an involuntary moan of relief floats from me. I didn't realize how cold my skin still was, or that the powerful streams of water that come from the walls would feel like a massage.

"You're all right in there?" Gavin asks.

"More than all right."

"Sounds like it. I told you."

"You did. See you tomorrow."

When I step out of the shower I feel like a new woman, worries washed down the drain and body ready for him.

There is a large counter with two sinks. Like Gavin's closet, all of his things are neatly organized on one side. If I had this much space, I'd fill it all, and I'd alternate between both sinks.

There is a small jade bowl with a bar in it and a shave brush next to it. I lift his bottle of aftershave and gently remove the top. It's his scent; standing on the edge of a flowing river, but on him, it smells even better.

Between the two sinks Gavin has left clothes. I slip on the royal blue shirt, which conceals all of my curves, and step into the gray pants that swallow my legs. The high-quality cotton feels like silk. This would be the perfect set of clothes if I wanted to curl up on the couch and fall asleep. But that isn't what I want.

I wonder if I can relight the sensual woman I'd once so readily embodied. I slip the pants back off, fold them, and put them back on the counter. My long bare legs stick out of the shirt. Am I brave enough to walk out to the living room in only this?

CHAPTER 20

$\mathcal{G}$lass clanks behind me, and I turn to see Gavin's eyes graze the length of me, no shame or need to hide it.

"I almost dropped these," he says. "And I think I just had a minor heart attack."

He sets the glasses down on the coffee table and fills each one with a generous pour. As he hands me one his lips part, but nothing is said. The desire in his eyes, the plea on his silent lips, makes me feel like a vixen.

"Shower is all yours," I say and bite my lip on purpose.

Gavin walks backward toward the hall, eyes on me until he disappears around the corner.

I sit down on the oversized couch which cradles me like an enormous cloud. Off the back of it I grab a white chiffon blanket, and from the coffee table I pick up a magazine. With my glass of wine in hand, I settle back and take a sip. This isn't the zinfandel we drank earlier, but it's familiar. I think it's one we'd had on our first date, the pinot perhaps.

Here I'm wrapped in the comfort of the quiet space, and the calm energy. It is nothing like the constant hum of living in the thick of the city or sleeping in hotel rooms where everything around you is open twenty-four hours a day. I feel warm and safe here.

I'm halfway through the article and taking my last sip of wine when Gavin returns. He's wearing the same shirt I am only black, and a pair of gray cotton shorts. These clothes complement the masculine curves of his body.

Under his arm is a laundry basket. "I'm going to toss our dirty clothes in the washer. Is your bra all right to go in with everything?"

"Yes, thank you." I set the magazine down on the table and take in the view of him.

"What?" he asks shyly.

"I liked you before, but seeing you with a laundry basket just put it way over the top."

"What? Why?" He laughs.

"Out of all the household stuff, laundry is the only thing I don't really like doing."

"I'll keep that in mind."

I pull the blanket around my shoulders and stand in front of the fireplace. We both know what we want, which should make me less nervous, yet it doesn't.

I hear Gavin's bare feet tap the wood floor with a length in his stride. He lifts the blanket and slips his hands from the crest of my backside up to my waist slowly as if savoring the way he can now touch me. There is nothing between his hands and me but his shirt. True, this is always how it is, a thin fabric concealing the private pieces of us, but now it feels sensual and insufficient at the same time.

We sit next to each other on the couch. I lean into Gavin and pull the blanket over us. Below it, Gavin lifts the hem of my shirt then places his hand on my bare hip. His fingers slide over the place where my panties should be.

He makes a low moan. "What would you like to watch?"

I let my eyes drift close so I can take in the sensation of his touch and nothing else. The pads of Gavin's fingers draw together, then as they move apart the back of his nails graze my skin. My body begins to pump some glorious chemical into my bloodstream, things in me reorganize, I'm becoming something else: eyes light, muscles soft, weightless.

I finally open my eyes to a movie I don't recognize. When did it start?

Gavin's hand stills. "I can't do this. It's wrong, Nyla, but I can't even pay attention to this movie with you here, touching me, and me touching you."

"Should I leave?" I squeeze my hand on his thigh, and he grips me tighter. "I'm kidding."

I sit up and stand in front of Gavin. He watches me with wanting eyes. I slide my knees on the sides of his hips and settle my butt onto his thighs.

"Nyla," he says. "You have no idea what you do to me."

In his ear, I whisper, "Oh, I do."

I spend a long time tasting his lips. His breath rushes around my neck as his lips threaten to devour me. Below my hands, I feel the roll of his arm muscles. My entire being is relaxed and ready for this man.

His hands slow, his lips leave my skin. I pull back to find that his eyes are closed.

"Have you changed your mind?" I ask.

Gavin's eyes open, revealing the red hot need that he's holding back, as if what he wants is a sin.

"If you let me do the driving right now we'll both be in trouble because I'm holding on by a thread."

The strain in his voice thrills me. I begin to lift his shirt and, taking my cue, he grabs the back of it just below the neck and slowly pulls it off. My hands trail the hem of the shirt as it goes, through the soft hair on his stomach, then chest, until I hit two bare patches, and my hands stop.

He drops his shirt to the side and nods permission in a way that says he trusts me. I lift my hands like book covers. Scars. My desire muddles with compassion because I know what these are. I curl my hands, then extend an index finger, and gently I trace the scar on the left below the collarbone. The skin is tight, an angry mass of scar tissue that looks like it tried to reopen.

Gavin tucks my hair behind my ear, and as he trails my jaw with his fingers, he says, "It was for a port. They used the same incision to put it in, and take it out."

I don't tell him that I know what it's from. This isn't the first time I've seen this scar, although his is no longer red and fresh like the one I knew which never had time to heal fully.

Gavin wraps his hand around mine and moves it, so my finger is on the other scar. "A PICC line, for the transplant," he says.

I bite my lip, so I don't let out a single word. This one, too, is healed, though the shape is a little different and smaller.

"The dots are from radiation," he says.

"Radiation? What dots?"

He points at two small gray dots a few inches below his clavicle on each side, then to another between his nipples. I can't see this one because his chest hair obscures it. Two more are on each side.

"So they could line up the radiation machine. Thirty treatments."

"Did it hurt?"

"No. My cousin Stephan is a tattoo artist. He thinks I should turn them into something, but I think these will be the only tattoos I will ever get. Do you like tattoos?"

"Yes. I'd never get one. But I like these." I run my hand around the circle touching each one. "These helped save your life."

"Kind of."

I kiss each scar and say a silent thank you. "The scars and the tattoos are beautiful, Gavin."

He hugs me gratefully, and there is a jiggle of laughter in his belly. "Thank you for kissing them. I'm self-conscious of them."

"Why?"

"I don't like to talk about it. But people like to stare at scars, and they aren't shy about asking, especially those who recognize them. Plus all this chest hair highlights them even more."

"I think your hairless spots are sexy."

"You do, do you?"

I run my fingers down the center of his torso to the top of his pants and slip one finger below the band. "I think this is sexy too."

"I've only got a single thread, Nyla, and it's unraveling."

I wiggle my hips feeling what he wants to offer me. "What if," I whisper, "I ask you to let go of that thread?"

Gavin clutches me to his body, stands, and carries me to his bedroom where he lays me down on the bed. I slide my foot up his leg and, with my toes, press the band of his pants down. The line where his oblique meets his hip is candy to my eyes. My body tightens all on its own giving me pleasure.

"Gavin, do you have a condom?"

He stills. "Ahhh, no," he says, though he doesn't look too deterred. "I know it looks irresponsible, but I haven't needed them in a very long time. And with us, I—"

I move off the bed, stand up, then jog down the hall to my purse. I return with a box in my hand.

"You have a box of condoms in your purse?" he asks, shocked or pleased, I'm not sure.

"I picked them up yesterday. I knew we might soon, so I figured I better, you know. I meant to leave them at my house, but I forgot to take them out. Good thing, I guess. I mean, if you want to have sex, that is."

I toss the box of condoms at him and pull off my shirt. He rips the box open, takes one out and sets it on the nightstand. Then he puts the box into the drawer.

He scoops me up and lays me down on the bed again. I watch Gavin, my eyes wide open, enthralled by the euphoric look on his face. It's like I'm his universe, and he's taking great care, restraint, to be gentle with me.

"I want you," he says between the kisses he trails down between my breasts. "Dearest love."

What courses through my veins is something that has not been translated into any language I know. There are no words to explain my thoughts . . . feelings . . . because there isn't a single one. I've become the desires of my instincts as if for a few brief moments, or an eternity, my being transcends the need for everything except this.

I'd forgotten my own body, but now a gentle tightening begins between my thighs . . . swelling . . . expanding . . . cresting. My toes point. Gavin keeps his eyes on mine, not once have we looked away. His mouth parts, and with a thrust that could shift the earth, total bliss melts over his face.

Slowly he releases the weight of his body onto me.

"Ohhh, Nyla . . . Nyla . . . Please let me keep you."

I'm exhausted, physically and emotionally, though my soul feels light. I curl into Gavin's side, and before I can utter how perfect it all feels, I fall asleep.

•••

My eyes flutter open to a pitch-black room. I'm curled on the edge of the bed, my knees pulled tight to my chest. This is how I always sleep, though it's not what I'd expect of myself when sharing a bed with Gavin. His hand is on my hip. His thumb moves back and forth methodically tracing an infinity sign. I stretch my legs out one by one and roll over, his hand floats over my body, brushing past a place that sends a wave of desire. I can't see Gavin, but I feel the warmth of his breath before he kisses my forehead and then finds my lips.

"Nyla, may I have you again?"

I slide my hand down the outside of his thigh, then up along the inside of it. He is all ready for me, and somehow I woke aching for him. I lift onto my knees, mount him, and slowly sink down allowing my body to melt around him. The covers fall off my body. The air of the house is cooler than when I fell asleep, but from below me, within me, his heat radiates and keeps me warm.

Gavin's breath picks up, his fingers grip my knees, and I move up and down slowly, relishing how he fills me. Nothing feels more powerful than this, the need of a man between my thighs, the connection of our energy honoring the purest drive in our bodies.

I lower my chest onto him and thread my fingers through his thick hair. "Gavin, I love the way you feel in me."

He holds me so tight I can hardly breathe, but my hips still move in the way my body demands.

"I feel like we are built to go together, Nyla, like a lock and a key."

"Mmmm," I lift my chest and put my hands on his shoulders, "I feel it, too."

I can't see them, but my fingers brush over his scars as I slide them lower to where our bodies connect. His hand finds mine, and I guide him to my clitoris and show him a rhythm that I like. I feel a little selfish, but I want all of him.

I lift higher on my knees, all of my energy floods to the center of my body, then I slide down him, and every cell in me pushes away from my core like an exploding star. It feels as if Earth lost her gravity.

"Oh, my love," his voice is rough and urgent.

He is not done. His hand grips my thighs begging for movement. I'm breathing, yet, there is not enough air. Somehow this feels okay.

"I can't move," I say.

Gavin holds me tight and rolls me below him. My limbs wrap around his body as tightly as a woman lost at sea would cling to the only raft that would save her life.

His careful control begins to slip. Gone is the cautious lover I enjoyed earlier. Now he moves with impassioned strength.

Gavin slows, and asks, "Are you all right?"

"Yessss." I hear the strain in my voice that sounds distant from my own ears.

Gavin moves again with renewed strength. I hear the sounds that escape me which could easily be interpreted as pain or extreme pleasure. How odd that these lines cross so often as if someplace deep inside, birth and death are the same.

"I want you," I say like a pledge. I nibble his neck and rub the side of his face with mine. "I want you."

Gavin squeezes me tight, I didn't know we could get any closer, but we do. My name is a prayer that he says as he releases. He melts onto me, and says, "I'm going to keep you." Even more quietly, "Dear love, please let me keep you forever."

CHAPTER 21

Faint rays of daylight filter in through the soft, gray drapes drawn over the bedroom windows. I'm curled on the edge of the bed again. Without looking, I know I am alone. I turn the clock on the bedside table toward me; it's only 6:55 a.m. Next to it is a condom wrapper that was hastily torn open last night.

My body flutters with a reminder of how good being with Gavin felt, but it's quickly erased with a wave of dread as I remember why there is only one condom wrapper on the bedside table.

I'm frustrated that I was so careless. I promised myself that I would always use two forms of protection. There is no room in my life for the responsibilities of children. Plus, I'm sure Gavin doesn't want to repeat his past. This morning I'll talk with Gavin about it.

I stand on my jellied legs and go into the bathroom. On the counter neatly folded is the royal blue shirt I wore last night and a toothbrush, still in the package.

The shirt is even softer than it was yesterday and it smells of our mingled scents. Brushing my teeth, I look at myself in the mirror. My hair is a full mass around me, my eyes are bright, and my body looks as relaxed as I feel.

It was the best sex I've ever had.

A swell of guilt slaps me because my thoughts and feelings are a betrayal to my husband. I can't allow myself to think that anything I experience is the best I've ever had without smearing his memory. I amend my thought to be that it was the best sex I've had in four years. Granted it's the only sex I've had. But now, thinking this while standing in Gavin's house, in his shirt, with a toothbrush he's left for me, I feel like I've accepted some level of adultery. I can't win in my head. I wish for the peace and presence I had last night when I'd managed to go an entire evening when everything was just about Gavin and me.

I walk down the hall and try not to disturb the quiet in the house. In the living room, Gavin is stretched out on the couch, one hand behind his head, a book in the other, and the chiffon blanket tossed across his hips. He's a vision of male perfection.

Gavin looks up, satisfied ease on his face, and tosses the book onto the table. He lifts the blanket and pats his chest.

"Good morning, beautiful," he says.

On the coffee table is a mug, empty except for a bit of coffee around the corners.

Gavin catches my hand and tugs. I look into his eyes and see a weight I'd not expected.

"Good morning, beautiful." He pats his chest again.

"Good morning," I say.

Just like last night, as I lay down on him, I find everything about our form molds together perfectly. I lay my head over his heart. The blanket tightens around us. He pushes my hair back from my face, tucks it behind my ear.

"You have the most magnificent body," he says. "But this," his hand dips into my waist, "these hips, and this," he grips my butt so hard my body is ready to surrender fully to him, "you are my goddess, you know that?"

Last night in the heat of connection Gavin said many things that I let slip in one ear and out the other. I've learned we aren't always supposed to hold tight to the words spoken in the heat of passion. I'm not sure what to do with these words, though.

"Thank you," I say. "You are an amazing lover."

He makes a grateful sound. "Did you sleep well?"

"Yes. You didn't though."

"What makes you say that?"

"It looks like you've been up for a while and I know you don't usually get up before seven. Do I snore? I don't think so. And I don't think I'm a bed hog."

"No. You sleep in a ball on the edge of the bed, and you're so quiet I wasn't sure you were alive. I lay in bed awhile before I got up."

I set my chin on his chest and look into his eyes so I can get a better idea as to what he is thinking. "Clearly," I say.

"Do you want to tell me why you sleep like that?"

"No."

"It doesn't have anything to do with me, does it? I just want to make sure, because I had you in my arms twice and as you pulled away from me you said you don't want to hurt me."

Sometimes we don't have control over our thoughts, our words, especially when we aren't conscious of them.

"It doesn't have anything to do with you, and I don't want to talk about it, especially when your hands are on my bare ass, and I'm between your legs."

He pulls me up his body until our lips come together.

"You taste like coffee," I say.

"You taste like mint."

"Yes, thanks for the toothbrush."

"Now you have a toothbrush here for when you stay, which I hope is every night."

I laugh and say, "You don't remember what I do for a living do you? You'll be lucky to get me once or twice a week."

The sexy look on his face falls into a firm pinch. "I will take whatever you'll give me, and I'll bend in any way possible so that we can be together."

An unspoken agreement passes between us.

"Would you like coffee?" he asks.

"I would love some."

Gavin picks up his empty mug and leads the way to the kitchen. He dumps grounds from the coffee maker and then presses a button on the grinder.

I muster the courage to bring up the condom issue. "I'm sorry about last night." I want to swallow the words back in.

Gavin stops and turns quickly. "What are you sorry for?"

"That came out wrong. I'm sorry that I didn't stop to put a condom on the second time. I got greedy and wasn't thinking. I had an IUD put in last week, so no need to worry, really. But, it isn't a 100 percent guarantee, so I need for us to use a condom every single time. My career is really important to me, as you know, and I don't want a pregnancy to derail my plans. Now or ever."

A sad laugh dies quickly in his throat as he turns away from me. He grabs a cup from the cupboard identical to the one he's using, black with a gold rim around the top. From the fridge, he grabs a small container of half-and-half, rips the paper top open, then pours just the right amount.

"You have half-and-half?" I ask, knowing he doesn't use it.

"I've been buying it since I met you. Figured at some point I might need to make you a cup of coffee here." His voice is flat, and his eyes avoid mine.

"Thank you," I say.

The silence is heavy, but I don't know what else to say.

The smell of coffee floats in the air. Gavin fills my mug and hands it to me with the handle turned toward me.

"I have something I need to tell you," Gavin says. "But this must stay between us because no one knows, and it's very personal."

"I'd never share anything you told me."

"I know, but it's sensitive for me, and I . . . ." He sips his coffee and nods. "I've tried to think of a way to tell you this earlier, but I couldn't. On the one hand, it felt presumptuous to bring it up, but I should have said something before last night. I am aware that you've put a lot of trust in me to be here now."

"You're freaking me out, Gavin."

"It's nothing. Hang on." He holds up his hand to reassure me. "It's . . . when I went through treatment, things weren't working. The cancer progressed despite the standard protocol of chemo. My doctors told me I needed a transplant and also strongly suggested using a new series of drugs. The regimen was still in a trial phase. But what they did know, based on the class of drugs, was that it had a higher likelihood of affecting fertility. But my life sounded like a better option, so I signed the waiver."

"How high of a risk?"

"They didn't know. It's still in the follow-up phase. I have blood work and sperm tests done every three to four months. A couple of weeks ago I was told I am still at zero. My doctor said that since my counts haven't started to at least rebound that it's unlikely, in her opinion, that they ever will." He sets his mug down and clasps his hands behind his head. "The doc said that the four-year mark is kind of the magic time when they determine if it's permanent. I'm almost to the four year mark, but I'll tell you that in my gut I already know. It's not happening for me."

"Oh."

"I'm not trying to scare you, Nyla, but I have thought a lot about the future with you. When we went to that store on Friday to look for something for your brother, it threw me, especially when that woman asked. I hate the thought that I can't get you pregnant. It sounds stupid, but it affects how I feel about myself. Still, it was wrong that I kept it from you."

What Gavin decided to do before he started treatment isn't any of my business, and it doesn't affect me at all, but still, I ask, "Did you bank before you started chemo?"

Gavin's lips draw back between his teeth and his nostrils flare. "I did. But then one day I found myself very alone and angry with the shitty hand I'd been dealt and had the sperm destroyed." He presses his hand to his heart. "I am so sorry I didn't meet you earlier in my life."

I'm lost with how to reconcile my past experiences with how I feel today. I don't wish to have met Gavin earlier in my life because I loved my husband and I was happy. Yet I am so grateful that it's Gavin here in front of me now because I do feel that there is something about us that goes together just right.

"I'm all in with you," Gavin says. "But if this is a deal breaker I need to know. Obviously, I'll try to change your mind. But you might want time to think about it?"

I'm filled with experiences and secrets I've tucked away, which I have no intention to share with Gavin, or anyone else, and I know he has these too. But are there things I have a right to know? And are there things I am obligated to share?

There is pain in Gavin's eyes and uncomfortable tightness in his body that I want to help relieve.

I place my hand on his back, and say, "Fucking cancer."

Gavin's chin trembles, eyes well. "Fucking chemo."

"But then again," I cup his cheek and stand on my toes, "thank you chemo."

Gavin nods and whispers, "Yes."

Looking at me, his tears fall. Each one I catch with my lips, then I brush away the trails of wetness with my thumbs.

"The thing about my cancer," he says, "is even though it's gone, it still feels like I can't get out from under a goddamn car that's landed on me."

Cancer has been eradicated from my life through death, from his body through treatment, and yet it continues to alter our lives like some cruel game.

"Gavin, what you just shared with me doesn't change how I feel about you. Us."

The calm I've felt as we've talked begins to crack. There is a bubble of emotions that I won't acknowledge.

Gavin looks like he needs more assurance, but I can't say anything. Perhaps it's wrong, but I decide to use my body to impart acceptance to him now.

I remove my shirt, drop it on the kitchen floor, and pull him all the way into the shower. I strip his clothes fervently, turn the water on, spin my back to him, and press my hands to the wall. A waterfall cascades down my back, and then it's only Gavin.

It's easier in life to pursue things that have a goal, like winning gold or sitting on an anchor desk. It's easier to slip on a pair of running shoes and release what I feel instead of doing something with my feelings. But when there are two people, when there is no end game, I don't know what to do.

There is much I am not ready for, there are things I never want again, and because of this, I don't know how to move forward with Gavin. Do I care that he can't have kids? Do I feel a loss because of it? Am I supposed to? Did the universe make me a widow to prepare me for him?

Gavin's release erases some of my pain, not all of it, but I am thankful that I have myself to offer him, or at least pieces of me.

He holds me, my back pressed against his chest for a long while before he turns me around. His smile falls.

"I can tell the difference between water and tears," Gavin says. "I am sorry. The last thing I ever want to do is cause you pain, but I'm a selfish man because I'm not willing to let you go. Please say you'll keep me."

Water pours over us, though it does not find a path between us because where we meet there's an airtight seal.

There are a lot of things I need to figure out, and I have no idea how long that will take me. But for some reason, though I don't know why, I can honestly say, "I will keep you, Gavin Boston."

The stitches in my soul are pulling tight, but I'll make them hold, I will ensure that I heal for him.

CHAPTER 22

*G*avin has asked me many times to visit him at work when I return on Fridays, but the timing hasn't worked. This morning, my quick flight from Seattle allowed for the perfect opportunity to surprise him.

The last time I was here at Boston Smith Company, it was night, and my SUV had been burglarized, the windows shattered. I didn't get a good look at it then, but now I take a moment to admire it. Gavin told me this building used to be a window factory that was abandoned sometime in the fifties. The structure is both artful and modern; bright white with windows trimmed in black steel and fresh wood accents all around.

Inside the clean, open lobby, it's bustling with people moving in all directions. The place is like Gavin's house, awe-inspiring. Immediately the blue-glazed cement floor catches my eye, it varies in color like the swirling ocean.

At the round reception desk, decorated for Thanksgiving with a scattering of fall leaves and an overflowing cornucopia, a woman smiles at me. "Good afternoon," she says. "Welcome to Boston Smith. How may I help you?"

"Hello. My name is Nyla. I'm wondering if you can point me in the direction of—"

"Nyla!"

I look over my shoulder and see Trace, arms open wide. "So great to see you. You haven't been here before, have you?"

"No. I thought I'd stop in and surprise Gavin. I got back this morning."

"Couldn't wait to see him? The truth is that poor guy can barely make it through Fridays anymore, anticipating your return."

He looks to the woman behind the desk and says, "Pat, this is Nyla Tripple, Gavin's girlfriend."

I've never been introduced as Gavin's girlfriend, and I don't refer to him as my boyfriend. We've been together for a while now, perhaps it's a fair description. I mull the two titles over in my head, but I feel too old for them. I wonder how Gavin refers to me.

Pat stands from her desk and pushes her glasses onto the top of her head. She shakes my hand like a mother grateful that her son finally has a girlfriend. "What a treat to meet you. Would you like me to show you to his office?"

"Is he free?" I ask.

"I'm not sure," Trace says. "His assistant would know, but I'm willing to bet he'd make time for you no matter what. I'll show Nyla to Gavin's office. Thank you, Pat."

Trace leads me up four flights of stairs which are an engineering marvel. They are constructed of thick wood planks that appear to float. We reach the fourth floor where there are several occupied desks in the middle and an area with a Ping-Pong table where there appears to be a friendly match underway. At the far end is a conference room with a glass wall, there is a full meeting in process. Offices, most with doors open, surround the perimeter.

We stop at a desk where a man about my age sits. Trace says, "This well-dressed gentleman is Alvis, Gavin's right-hand man, and quite possibly the only one in the office that might be a better dresser than Gavin. Alvis, this lovely woman is Gavin's girlfriend."

Alvis stands with an excited smile that consumes half his face. He is rather fancy in a navy suit and a pair of thick, black-rimmed glasses. "Nyla?" he asks.

"That would be me."

"It sure is wonderful to meet you."

"Is Gavin free?" Trace asks.

"He's on a conference call, but you can go in."

"I don't want to bother him," I say. "I can wait."

"No, really, you should go in," Alvis says. "He wouldn't want you waiting out here for him."

"He's right," Trace says. "And I'll see you tonight."

Today is the tenth birthday of Trace and Linda's son, Alex. Gavin and I have been invited to celebrate with the family.

"Did you hear the party has been moved to Gavin's?" Trace asks.

"I didn't."

"Alex thinks Gavin is the coolest guy on the face of the earth. When we asked him where he wanted to eat dinner, he said Uncle Gavin's house."

"That is sweet," I say.

"Yep, so Gavin got roped into grilling tonight."

"I'm sure he is happy to do it, and it's a beautiful day."

"Cool but clear." Trace looks a little uncertain for a moment, his eyes bounce to Gavin's office door and back to me. "Thanks for taking such good care of him. It means a lot to Linda and me."

"I'm the lucky one."

Slowly I turn the handle of Gavin's office door. It's strange to just welcome myself without knocking, as Alvis said to do.

The windows are unusually high, starting at nearly shoulder height and continuing all the way to the twenty-foot ceilings. Gavin's elbows rest on the ledge, his gaze in the direction of the Fremont bridge. It's a fantastic view. He leans his head on his thumb and index finger and makes a sound of acknowledgment. I want to see his face, but I'm enjoying this view. It isn't often I get a chance to observe him without him knowing, especially when he's in his work clothes: crisp white shirt rolled up to his elbows, navy vest, and brown slacks tailored perfectly. He's even got the wingtips on from the first day I met him. They have a soft spot in my heart.

Quietly I close the door and take a seat on the small couch that sits opposite of two matching chairs.

Gavin's desk, a solid piece with curved legs, is on the other side of the room, near the windows. Blueprints are rolled out with an open binder and a shiny gold pen on them.

The rustle of my jacket causes Gavin to look over his shoulder. He shakes his head as a smile slides onto his face.

"Yes, I'm still here," he says into the phone. "I'm sorry to cut this short, but someone powerful just walked in. May I call you back?"

"I don't want to interrupt you, Mr. Boston," I say.

Every week when I return, the first kiss is something that surprises me. There's an electric current in Gavin's lips that recharges me. I'm aware that my weekly absence adds to the heat of our reunions, but something in me knows that even if I weren't gone so much, we would still maintain the same fire.

"I missed you," he says.

"I was in the neighborhood and couldn't resist popping in. I've been so excited to see you, I don't know why."

"You don't?"

"Well, it's because I really, really like you. So I thought I'd take my chances at surprising you and maybe buy you a cup of coffee, or lunch if you have time."

"Lunch sounds amazing, I'm starving. I've only got about thirty minutes though before my next meeting. If it weren't with so many people, I'd cancel it and go home with you now."

He holds up my coat for me, the one I'd just taken off, then takes my hand and leads me through the office. I think he looks rather proud to have me here.

"I saw Trace," I say. "You're grilling tonight?"

He holds the front door open for me. "It will be fun. I'll get to use my new grill. I need to go to the grocery store when I get off, but I hope to be home by five. They're coming over at six."

Two blocks over from Gavin's office, we stop into a small sandwich shop called Between Two Slices. It's eccentric with bright pink walls and fifties diner-style tables and chairs. I order soup, because like usual I'm cold, and Gavin orders a sandwich. The food doesn't disappoint.

"I got on an early flight this morning back from Seattle," I say and smile. "It made me think of that first day we met. Do you remember?"

"Do I remember? I don't think you thought a thing of me then, but I was," he pauses, "ah, quite certain I'd need to see you again when you walked away from me, up those stairs."

"You did not."

"I had a feeling about you. Fate smiled on us. A series of unfortunate events that turned out to be fortunate for me."

Below the table, I slip my shoe off and run my toes along his pant leg, which makes him grin.

"If you tell me what you need at the store I'll go shopping. Maybe then we'll have a little extra time, to, you know."

Gavin reaches into his coat pocket, pulls out his key ring and removes one. "I had this made for you yesterday. I want you to come and go as you please at the house, to always feel like it's your home too." He shakes the key a little. "Are you going to take it?"

Reaching out to accept the shiny, new key, I ask, "Are you sure?"

"Am I sure? Positive. Now you can head over Fridays when you get home, anytime that works for you. And, it kind of thrills me to think I might actually get to come home to my beautiful woman. There's something quite sexy about that."

"Especially if I'm in something sexy."

"Anything you have on is sexy."

"Hand me your phone."

Gavin sets it on the table, enters four numbers, and slides it toward me. I look my name up in his phone book and note in my contact information the code to the keyless entry at my house.

"That's for my house. It seems less committal than a real key, though."

Gavin takes my hand and kisses my knuckles, then he turns it over and kisses the inside of my wrist. My breath becomes light and rapid.

As we walk back to my car, Gavin keeps me tucked close to his side, a place that has become one of my favorites in the world.

He opens my car door. "I'll see you at home then? Do I get to keep you all weekend?"

"All weekend?"

"You said it's a later flight on Monday. I'm hoping you'll stay three nights instead of your usual two?"

Every Friday when I get home, I unpack my bag from the week, then I pull out a smaller weekend bag which has a carbon copy of everything I need, and add clothes to it. On Sundays, I go home because I need to do laundry and pack again. Gavin usually spends the day with me, and we watch football. Staying at his house again would complicate my routine, but I love it there.

"I still have to pack for the week," I say.

"We can go to your house Saturday or Sunday and still do that. Or if you'd prefer, I can stay at your house Sunday."

"You'd stay in my rainbow sheets?"

"Of course! With you, I'll do anything."

"I do love your house."

"Just my house?"

I know what he's trying to get me to say, but those words feel like an impossibility. He says he loves me when we are in bed, usually at the peak of it all, and I let the words slip through my ears.

Last weekend though, he held my eyes for a long time after he said them, still inside of me. I couldn't repeat it back. Instead, I gave him a compliment about his excellent abilities in bed. This seemed to appease him.

As much as this all feels perfect with Gavin, I still need to figure some things out. Specifically, my heart, which feels like it's wrapped in a cast, still trying to heal. Why is it easier to give my body than my heart?

"Send me that shopping list so that you can get home sooner," I say. "Then, I'll really show you how much I've missed you."

"You'll have it in five minutes, and I'll be home by four, earlier if you're lucky."

"Oh, Mr. Boston, I'm feeling pretty lucky."

CHAPTER 23

$\mathcal{G}$avin's front door opens with a thud. The thunder of footsteps grows closer and closer until two children appear at the entry of the kitchen. The boy hops up on a barstool at the island where Gavin and I are working on dinner.

"Hi, Uncle Gavin," the boy says. He looks at me with unblinking blue eyes.

Gavin reaches across the island and gives him a high five. "The birthday boy. You look much older today, definitely ten. Alex, this is Nyla, my girlfriend."

That title again, straight from Gavin, does seem as strange as I thought in my head.

"Nice to meet you, Alex. Happy birthday."

Alex shakes my hand, making his ash-blond hair fall into his eyes. He pushes it back and smiles at me like he's ready for school pictures.

The little girl continues around the island, lifts her arms to Gavin, and says, "Up, please." She has delicate skin, like a porcelain doll, and a tiny nose. Her fine blond hair is falling out of her braid that almost reaches her shoulders.

"Emma, ease up on the grip, or you are going to rip my arm hair out," Gavin says.

She lifts her hand like she's touched something mysterious. "So hairy!" She rubs her hand quickly on it. "Daddy don't have hair. Why do you?"

"Just lucky, I guess."

"I'm five," Emma says to me.

"I am thirty-four, so on my next birthday I'll have a five in my number like you."

"When is your birthday?" Emma asks.

"My birthday is on Christmas day."

"Do you get even more presents?" Alex asks.

"Kind of."

"We watch you on TV," Alex says.

"You do?"

Alex holds up a football, and says, "Dad said you could teach me how to throw a ball better than him."

"I'll be happy to. You'll have to meet my brother someday. He was a quarterback in college and can really throw."

"That's so cool," Alex says with astonishment.

"Hey, you two," Linda says.

Linda sets a platter of fruit onto the counter and Trace sets down a bowl of salad. She looks between Gavin and me with a smile of satisfaction.

Gavin takes a plate of hamburger patties out of the fridge, and says to Alex, "Want to help with the grill?"

"Yeah!"

"Hold these." Gavin hands the plate to Alex, and out of the freezer he grabs a veggie patty.

"What's that?"

"It's a hamburger for a vegetarian." Gavin looks at me and winks.

"What is a vegetarian?" Alex asks.

"A person who doesn't eat animals."

Emma's face pulls like she's about to whine. "I don't want to eat animals!"

"Come on, Emma, you can help me too," Gavin says.

The kids follow behind Gavin.

"I should go help," Trace says and grabs the bag of buns and plate of cheese.

"Alex used to think Gavin was the coolest guy on the face of the earth," Linda says. "But now that they've been watching you on TV, you should hear him. Uncle Gavin's girlfriend is," she makes air quotes with her fingers, "'a football lady.' He thinks Gavin is some sort of god. You might ruin his expectation of women because now he wants to know why I don't watch football."

Dismissively, I say, "He'll be fine."

"Really, those two sit at the house and watch football, and each time you come on the TV, they lean forward just a little. Gavin gets this stupid grin on his face. You know which grin I'm talking about, right?"

"To me, all of Gavin's grins are sexy."

"I get it, I'm glad you feel that way. He's like a brother to me. We appreciate you two having us over. It means a lot to Alex, well, to all of us."

I've spent a lot of time in this house, but it's always been Gavin and I here alone. We enjoy this space together as a sanctuary, a respite from the busy world, and the busy lives that we experience outside of each other. However, as I look out the window, I see things differently. Gavin is next to the barbecue. He has Emma in one arm while his free one moves animatedly, as he does only when he really gets into a story. Alex watches him, mouth agape, captivated by whatever Gavin is telling him. This home is a place that is meant to hold life, not to just be a weekend retreat.

•••

I stand to collect everyone's empty plates. Gavin begins to stand, but I put a hand on his shoulder and kiss his cheek, and say, "I'll get it."

He squeezes my hand and kisses the inside of my wrist, like this afternoon. I've never had anyone kiss me like that there. It's delicate and feels like love.

In the kitchen, I load the dishwasher and begin to work on the hand-wash items. Linda grabs a clean towel from the drawer and starts to dry. Alex walks into the kitchen, looks at the two of us, then peeks into the sink.

"Can I help?" he asks.

"You want to dry?" Linda asks.

Alex looks at his mom and then back to me.

"That does help me a lot," I say.

"Okay," he says.

Linda hands Alex the towel and leaves us in the kitchen. He takes great pride in the job he's been given, ensuring the dishes are completely dry before he sets them on the counter.

"I was told," I say, "that you don't want a cake for your birthday."

"I don't like cake."

"What do you like?"

"I'm like Uncle Gavin. I like cookies."

"What kind?"

"I know Uncle likes peanut butter, but I like chocolate chip best."

"Should we make you some of those?"

He looks at me with round excited eyes. "Can we?"

"Of course we can. Would you like to help?"

Alex nods, then without saying anything, he runs out of the kitchen, the wet towel abandoned on the counter.

A couple minutes later, Gavin walks into the kitchen with a grin on his face. I wonder if this is the silly grin Linda mentioned, because to me it sure is sexy. He picks up the wet towel and hangs it on the oven handle, then begins to put the dishes away that Alex dried.

"We're baking cookies?" Gavin asks.

"I sure hope you have chocolate chips," I say.

"My mother likes to stock the baking supplies when she visits, so I bet we'll get lucky."

Gavin opens the pantry and pulls down a plastic bin then tosses a bag of semisweet chocolate chips onto the counter. "Look at that, we are lucky."

"Very," I say.

Gavin draws me to him and kisses the curve of my neck. "Have I told you how much you amaze me?" he asks.

Alex runs back into the kitchen and climbs onto the stool. He spots the bag of chocolate chips, reaches across the counter, and grabs them. "Uncle Gavin, I'm ready now. Nyla, we have some."

I put the last plate in the dishwasher. "Thanks to the way-cool Uncle Gavin, we do have chocolate chips." I open the pantry and pull out the other ingredients, handing them to my little helper who is very excited to be making his own birthday dessert.

"Since Uncle is my uncle, can you be my auntie?" Alex asks. "I don't have any aunties, just four uncles."

Gavin pops up from behind the island with a mixing bowl in hand and gives a questioning look as if I'm the one to make such a determination.

"Ah, you know, that is all right with me, but just be sure it's okay with your mo—"

Alex turns and sets the bag of flour on the counter, then runs out of the kitchen hollering, "Mom."

Gavin says, "Linda will say it's fine, so hopefully you really don't mind."

"I've never had anyone call me—"

Alex returns sliding along the tile floor in his socks. "Mom said it's fine. Now I can tell people my auntie is on TV."

To think only a few hours ago that it was the first time I'd heard myself referred to as Gavin's girlfriend. Now I've somehow gotten attached to his second family. It feels like I've gone through some sort of time warp knowing how I got here, and yet not entirely sure. In my head, I try to attach the word boyfriend to Gavin. I think of my little niece on the way and wonder if someday she'll call Gavin uncle. My belly rolls at the thought. Girlfriend, house keys, auntie . . . Something tells me Gavin has an idea of what I'm thinking about as he sits down on the barstool across from Alex and me.

Alex is a great little helper, eager to do anything that is asked of him. It takes me longer to make the cookies with him, but it's a lot more fun with his help. He carries three dough balls out to the living room for his family.

Gavin stands up and pulls me into a little corner of the kitchen tucked away from the door. He kisses me, flicks my earlobe with his tongue, and says, "I was told you looked a little shocked to be introduced as my girlfriend today."

"Did I?"

He shrugs.

"It might have surprised me a little."

"Maybe I should have officially asked before you became the auntie match for this uncle."

"Uncle Gavin?" Emma says.

Unlike her brother, Emma moves silently. With one hand, she tugs on the leg of Gavin's jeans, in the other is a doll. Reluctantly Gavin releases me and swoops her up into his arms. She lays her head on his shoulder and sticks her thumb into her mouth.

Tonight is the first time I've seen Gavin with kids. It makes me wonder how fate twisted so cruelly that this man will not be a father when it's clear he should.

"Should we have Alex open his gift while the cookies are baking?" I ask Gavin.

On the deck outside, Alex bounces back and forth between his feet while he watches the city below.

"Alex," Gavin says. "Do you want to open a present?"

He runs into the living room and sits across from me on the floor. I hand him a box wrapped in paper the color of the sun.

"You got me something?" Alex asks with large round eyes as sparkly as his mother's.

"It's from Gavin and me."

Alex tears open the wrapping paper that falls to the ground in small pieces. He can't get the flap open that is closed with a bit of tape.

Linda says, "Here, buddy," and holds her hand out.

She cuts the tape with her fingernail and hands it back. Alex opens the flap and dumps the football out onto his lap. He picks it up and turns it until he sees the Seattle team logo.

"It's signed by the starters from this week," I say.

Trace looks at me, his mouth half open, then to his son, and says, "That isn't something to play with. Do you understand, Alex? Be careful."

I'm around football players all the time. I forget how much people look up to them. For me, it is just a signed football from the men I talked to that week.

Alex holds it like a prized jewel. "Is it really?"

The excitement on his face is something that makes my heart swell. I can see why parents want to do so much for their children. This kid isn't even mine, and I'd get another football signed for him just to see that pure wonder on his face. When an adult gets an autograph, there is a sense of value in their eyes. But him, I can see that this means everything in his ten-year-old world.

"That's incredibly generous of you," Linda says.

"We'll put it in a special box," Trace says.

Trace reaches for the ball, but Alex pulls it away, runs to me and throws himself into my arms, knocking me from my upright position.

"You like it?" I ask him.

He squeezes my neck with his free arm.

"I'm not sure he'll ever let that ball go," Linda says.

Alex holds onto me, his arm tightens, then Trace says, "You have to let Nyla go, buddy."

Reluctantly Alex releases me.

"I like the birds too!" Emma says.

"You do? When is your birthday?"

She turns to look at her mother and then remembers on her own. "July two."

"Second," Linda says.

"Second," Emma says.

"All right, I'll remember for July second."

"But I like the one with the dolphin too," she says.

"She just goes by the mascot right now," Trace says.

"That is a good method," I say.

Alex runs his small hands over the signatures of the ball and sits down alongside me. "Can you read them to me?"

"They are kind of messy, aren't they?"

I read each one to him. We talk about their position and their purpose, and then I give him my inside scoop on each player. When we are done talking, I look up and realize everyone is listening.

"I love you," Alex says as he hugs me tightly again, though he doesn't knock me to the ground this time.

I wish it were easier for adults to say these words, for us to express this feeling, without being so afraid of the consequences. I can't remember the last time I told someone I loved them, even though I love a lot of people.

I hug him back, and say, "I love you too."

"Can I go to a game with you?" he asks.

"Maybe someday everyone can come."

"Okay. Will you teach me to throw the football now?"

Trace holds out his hand. "Not with that one."

Reluctantly Alex gives it to his dad. Trace carefully slips it back into the box and closes it. Gavin helps me up off the ground.

"Go get your other one and let's go out back," I say.

•••

At the end of the night, Emma insists that Gavin carries her out to her car seat. I wave goodbye to the Smiths as they walk out to their large SUV and then go back inside.

It's silent now, but the house still hums with the happy energy of the celebration. This is a place meant to hold people, and it's a place where happy memories are supposed to be made.

Gavin comes back inside, and with a brightness in his eyes, he grabs my hand. He leads me through the living room, into the kitchen, and back into the little nook where we'd be away from prying eyes if there were any.

"I'd like to finish our conversation."

"Here?"

"I just want to regain the same momentum we had."

"Was there momentum?"

"There was. So I was saying, perhaps I should have asked you if you wanted to be my girlfriend before everyone, including me, just started calling you that."

"No, you said something about auntie match for this uncle."

"You're right. Either way. It leads to the same question. Nyla Tripple, will you be my girlfriend?"

"I feel too old to be a girlfriend?"

"Wife then?"

I laugh, sure that was not where I was going with that.

"Ah no. That requires too much paperwork."

"Girlfriend then? One step before the other."

"You really want me to refer to you as my boyfriend?"

"What else do you want to call me?"

"Well, I was considering sexiest man alive, sex god, sexpot works too."

"I'm not opposed to any of those when it's just you and me. You might make me blush if you said that to others with me there."

"True and I don't want to entice other women to try and pick you up. Boyfriend, I guess. There is always my friend."

"Not enough for me now." He grabs my thighs and lifts them around his waist. "Isn't there a requirement to consummate the relationship to make it official?"

"I don't think that is a requirement for this."

"Well, let's just pretend it is. That way you can make your sex god happy."

CHAPTER 24

$\mathcal{G}$avin sits at the kitchen island, dressed and ready for his workday. He looks up from the newspaper in his hand and sets it down. Appreciatively he looks me over. This morning I slept in, something I rarely do. I'm still in his T-shirt, my hair is a mess, and my eyes are only half open.

"Good morning, beautiful. Would you like some coffee?"

"Morning, handsome. I'd love some, but I got it, don't get up."

I stand behind him, slip my arms over his shoulders, and down his chest over his vest, feeling the gentle curves of him. Then I kiss his neck just above his collar.

"What do you have on the docket for this Monday?" I ask.

"I have a breakfast meeting, need to work on permits and the plans for the Yamhill building, and interviews. Trace insists I sit in on these last few candidate interviews for those positions I told you about. I don't like the HR side of the business all that much, but he's right. I need to help make sure we've got the right people." He leans back into me and closes his eyes. "And you are off to San Diego."

"The big Thanksgiving Day game. It's exciting. I got a hotel near the water so I can run on the beach in the morning."

Gavin's eyes open slowly. "I love when you look at me like that."

"Like what?"

"I don't know. Like you're either going to pounce on me, or melt into a puddle."

"Not time for either of those things right now, unfortunately. I think rebounding from a puddle would take me too long. This is nice though, being able to talk to you in person, before we head off for our day, or rather, the week. Kinda feels like an upgrade from the weekend girlfriend status."

He sits up, slowly stands. "I heard you say that to Linda, weekend girlfriend. Frankly, it pissed me off and hurt my feelings."

"Gavin," I pat his arm a couple times and move toward the coffee maker, "I don't mean anything by it. But it's kind of true because I'm only around on the weekends. I mean it tongue-in-cheek, of course."

I pour my coffee add the half-and-half, and turn around to see the light that was in Gavin's face has dimmed. He yanks his eyes away from mine, stomps on the foot pedal of the trash can, and throws his apple core in.

"I didn't sign up for a weekend girlfriend. That makes me sound like I don't care, or you don't."

He moves around the kitchen, takes the last sip of his coffee, rinses the cup, and washes his hands. In this stretch of silence, it seems as if Gavin's broad shoulders are expanding, yet he struggles to control it.

I take a deep breath, try for an apologetic smile. "I wasn't trying to be rude. I'm sorry."

"Is that what you signed up for?" He pulls the towel from the rack, dries his hands, and tosses it down on the counter. "A weekend boyfriend?"

His words *weekend boyfriend* are loaded with implications which make me feel as if I have done something wrong. I try not to let this show, to stay calm.

"Gavin, until this weekend I hadn't even thought about titles or expectations because it's just . . . but now that you say it that way, I understand what you're trying to get me to see. You know it's just us, or I think it is?"

"Of course!" Gavin shakes his head at me.

"What?"

He makes an exacerbated sound. "Are you ever going to really let me in?"

With a little laugh, I say, "Gavin, I've let you in as far as I can, trust me. Where is this coming from? Why are you so frustrated?"

"It's not hard for me to see that what you think, or feel, and what comes out of your mouth doesn't always match. You plaster on that perfect facade, which is okay for the outside world, but not me. Not us."

Gavin's phone rings. He picks it up from the counter, presses a button, and puts it in his pocket. "I need to go."

The truth, while out of left field, burns. It makes me angry that he's never said this before. And it scares me to think of what he sees in me.

"I'm not the only one at fault here, Gavin. You can't even talk about your emotions unless you've just come in me. Or apparently, if you're pissed at me."

His eyes burn into mine. "At least I talk about them! Someday, you'll have to dig a little deeper for us."

"I've given you everything! I give my weekends, happily, to our relationship. I'm here. I haven't spent a night at home in two weeks, Gavin. Maybe this isn't enough for you—"

"I'm not worried about physical space or time. Those things I can work with. What I can't work with is how you've sealed pieces of yourself up. Pieces I need to feel comfortable in us."

"What pieces?"

He shakes his head again. "This is getting derailed, Nyla. Let's talk about it when we—"

"This is me getting emotional, Gavin, exactly what you asked for! Tell me what you want from me. Because I am lost. I've climbed an emotional mountain to be standing here in your house, your shirt, to open my body to you! What else do you want from me?"

His shoulders sink. "I want you to think more of us without me having to ask for it all the time. I just want you to be brave enough to love me, someday, even if it hurts a little."

"Love isn't supposed to hurt."

"I don't know. I love you, and I'm in quite a bit of pain."

"Gavin."

"It's scary to be in an imbalanced relationship. To know I care more."

"That isn't true."

"Do you realize I'd do anything for you. I'd give up anything for you. If I could bring Lorenzo back so that you didn't have all this pain, and your beautiful heart wasn't locked away, I'd do that, for you. If I could go back in time and meet you before him, so we would have been together through the ups and downs, and I could have been able to protect your heart . . . I'd do that for me. But I can't fix anything, Nyla."

My lips tighten, my body follows their lead, I cross my arms over my chest.

"I'll stay in this one-sided relationship because I love you, with everything I am. But what I need from you is to not think of this, me, as just a weekend boyfriend. And, you'll hate me for saying this, but I need our relationship to be only us. I see his name too often in your eyes, and I hear it when you sleep in a ball on the edge of the bed and—"

Gavin's phone rings again. He pulls it from his pocket and not looking happy he takes the call. "Hey, yes. But I need to call you back in sixty seconds." He looks straight at me, silently communicating that is all he has left for me too.

He ends the call, and says to me, "At this breakfast meeting I'm speaking about the future of city development for more than a hundred key players in Portland. If it didn't affect my business so much, I'd stay here, and continue this conversation."

I'm a volcano, heat and steam rising, swirling lava leaking from protected stones. "It's not a conversation. It's an argument. Doesn't matter though because I've got a plane to catch."

"I'm not happy leaving us like this," he says.

"Makes two of us."

He lets out a long breath and walks out of the kitchen.

My ears demand all of my attention. I'm acutely aware of Gavin's footsteps. He walks to the bedroom, back, drops his shoes on the entry floor. A second later, I hear the coat closet open, then close.

Gavin returns to the kitchen, pulls on his jacket. He's wearing the fancy wingtip shoes that first caught my eye. I remember how struck I'd been by his kindness, and even now I continue to marvel at his attention for the sweetest and tiniest details of our life. He puts love in everything he does for me, us, it isn't even just his words.

The downward corners of my mouth lift, my entire body softens. The anger in his face drains to sadness, maybe exhaustion. I feel horrible knowing I am the cause.

"Please don't do the laundry when you leave," he says.

His request surprises me, shocks me actually.

Each Sunday, I strip the bed of the sheets, gather the towels and wash them. Then I make the bed and fold the laundry. The house is always so clean, but I want to help earn my keep so to speak. Although he never asks a thing of me.

"It feels like every time you leave you make an effort to erase your presence. You clean everything that smells like you. You pack every single belonging. When you do this, all trace of you is gone and then, yeah, maybe I do feel like I only have a weekend girlfriend. And that's not what I want. It might make me sound like an animal, but I'd like to smell you on the sheets. I'd like to see your towels, all those little bottles you have, and your hairbrush in the bathroom. Maybe then I can start to trust that you'll return no matter what, and loving you won't feel so scary."

"You don't think I'll come back?"

"You live an exciting life, around a lot of exciting people. I'd be a fool not to wonder, just a little, if this is enough."

He looks around the kitchen, then at my bare legs that stick out from his shirt, the only thing I ever wear around the house in the mornings. Walking toward me he buttons his coat, adjusts the collar. He stops, grips the hem of the shirt and tugs at it as he kisses me possessively.

"Don't wash this either, please," he says.

As I listen to his footsteps walk out the door, his truck start, and the sound of the engine fade, I pray this is not a preamble to the ending.

The bedsheets are a twisted mess, I resist the urge to strip them, and make it instead. It smells like us in here, a dance of Gavin's cologne and my shampoo. It's like standing in a lavender field along the river's edge, if such a thing exists.

I fold the shirt I'm wearing neatly and set it on the bed.

We've spent a lot of time in here, and the shower, in the throes of passion. I give him my body when I see the pain in his eyes, frustration, and sometimes when he wants an answer that I don't have. When he whispers loving confession in our most intimate of times, when there should be no barriers between us, I let them slide in one ear and out the other. In the beginning, I just assumed it was words of release, but in my heart, I've known for far too long that he's been baring his heart to me.

A thousand-pound weight lands on me, and I realize I haven't climbed an emotional mountain, I've just become good at using our intimacy, my body, for distraction. Not only for Gavin but myself.

On the bathroom counter, all of our stuff is neatly organized, and the two sides look balanced. Our towels hang next to each other. It appears two people live here.

After I get ready, I try to leave my things, all those little bottles which should mean nothing, but I can't do it. I don't know why. I pack them slowly, maybe I'll leave my hairbrush. No, I can't do that either.

The bathroom looks empty without these things.

Every week I drop into, and then quickly disappear from Gavin's space. I'm so used to my life on the go, packing and unpacking, that it feels normal. I always see Gavin happy with my arrival, but I'd never thought about what happens when I leave no trace of me behind in the spaces he continues to live in.

I realize I've even packed the toothbrush he gave me that first night I stayed. I take it back out and put it in the cup next to his.

My hand shakes as I zip my weekend bag and put it on my shoulder. I don't think we just broke up. But then why do I feel like something is final about my departure?

I lock the front door with the key Gavin gave me. I turn it over in my hand. It's so shiny and new. I should leave it for him. What if after today he realizes he doesn't trust something in us and wants it back? I unhook it and stick it under the mat.

I drive out the private road, but halfway down I feel like I've reached the end of a line. I can't imagine sending Gavin a message that says, "key is under the mat." How cowardly would that be? To leave the scent of me behind, the toothbrush, and the key. I reverse my car and drive back down the road. It's the longest I've ever driven backward.

CHAPTER 25

*T*he ringing in my ears wakes me.

It stops.

Then starts again.

It takes me a few moments to float up from the fog of sleep, curled on the edge of the king-sized bed at a nice hotel in San Diego.

I reach out and slam my hand down on the alarm clock. The ringing doesn't stop. It's my cell phone on the desk. With all my effort, I drag myself from the bed just as it stops ringing. I don't even bother to check who it was. Nature's call is more urgent.

The first thing I do each morning is put on my running clothes with sleepy arms that feel like a thousand pounds, drink a bottle of water, then stretch on my yoga mat. Slowly I wake, and my body loosens. About thirty minutes later, I'm ready for my run.

Just as I tie my second shoelace, my phone rings again. It's Wednesday, just after seven, which is much earlier than when Gavin usually calls. I pick up my phone from the hotel desk and turn it over to see Perry Taklin's name. He is someone that calls obscenely early sometimes. He's a big fan of the "early bird catches the worm" idea.

"Happy day to you," Perry says.

"You're awfully chipper for 7 a.m."

"I'm starving, and I bet you haven't eaten yet. How about you meet me for breakfast."

"When?"

"Now works for me. How about you?"

"I was just heading out for a run," I say, though we both know I'd cancel anything to meet with him.

"Well, how about you run on down here to Omelet. It's just down the street from you."

"Okay, I'll be there in fifteen minutes."

I run down to the restaurant and spot Perry through one of the windows laughing, his hand on his jiggling belly. Across from him, I see someone, but they're obscured by the morning light bouncing on the window.

Inside, I tell the hostess I'm joining a table and head into the main dining room which is full. It's Darren Dryer at the table with Perry. Darren's hands move all over the place, as usual, his voice escalates like he is about to deliver the punch line to a joke. I hadn't expected anyone else to be here, but the fact that it's Darren with Perry is quite curious.

I pull out my chair. "Good morning. You two got a great spot."

Both men stand, hug me, then return to their seats.

"How's the run so far, kid?" Perry asks.

"Short, but good."

"It's at least what, a mile?"

"Maybe a half."

"That's a full run for me," Perry says. "Not like the old days when churning the legs was easy. Though I'm packing a few extra pounds. Not like you trim young'uns."

"Some days I don't feel so young anymore," Darren says.

"You look like you were out for a run this morning," I say to Darren.

"I went out for a walk. If I were running these days, I'd call you. But my damn knee only handles walks now and that," he makes a wheel motion with his hand, "you know that machine you can use that's like running but easier on the joints."

"Elliptical," Perry says.

Darren snaps. "That's it. My wife got me one of those a couple years ago. It's the best. Kids love it too."

These two men crack me up, and indeed are two of my favorite people in the business. But, I still wonder why the three of us are here. Darren and I in workout clothes and Perry in an unusual combination of shorts and a casual shirt.

"You're coming tonight, right, Nyla?" Darren says. "To the pre-Thanksgiving shindig?"

"I'd forgotten about it," I say. "But I did RSVP a while back."

"Marlena and the kids are coming. Is your wife coming as well, Perry?" Darren asks.

"Yes." Perry leans closer to me. "My wife is quite excited to meet your new beau."

"Ah, she'll have to wait then."

Darren, with a confused expression, says, "You didn't invite him?"

"He had other plans already, with family."

A couple of weeks ago Gavin told me he was going to his aunt and uncle's house for Thanksgiving dinner and that his parents were flying in. I didn't even extend an invitation for him to join me here. Now, I look back and see he was feeling my response out. I've never thought about inviting him to travel with me. I understand even more now what he was talking about. The invite into this side of my life would have been a good idea.

"All right guys, what's up?" I ask.

"We are here," Perry leans forward and looks around, "because as of this morning, Darren's co-host has been released from his contract."

"What happened?" I ask.

Perry shakes his head and squeezes his temples. "It's going to be a damn scandal, and I don't really want to go into it. But it amazes me still how many men are disgraceful boys when it comes to manners with women. Well," he presses his hands together, "it's worse than that, unfortunately. But on the flip side of it all, is an opportunity. Immediate."

"Which means I need a co-host," Darren says. "I know we'll be great together. What do you say?"

"Permanent post?" I ask.

"Of course," Darren says. "Right, Perry?"

"You know where I'm at with this, kid. Most definitely permanent."

Excitement vibrates inside of me. It takes all of my self-control to not jump up when, I say, "I'm thrilled, honored, and grateful."

"Difficult spots make way for better ones," Perry says. "Especially in this case. You'll do a great job."

•••

I finish my extra-long run, take off my running shoes, and walk to the ocean's edge. Water slides over my feet and pulls the sand from below me.

The beach is busy: kids play in the sand, the water is dotted with swimmers, shade tents are being erected for a leisurely day.

I'm here alone, a thousand miles from home and from everyone I'd want to share this news with. I've spent nearly my entire life focused on my goals, but as glamorous as it might all seem, this career, as well as my previous, is a lot of time by myself. Millions of miles flown, thousands of hotel rooms, endless hours in cars.

Lorenzo sacrificed a lot for me, rarely was I alone when he was alive. He built his goals around mine and worked around me. Though it was a strain sometimes, it worked for us. Really, we were always happy. Even in the end . . . mostly.

A ball lands in the water next to me. A large chocolate lab bounds up to get it, its backside knocks into my knees in his excitement.

"I am so sorry!" a woman says.

Her cheeks have the glow of a satisfied woman. The man who holds her hand has a similar glow.

He says, "She is just a year and doesn't realize how big her body is."

The lab drops the ball back in the water at my feet and bounces back and forth. I pick it up and ask the couple, "May I throw it for her?"

"Yes," the woman says.

I pitch the ball down the shoreline and the chocolate

lab jets off. Its long body stretches out and floats momentarily over the earth between each step. I feel the love the dog has for the run. I, too, relish those moments between footfalls when my body feels nothing but air.

"Damn," the man says. "Great arm. I wouldn't have to throw the ball as much if I could do that."

"Have a good day," the woman says.

Is it weird to feel envious of them as they walk away? They have the ocean, each other, and their dog on a lazy start to the holiday weekend. I've never thought about having a dog. My job would not be conducive, but I think it would be fun. I'd actually rather have the guy, not that guy, my guy.

Since Monday, when Gavin and I departed on less than ideal terms, we've talked every day at our usual times (in the morning and the night), but we've not broached the subject of our argument or the future. This morning he left me a message while I met with Perry and Darren. I haven't called him back yet.

I've thought a lot about Gavin and me. With his business and my career, and no sign of either slowing down, what options do we have?

As I stand on the edge of the land, alone in my good news, I long to feel Gavin's protective arms around me. I want to celebrate our lives together, I want to share them. I don't want to just be his weekend girlfriend.

I've never called him during his work hours. I cross my fingers and hope he'll answer.

"Hey, Nyla," Gavin says quietly. "Hang on." There are sounds of movement and voices in the background like someone is presenting, then it all fades. "Sorry about that."

"I'm sorry. It sounds like you're in a meeting."

"Don't be. I'd rather hear your voice than his anyway. Everything all right?"

"I'm sorry I missed your call. I was at an impromptu breakfast meeting with Perry and Darren."

"Impromptu?"

"You're never going to believe this. I'm the new co-host on the desk with Darren. His old co-host got ousted. Now, it's me!"

"That I can believe. I'm really proud of you."

"You're the first person I wanted to tell, Gavin."

"That means a lot to me. How are you feeling?"

"Like there's enough energy in me to light the entire city, maybe the whole state of California."

Gavin's laugh is deep and rich, I love the way it sounds every time. I close my eyes and see his smile that goes with it.

"I'm also a little scared," I say like it's a secret I hope the ocean will absorb, so no one else knows. "That's also how I feel. Between you and me."

"Nyla," he moans quietly. "Where are you?"

"San Diego."

"I know that. Where exactly?"

"Where the earth meets the ocean."

"That's what I hear, the water."

"I've walked a little further in, now it's up to my knees."

The chocolate lab bounds back to me, the ball in her mouth, and drops it in the water next to my leg. The man, who is running at what looks like his full speed, hollers, "Lily!"

Playfully, I say, "Your name is Lily?"

"Lily?" Gavin says in my ear.

"This big chocolate lab wants me to play with her. I threw the ball, and she's now brought it back."

"Miss, I'm really sorry," the man says.

"Don't be."

"Do you have a dog?" he asks.

"Never have, but I bet it's fun."

The woman leans heavily on the man's shoulder. "And a lot of work."

"Worth it though," the guy says with a happy smile.

She fixes him with a questionable look. "Debatable."

The man clips a leash onto Lily's collar, and I hand him the ball.

"Thanks," he says.

I lift my phone back to my mouth, and say, "Sorry Gavin. Where were we? Oh, I was going to tell you, I really wish I could hug you right now. That we didn't always have to wait for the weekends."

"Give me five, six hours tops."

"For what?"

"I'll have you in my arms."

I laugh. My laugh fades. "Are you serious? How? There is no way. No, I can't ask that of you Gavin. It's impossible, today is—"

"Do you want me there?"

"Yes, more than anything."

"Then I'll be there."

"How?"

"Magic."

I should protest, the airport will be a mess with it being the morning before Thanksgiving, not to mention there is a high likelihood everything is booked. But selfishly I want him to share in this exciting time with me. And if he wants it, too, he apparently has some magic.

"Tonight is my work Thanksgiving thing," I say. "People are bringing families that traveled with them. Would you want to go with me?"

"I'd love to. Send me your return flight so I can book that back with you. Are my work clothes enough for tonight?"

"I'm a sucker for what you wear to work, you know that?"

"I didn't, actually. You like my vest?"

"I don't think I tell you enough. It's the vest, the way you roll your sleeves up and your strong forearms show with the dark hair on them, and your pants, the way they hug your ass. And then sometimes, you wear those wingtips, the ones you wore the first day I saw you. I guess I love them so much because they made me notice you that first day."

"What did you think of me that first day, Nyla?"

"I was struck by your kindness, your size, how handsome you are. Also, I thought it was unfortunate you didn't notice that woman hitting on you."

"Oh, I noticed, but I already knew I had my eyes on someone special."

As we hang up, I almost say I love you without a thought, and I don't know what stops it, or why I was going to say it. Actually, I do. My heart beats faster at the thought, the honesty in me, but the sound of the rolling waves calms me. I don't know what it is about the ocean. I feel safe here, even though the current in the water feels strong enough to pull me under.

CHAPTER 26

*M*agic happened.

When I get back to my hotel room, the most handsome man is there stretched out on the couch talking on the phone.

Gavin says, "Mom, I need to get going. My beautiful girlfriend just got home."

I've stayed in thousands of hotel rooms, from the budget-friendly to the fanciest of suites, but they have always been temporary shelters. Although, hearing Gavin say "home" I feel for the first time like this hotel could be just that, because like they say, home is where the heart is.

"You want to say hi to her? Ummm sure. But don't say that to her, you might scare her away. No, yes I will, but not now. Please." He sets his phone on the table, turns on his side, and pats the cushion. "You're on speaker, Mom."

"And Dad," Mrs. Boston says. "You're on speaker too."

"Hi you two," Mr. Boston says.

"Hi, Mr. and Mrs. Boston."

"Kathy and Richard," Kathy says. "Please."

"Hello, Kathy and Richard," I say.

"Gavin just shared your exciting news, congratulations."

"Thank you very much. I'm excited both about the debut, and that Gavin can be there with me."

"Will he get a good seat?" Richard asks.

"If he doesn't mind standing, he'll be on the field with me."

"Wow, Gav. There's a once-in-a-lifetime experience."

Gavin mouths *really* and I shake my head yes.

"If he doesn't want to stand, I'm sure I can find him a great seat."

"I bet he'll stand," Kathy says. "He's—"

"Mom," Gavin says. "Please."

"Please, please. Gavin thinks I embarrass him sometimes," Kathy says.

"I don't, Mom, but we have to get going because we need to be downstairs in five minutes."

Gavin hangs up the phone and sets it on the table. I lay my clothed body onto his and kiss his lips in a way that I hope conveys my gratitude.

"Thank you," I say. "It means so much to have you here. To know that you want to be here too."

I walk across the room to the closet where my dress hangs. Out of the corner of my eye, I see Gavin move toward me like he wants something.

"You gotta stay in your chair, handsome."

"I don't think I have to anymore."

He sits on the edge of the bed within arms reach. I take my clothes off, a bit slower than needed. I can feel his eyes on my back, and it makes me want to do certain things.

"Want to help me dress?" I ask.

The dress is simple, light purple with clean lines and a fuller skirt. I hand it to Gavin, then I reach my arms overhead. He slips it over my body, places one hand at the base of the zipper and takes his time to zip it.

Short on air, I say, "You really are magic."

"Mmm. So are you."

"Your parents sound nice."

He squeezes my hips and slaps my butt. "I do actually have very cool parents."

•••

On the second floor of a popular restaurant in downtown San Diego, called Mission Grill, a private dining room is set with several round tables. Each has formal place settings and menus laid on top.

Between our crew and their families, there are at least fifty people here. I've been to many of these celebrations over the years, yet I've never stopped to consider how much this feels like my extended family. With Gavin here, it feels like I'm blending one piece of my family with the other.

Across the room, Perry winks at me, and with a discreet finger he points to Gavin and tips his head to the side just a fraction in question. I nod yes, and he takes his wife's elbow and leads her toward us.

"Gavin, this is Perry and Janaka," I say.

"It's Jan for family," Janaka says and gives Gavin a hug.

"You must have just flown in?" Perry says.

"Yes, just arrived a couple hours ago," Gavin says.

"How was the airport? Crazy I bet," Perry says.

Gavin looks at me like a man forced to reveal his secret. "I didn't have to deal with the airport."

"Good man," Perry says. "I prefer private as well."

"And here I thought you arrived by a magic flying horse," I say.

Six waiters come into the room carrying two bottles of wine each.

"Looks like dinner time," Perry says. "We're all at the table there in the back with Darren and his family. Those kids are growing up."

Darren's two daughters are no longer kids. The oldest is thirteen, and the other is twelve. They both look like their dad, with softer features and larger cheeks.

Darcy, Darren's oldest, sits down next to me, and says, "Nyla, I joined the track club like you said, and I love it. Not to brag or anything, but I am the fastest." She looks across me to Gavin, and says, "Hi, I'm Darcy."

"Nice to meet you, I'm Gavin."

"This is my sister DeDe, my mom Marlena, and you know my dad."

"Just dad I guess," Darren says. "It's Darren, though. Good to meet you, Gavin. Welcome to the Thursday family."

"Thank you," Gavin says to Darren.

The evening is filled with laughter, plenty of food, and much to be thankful for. The tea lights on the tables burn through all of their wax and slowly, one by one, go out on their own and send little streams of smoke up in the air.

•••

Gavin and I go back to the beach where I'd run this morning. The full moon hangs in the east which gives enough light to see our way. There are a few people on the sidewalk, but no one on the sand.

Gavin takes off his fancy wingtip shoes and rolls his pants up to his knees. I slip off my shoes and pick them up.

"I'll carry those," he says. He adjusts the two pairs in one of his large hands and then takes my hand with his other. "You look even more beautiful than I'd imagined on the beach." Gavin kisses the inside of my wrist.

"I love when you kiss me there."

"Your skin feels like silk here." His thumb sweeps the inside of my wrist. "Just like another part of you." He grins mischievously. "It's not socially acceptable to kiss you there, in public."

"I'd think not."

Gavin lifts my wrist to his lips again. "But here," his breath rushes over my soft skin, "I can always kiss you. Now you know that I might be thinking about other things."

"I already knew you were. I feel it on your lips."

The wind whips my hair from my neck, I tame it with my hand as a shiver runs from my shoulders through my arms.

Gavin lets go of my hand and wraps his arm around me. "I don't know why, but I always think of San Diego as nice and warm twenty-four seven. Are you warm enough?"

"I'm perfect."

"You really are."

We walk closer to the ocean, where the sand firms below our feet, then to where the water washes around our ankles and splashes up on our legs.

"I had a lot of fun," Gavin says. "It's nice to see you have a good group of people around when you travel. Darren reminds me of your brother."

"He is a lot like him. We have fun. Sometimes we even toss the football around, and it reminds me of when I was a little kid playing ball with Kevin."

We walk back to dry sand and sit down. I shimmy back against Gavin between his knees and tuck myself into the warm shelter of his body.

"I'll send you my schedule for the rest of the season," I say. "If there's anyplace you want to join me, I'd love to have you. But, there is no pressure."

"Even if it's just for a night, I'll make it to as many as I can. Is staying the weekends at my house becoming too much? I mean, not being together isn't an option for me, but I'm happy to stay at your house. What would make things easier for you?"

"I don't know what it is about your home, Gavin, but I love it. When I'm there, something feels right. I feel at peace."

"When I found that house, I knew right away it was special. Something in me said I was supposed to make it my home. But, I don't know how to explain this, that first night you stayed it finally felt . . . whole. Full in the way it's supposed to. With us in it."

"I feel the same thing."

"That's why each week when you leave and everything is gone it feels so empty. Like I've been left. The first time I didn't think much of it, but once I saw it was your pattern, it stung. And I wondered if maybe I was missing something about how you felt about me, or us. I should have said something instead of letting it stew, though. I'm sorry."

"I spend more time on the road than not, and I'm used to packing up everywhere I go. I hadn't looked at it from your side, and I didn't know it bothered you. I didn't wash the sheets."

"I know. They smell good. And you left the toothbrush."

"Careful what you wish for. You might find a hairbrush next week."

"Oh, please don't tease me like that."

I love the way silence settles between us, like a perfectly placed comma that lets us both breathe. In that space is the comfort that we know we're still talking.

"Also," I say, "I'm sorry for being disrespectful about the sweet things you say when we're close."

"I've never said anything I don't mean to you, and I promise I never will."

I turn to face him, threading my legs over his. There isn't a soul near us. It feels like we own this corner of the earth in the dark, lit up by the moon over Gavin's shoulder.

"I love you, Nyla. I don't expect you to say it back or feel the same way, but I want to say it not just when I've," he hesitates and lifts his chin, "you know." He steals a quick kiss. "Though it's hard not to say it then, because in those times together, with nothing else distracting us, I feel it in every cell of my body. Almost like I am nothing else but that feeling."

"Gavin—"

"It's all right, Nyla, knowing you want me here is enough."

When Lorenzo died, it felt like my heart was wrapped in a cast which was impossible to remove. Then today when I hung up the phone, as I stood on the edge of the ocean and the current swirled around my feet, I realized it was me that kept my heart bound with threads of fear and grief.

I press one hand over his heart. "Gavin, I love you."

Gavin's mouth opens, then his lips pull back together, and he smiles. He presses his hand against mine and breathes into us.

The first time I'd fallen in love, it was easy, because Lorenzo and I were young and innocent. We had no idea how life would test us, or that our love, which becomes a part of who we are, would not be enough to keep us together.

Now, I know love may not save us from fate's hand, and yet it requires us to surrender as if floating blindly in space where asteroids, planets, suns, and moons swirl around us. It seeps into the cells of our body—blood, bone, and skin—and gives life an entirely different texture.

The second time I fell in love, it was not easy, because I knew how far I could fall and how much I could lose. Yet, more importantly, I know how much I've gained. That is why I choose to love bravely.

CHAPTER 27

"Almost there," Gavin says.

He turns the rented SUV onto a one-lane road. Gray clouds billow above us, but the blanket of snow all around makes things feel bright. Along the sides of the road, the snowbanks reach the bottom of my window.

"Dad has an old red pickup that he's mounted a plow on. He does his best to keep the road clear, but he said with the constant snow this week it's been impossible. You can't tell now, but once all this snow melts there is enough room on this road for two vehicles."

The steering wheel has turned into Gavin's impromptu drum, and occasionally he catches the chorus of the song. He has a powerful set of pipes suited for rock music and slow ballads of sorts. It's husky, almost a little gravelly at times, although there's no trace of it when he talks.

It reminds me of the first time I got him to play his guitar for me, the day after we had sex for the first time. Now to get him to play I just bat my eyes and ask really nice. He always obliges, which means he sings a lot to me.

I always let him choose the songs he wants to play and so far none have been his brother's.

"What inspired you to learn to play and sing?" I ask.

Gavin's hands stop drumming the wild beat, and his lips pull to the right. "When I was a sophomore in high school, I liked a girl, but she told me I was too nice. Why do girls do that, tell guys they're too nice?"

"That's a complex topic. But your kindness is one of the many qualities that I love about you."

"Note to self, do not become a self-absorbed rock star."

"Yes, I like you just the way you are."

"Thank you. But, back then I thought I could shape this bad boy image and win her over. I learned two things. One, I am nice, and there's no changing that. Two, I don't like to be the center of attention. I do like to sing and play at home for you, and you seem to like it, but I don't want to play for anyone else."

"I love when you sing. I told you that all I want for Christmas is you singing to me in your birthday suit next to the fire."

"That's a Christmas wish I'll grant, but it has to wait until we get home. I'm not sure anyone else wants to see that but you."

This week Gavin traveled with me to Denver. On Christmas we celebrated my birthday and nothing else. Today is effectively our Christmas Eve. This worked out perfectly for the rest of Gavin's family because Jax worked on Christmas day too.

This morning Gavin and I boarded a flight bound for Sea-Tac, where we took a connecting flight to Pangborn Airport, just thirty miles from his family's cabin in Leavenworth, Washington.

"What are you grinning about?" I ask.

"Our amazing life together. I'm excited that my family finally gets to meet you. What are you grinning about?"

"This amazing winter wonderland, and being with you."

"What about my family? Are you excited to meet them?"

"Of course, but I will admit on the flip side of that coin I am incredibly nervous."

"Triple Threat Nyla gets nervous? I'm kidding, love. But really, why are you nervous?"

"You had it easy. My family already thought quite highly of you."

"Um, if you think going to Samuel Tripple's office to ask if I could date his daughter was easy, you are mistaken. He might have thought well of me as a business associate, but that didn't make it any easier. In fact, it might have made me even more nervous. You do know how intimidating your dad can be, right?"

"What did Pop say when you asked him?"

"I think that should stay between your dad and me. But suffice it to say there was a legitimate threat in there."

"No, I want to know."

Gavin shakes his head no.

"You weren't threatened into liking me, were you?"

"Not at all. Actually, the opposite." He takes a deep breath. "He threatened me, as he should, if I hurt you. I'll do the same if I have a daughter someday. But he also warned me that you weren't exactly easy to reach, regarding your heart, and that I shouldn't get my hopes up. That's as much as I am saying though."

The comment of *if I have a daughter someday* rattles around in my head. Just as I open my mouth to ask him what he means by that, he says, "What the hell?"

We've turned a bend in the road at the end of which is a log cabin, aged wood brilliant against the snow with smoke lifting from the chimney. In front of it is something that interrupts the idyllic scene: an ambulance.

Gavin steps on the gas. The tires lose traction on the packed snow. He eases the SUV back into its slow and steady pace.

"Sorry," he says.

The back doors of the ambulance close. A paramedic jogs around to the driver side and hops in. Gavin pulls the SUV over along the narrow road pushing the passenger side into the snowbank. The paramedic driving is a man with pitch-black hair and a beard that matches. He nods and looks down to the side of ambulance carefully maneuvering the tight space. There is just an inch between the two side mirrors.

The porch along the front of the cabin is wrapped in white Christmas lights. Jax, whom I recognize immediately from pictures, squeezes a woman with blonde hair against him. I assume she is his girlfriend, Brooke. While the brothers share little more than a family resemblance, the look of worry is identical.

Gavin stops the SUV at the bottom of the stairs, throws it into park, and pushes his door open so hard it rocks the vehicle. Frigid air rushes in. Before he's even entirely out of the vehicle, Gavin yells, "What happened?"

Brooke gives a quick wave and runs into the house.

Jax says to Gavin, "You drive. Brooke is getting our coats." He walks down off the porch and holds his hand out to catch a few flakes of snow. "I have a feeling the snow is only going to get heavier. Let's take Dad's truck. He has studs on it."

Brooke, who'd just come out of the house, says, "I'll get the keys."

A moment later she tosses them to Jax, who throws them to Gavin like a hot potato. Jax opens the back passenger door of a sleek silver pickup, and says, "Babe." Then he opens the front passenger side door, gives me a quick hug, and says, "Nice to meet you, Nyla. You ride up front with your man."

The engine roars, we start back down the road, and Gavin asks, "What is going on?"

"Can you catch up with the ambulance?" Jax asks.

"Of course, but can you please tell me what is going on?"

Jax drags a hand down his face and stops it over his mouth. "We think Dad had a heart attack."

The corners of Gavin's eyes slide toward his cheeks, nostrils flare, lips bunch.

He drives a reasonable speed down the snow-packed road, but as soon as we reach the main highway that is plowed and graveled, he speeds up. I almost tell him to be careful, but I don't think this would do anything but make him angry, so I bite my lip.

Gavin's lips soften once we catch up with the ambulance. "All right," he says, "will you please tell me what exactly happened?"

Jax says, "When we got here last night, Dad didn't look well, and this morning he didn't look much better. After breakfast, he laid down on the couch to watch a movie."

"Dad laid down on the couch to watch a movie?" Gavin says.

"An hour later he got up complaining that his chest felt tight. Mom asked him a million questions. You know how she gets. Since Uncle Fred, she's been on Dad to get a physical done."

"I know," Gavin says. "He's stubborn."

"Then, as he walked into the kitchen, he stopped, gripped his chest, and nearly fell to the floor."

"Jax caught him," Brooke says.

Gavin presses his hand to his forehead then lets it fall onto my thigh. "Did he say anything after you caught him?" he asks.

"Yeah, he said maybe you should call an ambulance," Jax says.

I lift Gavin's hand and kiss his knuckles, then turn his hand over and kiss the inside of his wrist. Even though this affection has become something he regularly does to me, I've never done this to him. It feels intimate in the most profound way.

He mouths *I love you*, and I mouth back *I love you too*.

We pull into the hospital parking lot, follow the ambulance around to the emergency room, and Gavin puts the truck in park. There is a sign that reads No Parking. Gavin's lips press into a hard line, and he makes a low grumble sound.

I say, "Go on. I'll park the truck."

Gavin grabs my chin with a tight grip and moves so quickly to kiss me that our teeth smack.

"Sorry." He runs his thumb over my lips.

"You're fine. Go, please. If you need anything, I'll be in the lobby."

The brothers run to the ambulance where Gavin takes his coat off and wraps it around a woman as she gets out. I know immediately this is Kathy. She is a tall, slight woman, and Gavin's jacket swallows her like a kid wearing her parent's clothes. Stretcher legs drop from the ambulance onto the pavement, and the three of them begin to follow it. Kathy stops and grabs Gavin's arm.

He points over his shoulder to the truck, and she waves a weak hand to me, then Gavin leads her into the hospital.

From the back seat, Brooke says, "If you don't mind, I'll hang with you. Brooke by the way."

"I'm Nyla. It's good to meet you."

The emergency room waiting area is packed.

Brooke points to two chairs across from the vending machine, and says, "There are a couple spots."

Even though I've sat most of the day, I collapse into the chair as if I've been on my feet for twelve hours.

Brooke holds up two magazines. "Not much of a selection, but take your pick."

Both covers are well worn, and more than a year old. I choose the one with a friendly looking sloth face. I don't have the energy to read, but the pictures are a welcome distraction.

"Have you ever seen anyone have a heart attack?" Brooke asks.

"I haven't seen a heart attack, a lot of other stuff though. How about you?"

Brooke shakes her head displacing the thick blonde hair tucked behind her ears. "Not until today. It was terrifying." She pulls a hair tie out of her coat pocket and gathers a ponytail at the nape of her neck. "I've only seen Jax scared like this when Gavin was diagnosed. Jax and I weren't together, but he called when he found out and came over to my house. Jax usually acts like he can handle everything, but that day was the first time he showed me he didn't think he could. Today was the second.

"This family has always welcomed me as one of their own, no matter if Jax and I were together. His parents send me cards on holidays, sometimes gifts. Gavin, he's like a big brother. They are tight you know, and take care of each other. I can't imagine . . ."

My mother passed away earlier this year. An aneurysm stole her before my father found her. There was no experience like this, the hope of survival or moments for last words.

It was a Tuesday. I was in Green Bay standing on the practice field, analyzing the route a wide receiver was running when Pop called. He tried to keep his sorrowful voice even enough to tell me about mom. I'm not sure how it happened, but I found myself in Brad's arms. He took me to an unoccupied room where my tears soaked the shoulder of his shirt, and he held me until I could stand again. He drove me in my rental car back to the hotel and helped me load my bags into it. Then he took me to the airport, returned the rental car, and caught a taxi back to his hotel.

I don't think I ever properly thanked him for that. I will, the next time I see him.

CHAPTER 28

Late in the evening Gavin, Jax, Brooke, and I return to the Boston family cabin. In the kitchen, Brooke opens the doors of a china hutch and pulls out four rock glasses.

Jax reaches over Brooke to the top shelf where he pushes a few bottles around, and says, "Here it is." He pulls down a faceted crystal decanter that's filled with brown liquid. "Dad's orders were to go home, drink two fingers of whiskey, and get in the hot tub."

"What is two fingers of whiskey?" I ask.

Gavin holds up two fingers, then sets them down on the table next to a glass. Jax pours the whiskey to the same height as Gavin's fingers.

"I get it, two fingers. This measurement could vary greatly depending on the drinker's hand size. That might be more than I need."

"We are going with my fingers." Gavin hands me a glass then holds up his. "To our family that makes it through shit together, for Dad whose ticker is still working, and Mom who has never been anything short of a saint."

"And," Jax says, "to our two beautiful ladies who sat in horribly uncomfortable waiting room chairs for ten hours, reading out-of-date magazines."

Gavin and Jax toss their glasses back like a shot. Brooke and I sip ours a bit more cautiously.

I have no idea what brand it is, and it doesn't matter, but I venture to guess this is quality stuff, smooth with caramel sweetness. Within minutes warmth spreads throughout my limbs.

Jax refills Gavin's and his glasses, then holds up the bottle to me. I wiggle mine to show I still have plenty, but he takes this as a request for more and adds yet another glug.

Richard will be in the hospital for the next few days, but the doctors are hopeful that medication will take care of him.

Unfortunately, I wasn't able to meet Richard and Kathy today, because the emergency room only allows immediate family. Tomorrow we're supposed to visit. I'm not sure it's the best time to meet them, but Gavin is insistent that I go. I'll trust his opinion.

I change into my swimsuit, wrap a robe around me, and go out back where Gavin and Jax are removing the top to the hot tub. Quickly I get in and melt into the warm water. Gavin settles in beside me and holds me tight. A canopy protects the hot tub but occasionally drifts of snow float in with a change in the wind.

Across from us, Jax nuzzles the side of Brooke's cheek. He hasn't been able to keep his hands off her tonight, it's like he thinks she'll float away if he doesn't hold onto her.

"Gavin," Jax says, "when you were sick, I never once thought you were going to die."

The corners of Gavin's lips lift into a smile that fades quickly. Hesitantly, he says, "That's good to hear."

"But today, when Dad was loaded into the ambulance, I felt this knot in my belly that made me think, what if?"

"What if, indeed," Brooke says. "Not just at his age, any age, right? Sometimes there is no rhyme or reason."

"Did you think you would die?" Jax asks Gavin.

"In my gut, I knew I wouldn't. But in my head, I feared that I might."

"How much time do you think we could save if we no longer feared anything?" Jax asks.

I say, "You can't save time. It's something that slips through our fingers at a constant speed, no matter what we do. The belief that we can have more or less is just an illusion."

"No, well, yes, Nyla, well put. But your experience of time changes, right? Sometimes it seems to stretch, other times it seems to," he snaps, "disappear."

"Perception," Gavin says. "The only way it doesn't seem to disappear or stretch out painfully is to stay present to the true rhythm of life."

"To not live here," Jax taps the side of his head, "where fear lives. But here." He sweeps his arm wide then taps his chest. He takes a deep breath. "What if we didn't care at all about dying? If every night we laid our head on the pillow we were at peace knowing that we've lived life fully."

"To always know it was a life well lived," Gavin says.

"Yes, brother." Jax's eyelids move like his long dark eyelashes have weights on them. "We do need to sit down for another jam session. I feel we've got more words in us. More hits."

"More hits?" I ask.

Jax laughs through his nose and shakes his head slowly. "You still haven't said anything."

"Not now," Gavin says and kisses my temple.

Jax taps the side of his head again.

I'm curious, but this isn't the moment to push my curiosity. Between the long day and stiff pours of whiskey, my eyelids are as heavy as Jax's. I stand, and say, "I need to go take a quick shower and get to bed. It's been a long day."

"I'll be right behind you, love," Gavin says.

Upstairs are three master suites and two more rooms which share a bathroom. Our space is cozy with red and blue plaid bedding which suits this place perfectly.

From the window in our room I hear voices. I walk to it and see we are directly over the hot tub canopy.

Jax says, "I can't believe you haven't said anything to her."

It's probably the whiskey which has turned up his volume.

Gavin's reply is hushed, and I can't hear everything he says, ". . . dare. I'll tell her when I'm ready."

"It isn't a big deal. She'll think it's a compliment. It will probably turn her on."

"I'm not so sure about that. It's her favorite song of yours. I'd rather just keep it that way," Gavin says.

"She really should know, 'Mystery Girl' is your song, and that she's yours."

I've never been one to eavesdrop or try to pry secrets from people because while I am good on camera, I am not a good actress. I can't fake surprise when people tell me something I shouldn't already know.

In the shower, the chorus of "Mystery Girl" plays on loop in my head:

And I had no idea at the time,
How or why I stayed alive,
But, I think it is for you, my mystery girl.
For you, all the reasons I survived.

254 ~ *Nicole Dwigans*

It's a song about surviving that which should kill him because he's destined for a woman who needs him.

I remember when I told Gavin my favorite song of Jax's was "Mystery Girl." He'd been shy about it, and at the time I thought he didn't want to be overshadowed by a famous brother. But now as I look back, I see it with new eyes. He didn't want to talk about it because it was personal to him.

I dry myself off, wrap the towel around me, and plug in my blow-dryer.

"I wasn't quick enough?" Gavin says with a frown.

"I shower quickly when you aren't here to slow me down."

"I never slow you down."

Like a man who has plans, Gavin grins as he sheds his swim trunks and gets into the shower. He hums. The scent of his shampoo, something of tea tree, lifts into the air. Steam fogs the mirror.

Gavin turns off the water, then pushes the shower curtain back. I see him in the reflection of the mirror, and even though I've seen him many times like this, entirely bare, I know I'll never get tired of the sight.

He dries his body with a periwinkle-blue towel, wraps it around his waist, and tucks the corner to keep it in place. He sits on the edge of the tub and reaches for me.

"Will you dry my hair too?" he asks.

I run my fingers through his hair, the color of roasted coffee beans with flecks of caramel. He's grown out the top since we started sleeping together because I love to wrap my fingers in it.

I gather all of my courage to say, "Can I ask you a question? It might be a little inappropriate right now, but it's rattled around in my head off and on all day. Maybe because I had too much time to think."

He rolls his head below my hand. "You can ask me anything."

"You said this afternoon, 'if I ever have a daughter.' What do you mean?"

His eyes open. "I may not be able to give the seed, per se." His eyes are vulnerable as if he's opened the shades directly into his soul. "But I can still be a father. It's something I want to do . . . with you."

"Gavin, I know there is a future for us, but I'm not sure I want to have kids."

"Did you want kids, before, with Lorenzo?"

I nod yes. "But, now I'm in a very different place in my life. This life is demanding of my time."

He looks down at his hands on my waist. "I'm happy to write our future together in any way you want, but remember time and space are things I can solve. You just have to decide what you want."

Gavin's hair is dry, a fluffy mass atop his head. I turn the blow-dryer off and set it on the counter.

"I know you aren't there yet, Nyla, but do you think it's something you want in the future?"

"Which part?"

"All of it?"

I bump his knee with mine and smile. "Maybe we should talk about living together first."

"Let's talk about it."

Sometimes I feel like I'm in a hot air balloon. I let my mind fill with ideas, I dream about moving in with Gavin, wearing a band on my finger again, always coming home to him. But then I wake up only to realize I'm tethered to a mass called the past.

"I have things I need to do before I can do that, Gavin," I say.

"We practically live together already. I think you even bought a full-sized shampoo and left it at the house."

"You noticed."

"Do what you need to, Nyla, please?" Gavin reaches up, and pulls the towel from my body then kisses the ridge of my hip bones, top to bottom. "I thought a lot today. And most of it had to do with us. I don't know how much to push you, Nyla, or how long I'm supposed to wait. But with an acute awareness of the fragility of life, I don't want to wait too long for anything."

It's like someone pushed a fast forward button and I've found myself stopped in a spot I wasn't expecting when the day started, or even thirty minutes ago. I want to be brave enough not just to love Gavin, but to live our life together with nothing between us.

"If you keep kissing me there, ohhhh, I won't be able to . . . what were you asking me?"

He pushes my thighs apart and gets down on his knees. "I was asking you if you'll explore this life with me?"

"Gavin? Why are we having a serious conversation and doing *this* at the same time? And perhaps I've had too much whiskey for this."

"Too much whiskey for this?" he asks, his words muffled.

"No, just enough for—" An embarrassingly loud moan escapes me, and I feel his smile on my southern lips. "Enough to let you do that for sure."

I grip his hair and admire him as he works me. The ridges of muscles on his shoulders, back, and neck shift and define with his effort. The sum and the parts of Gavin are everything I find attractive in the male form. The Universal Architect created him just for me.

His fingers slip into me. My knees tremble. The center of my body pulls in, lifts toward my heart, and I have no idea what I say, things just pour from me. I don't think I even make sense. It's the whiskey, right? Just the whiskey?

"I love when you lose control," Gavin says. "Sometimes your best words come, well, when you do."

"You're trying to disarm me."

He stands with the grace of a lion, licks his fingers. "I shouldn't ever need to disarm my future wife. You should always come to me, armor shed, heart open."

"Heart open?"

"I do the same for you, already, every day."

"You do."

"I want you to do the same for me."

I pull his towel off and look down.

"No, no," he says. "You can't talk with your mouth full."

"I can't, can I." I grin.

He walks me back into the bedroom like we're dancing and lays me down on the bed.

"I need you," he says.

"Mystery Girl?" I say.

Gavin runs splayed hands down my thighs, around the curve of my calf, then cups my heel. "It's about you." He pushes my legs back and angles my hips perfectly. Slowly he sinks into me watching my face melt. "When I was sick I had a dream as real as we are now. It was the best sex of my life, but more than that it made me realize I'd never experienced real love. When I woke up, I wrote it down, and there I had a rough draft of 'Mystery Girl.'" He kisses my collarbone and presses my leg into his waist. "The first time I held your hand and felt your skin, that dream came back to me in a rush. Do you remember that night?"

"I do."

"I was so thankful for the shelter of the darkness next to you because I was afraid you'd see what I felt. Then the first time we made love, I'd never believed in the ability to see the future until that night. It was truly a dream come true."

"Will you sing it to me?"

"Right now?"

"Please?"

Some of the song Gavin speaks like a poetry reading, there's tone and rhythm. Then other places he finds the tune and sings it beautifully.

Tears bloom in my eyes as I pull his ear next to my lips, and whisper, "I want you to be in me forever . . . I want to be yours forever."

There isn't another word spoken. Not another word is sung.

Gavin moves in me like a man gifted with all the time in the world, as if the goal of this union is not ultimate release, but eternal pleasure.

CHAPTER 29

The smell of hospital—disinfectants, plastic, and metal—permeates everything. There's a silver box, two feet wide and four feet tall, that looks like a mini fridge, but I know from my experience that inside are warm blankets. Above me, the lights are long and eerily bright.

Memories I'd forgotten, or maybe locked away, rush back to me. With every step, it feels like five pounds of lead is added to the soles of my sneakers. My hand in Gavin's begins to tremble. I pull away from him. Ahead of us Brooke and Jax walk alongside each other.

"Hey, guys," I say. "I'm going to stop here." I point to the door of the restroom. "You all, go on ahead."

Gavin nods to his brother and Brooke. "Head on down there. We'll be right behind you."

"You can go too," I say to Gavin.

"I will wait for you."

I close the restroom door and lean back against it. The cold metal is a relief to the rising temperature of my body. If I didn't know better, I'd think I am spiking a fever. I grab a towel from the dispenser and wet it with cool water, then press it to the back of my neck.

This space looks just like the bathrooms at Lorenzo's hospital: cream and blue tiles, white walls, and a gray string hangs next to the stainless steel toilet that will call someone if you need help.

Memories invade my mind, then the fabric of my body, and I suddenly find myself pulled back in time.

•••

Lorenzo's arm is around me as we step into the bathroom. We look like two young lovers out for a walk, but he needs me to stand and push the IV pole which is laden with bags of clear liquids. The simple task of going to the bathroom zaps all of his energy. His hands shake so badly he can't get his pants tied.

"I'll do it for you, hon," I say.

He drops his hands from the strings, anger consumes his face. As I tie the pants he grips my shoulder.

"Thanks," Lorenzo says. "Remember when it used to be sexy dressing and undressing each other. Fuck I'm so sorry, Nyla. I never expected this."

•••

When I first started dating Lorenzo, it felt romantic to need each other. It was easy to vow in sickness and in health. But the day came that tested our promise, and we learned there is nothing romantic about needing someone when you need them for everything.

It was harder on Lorenzo that it was me to care for his failing body. What was harder on me, was watching the bright blue eyes I'd fallen in love with dim with humiliation and anger. It was nothing in particular, and yet, it was everything.

Those dimmed blue eyes still haunt me in my sleep.

I step back out into the bright hallway bustling with two-way traffic. Across the space Gavin leans against the wall. His body is incredibly solid, the contours of his face and body are rounded with a small bit of fat that makes him look healthy. I wonder if he had the support he needed when he walked down the hall in the middle of the night. Who tied his pants? Who does these things when the one person who promised leaves?

"Did you get the breath or two you needed?" he asks.

"Kind of."

He swings my hand back and forth like we are walking through an open meadow.

"I'm at the hospital every three or four months for scans and tests. I don't associate all of this with just my transplant and bad days anymore. I see that isn't the case for you yet, but perhaps today will help. Someday, when you're ready, maybe you could go with me to an appointment, and we'll do something fun while we are there. That way you can have some positive associations with places like this."

I both love and hate that Gavin can look at me and read things I can't even articulate.

"What could we possibly do that would be fun at a hospital?"

I see a naughty glint in his eyes.

"Oh, Gavin." I shake my head no. "When are your next tests?"

"February. Would you like to know about my tests, how things are, and stuff?"

"Of course. I'll be with you wherever you want me, or need me."

Gavin pulls me to his chest and cradles my head against his shoulder as if I need comfort for something. He nuzzles his face into my hair.

"I love you," Gavin says. "It means everything to me that you waited all that time yesterday, and that you've come today. My mom and dad appreciate it too. It's nice to have visitors to cheer the day and distract from the stresses at hand."

He places a crooked finger under my chin and kisses my lips so gently that it feels like the tickle of bird feathers.

"You know I'll go wherever you need me, right?" I say.

"Yes. And I'll go wherever you need me."

"Space and time are irrelevant. I know."

"You've been listening."

He puts his arm around my shoulders. We are just two lovers walking down the hall, ones that don't need each other yet.

"Dad is in room 831, the day I met you, and my world began to change."

"Or, your birthday."

"The best birthday present I ever got was from you that day."

"What was that?"

"The grace of your company, the brightness of your smile."

He melts my heart with how tender and honest he is. I've never been around someone like him.

I push the door open to room 831. Kathy is seated in a chair next to the window. She has shoulder-length hair the same color as Gavin's, but aside from that, he looks nothing like her.

"Good morning!" she says brightly.

Dark smudges below her eyes and the lack of color in her cheeks tell me it was a sleepless night for her. I, too, have looked like this many mornings.

Kathy stands and puts one arm around me, then reaches her other up for Gavin. She has motherly energy. Her cheek is soft and warm, just like my mom's. I hug her back, probably too tightly for two that are strangers.

"What about the old man?" Richard says. "Both of you, come on."

Slowly he gets up from the bed. His blue hospital pants hang like empty bags from his hips. His head is bald, except for a little hair on the sides which is gray. In the face, he looks like Gavin: almond-shaped eyes, strong brow bone, fuller bottom lip. Although it all has a mismatch quality because he is much thinner, his skin is pasty as if it lacks oxygen, and his lips are dry.

Gavin told me that when he was sick he'd lost a lot of weight, but I couldn't imagine Gavin as a thin man, absent of muscle and the bit of softness I love. But seeing Richard ill, I can unfortunately now imagine Gavin as a sick man. I don't know if the nauseous flip in my stomach is sympathy for Richard, or for Gavin.

Richard's arms fall from me.

"Get back in bed," Gavin says. "You should be resting so you don't look like a ghost anymore."

"No ghost here," Richard says.

Gavin slides the last free chair in the room up to the head of the bed. He sits and pulls me onto his lap. Brooke is in a chair on the other side of Richard while Jax stands next to her.

"How are you feeling?" Gavin asks.

"Better than yesterday, hopefully better tomorrow, though."

"Do not ask him on a scale of one to ten," Kathy says.

"I hate that question too," Gavin says.

He pats his father's forearm. Richard catches his hand and holds it. They look like two men who didn't think this moment would be possible.

Kathy's eyes dart around like she's trying to dry out her eyes. She lifts her chest optimistically, but I can see it's hard for her to breathe. "We were just talking," she says. "Jax and Brooke can stay through next weekend. Perhaps it will work for you two as well, and we can celebrate Christmas then."

"That works for me," Gavin says. "I just want to fly out and spend New Year's with Nyla. I'll be gone the one night."

"That works great for me as well," I say. "I'll fly back on Friday."

"And I'll pick you up at the airport," Gavin says.

"See, Richard, nothing lost," Kathy says. "He is worried he ruined Christmas. I tried to assure him that he hasn't."

"You are our Christmas present, Dad," Jax says.

Richard swipes a tear quickly from the corner of his eye. "You know what. Your mother picked up a deck of cards from the little shop downstairs. How about we try a few hands of friendly poker?"

"Friendly? Are you getting so soft you can't place a bet now, Dad?" Gavin says.

"There's no place for a wallet in these pants, as comfortable as they are."

I say, "Friendly sounds like a good idea to me. I don't know how to play."

Gavin pulls his head back. "Are you kidding?"

"I've played before, but I hadn't a clue what I was doing."

"How about we play together first then, and I'll teach you," Gavin says.

Kathy stands, and says, "You know, I think I could use a walk. Would anyone like me to grab them a coffee on the way back?"

There is a unified "yes" of four voices.

I stand from Gavin's lap. "Actually, if you're up for some company I'd like to walk as well. Then between the two of us, we can carry all the coffee."

Kathy and I walk alongside each other silently until we get to the elevator.

"Thank you for everything," Kathy says.

I am not sure what she means.

She nods as if seeing my silent question. "When you and Gavin first started dating, I could immediately hear the smile in his voice. When we visited him a couple of months ago I saw the light back in his eyes. I'd worried it had burned out altogether. His experience strained him." She touches the side of my arm, then gives me a little squeeze. "But to see him near you. You've brought him back to life. It's a debt a mother can never repay."

"You've raised a wonderful man who has brought me back to life. Thank you."

We take the elevator to the first floor and walk through the crowded lobby out to a courtyard. Along the path, yellow cones with a slipping man reads Caution. Since it's been salted, we decide to give it a shot.

We haven't made it far when, Kathy says, "Perhaps we shouldn't risk a broken arm."

"We could walk the halls a little."

"The problem with hospitals is a walk in the hall doesn't feel like much of a break, certainly not any fresh air. But it's too cold to stand still out here."

We go back inside and stand at the window looking out to where we'd just been. We watch a couple other people attempt to walk, and look just as disappointed as I felt when they turn back to the door.

"Is there anything I can do you for you, Kathy? I know it's hard when your husband is sick. Of course, I also realize it's hard when your child is sick." I feel horrible for saying what I had, it came out all wrong.

Kathy smiles. "It's very different. Taking care of my son was the hardest thing I'd ever done. But he's a big boy, and our lives are separate in a lot of ways. I was thinking this morning how intertwined Richard's and my life is. He is everything to me. I hadn't thought about it, as silly as that sounds. We do everything together, and we share our dreams. It is hard."

I put my arm around her shoulders. We are just two women, nearly strangers, who don't need each other, but there is a shared understanding, and there is comfort in that.

"Sweet girl," Kathy says. "You're a strong one."

The space between her eyebrows begins to shake, then her cheeks. I pick up a box of tissues and hold it out to her. She takes one and dabs the inner corners of her eyes.

"They said he would be fine," she says.

The center of her chin collapses in.

"That's good."

"Did the doctors tell you that in the beginning too?" she asks.

I used to be one of those people that would say, "don't worry everything will be fine," but I've learned that we shouldn't try to feel better by gripping to a vision of a perfect outcome. It distracts from the time at hand. It's best to accept right away that this situation will end, one way or another. Though you have no control over how it does, there is ownership in how you experience it. Learning to stay peacefully in the present moment is hard. And being honest with people at their most challenging time is hard too.

"Yes," I say.

CHAPTER 30

"Well, well, well. Look what the wind blew in," Ms. Marshall says.

I can hardly hear her through my hood, which I've pulled tight around my head to protect me from the strong easterly winds that have dropped Portland well below freezing.

"Why on earth are you out walking at this hour and in this frigid weather?" I ask.

I hurry around the side of my car and open up the back to get my suitcase.

"If that weatherman gets it right, I might not get out for a walk tomorrow, so I figured I should take advantage while I can." She pulls her fluorescent pink cap lower over her ears and eyebrows. "They're calling for six inches tomorrow."

"Six? I thought I heard only three?"

"I don't think they know what's going on, as usual. But even if we get a dusting, we all know the whole city will shut down. Are you headed up to Gavin's house tonight, or will you be around tomorrow?"

"I'm supposed to head up there tonight, but I'm flat exhausted from a messy travel day."

Today I flew back from New Orleans. I was there for the last two weeks working on coverage for the final game of the season, the Championship Game. While there I did player interviews, commentary for the nightly sports shows, and wrote countless articles. Between all of that and the rough trip home, my mind and body feel like I've been through the wringer.

"If you happen to be around tomorrow, stop over for a cup of tea," Ms. Marshall says. "I miss seeing you around, and it would be great to catch up."

"That sounds wonderful. Thank you for the invite. Goodnight, Ms. Marshall."

I open the front door of my house. It smells stale, and it's almost as cold as it is outside. To the left of the front door is a basket which catches letters from the mail slot; it's overflowed. One envelope slid across the room and under the area rug, only a corner sticks out. I know from the return address this is one of the monthly bills for the Bainbridge house, and it's likely the others due are here too. I gather the wayward letters, pick up the basket by the leather handles, and carry it upstairs to my office.

Next, I take my bag up to my bedroom and unzip it. I sort all of the dirty clothes into piles on the floor. My phone starts to ring. I run down the stairs. When my foot hits the wood floor, I nearly face plant, but I get to the phone and answer just in time.

"Hi, love. I wanted to be sure you're all right," Gavin says.

"I'm sorry, Gavin, everything just seems to be off tonight."

"Are you all right?" he asks.

"Yes. Thank you for checking on me. I'm just worn out from a long week and travel issues. I didn't realize how late it is."

"I miss you," Gavin says.

"I miss you too. It's just . . ."

"Please don't make me wait any longer to see you, Nyla. It's been two weeks."

"I'm sorry. I'm grumpy because I'm tired and hungry."

I pull open my fridge. There's an old box of baking soda in the back, two beers, and yogurt that expired last month.

"I'll make you dinner," he says.

The strain in his voice grips my heart. I want to see him badly too. I take a deep breath and try to see if I can muster the energy to pack again.

"I love you, but I just don't think I can pack again tonight. I have on my last clean pair of underwear, not that you want to know that."

"May I come to you?"

"You're willing to do that?"

"I'll pick up dinner on my way, and be there in an hour, less if I can."

Instantly I feel relaxed. "Have I told you I love you?"

After I hang up the phone with Gavin, I go upstairs and into my bathroom. I strip off my clothes that smell stale and step into the warm stream of water. For thirty minutes, I stand in the shower rinsing away the weight of travel delays. When I get out, I feel refreshed but still weary, and a lot more hungry.

I fill a laundry basket and carry it down to the basement where my washer and dryer are. When I return to the first floor I hear Gavin's truck pull up. I peek out of the window and watch him. He puts a small duffel bag on his shoulder, grabs a garment bag, then a sack.

I open the door, and as he walks up the front steps, I admire him. "Gavin, you are even more handsome than I remember."

His face lights up. He hurries to set his things down and pulls me to his chest. "You are the most beautiful woman on TV, but it never compares to the sight of you in person. Two weeks is too long. We can't do this again, go this long." He lifts me and wraps my legs around him. "There is nothing on below this robe."

"There isn't. If you're quick about it, you can take advantage of that because I'm hungry in two ways."

He puts my back against the wall and with his other hand, works himself free.

•••

Forty-five minutes later, I feel like an entirely new woman; both of my hungers satisfied.

"All I ate today was a bag of almonds, coffee, and one of those cheese and fruit trays on the plane," I say.

Gavin reaches across the table and takes my hand. "That's not enough nourishment."

"I get grumpy when I'm hungry. I'm sorry."

Gavin nods. "Busy week with a lot going on. I'm always here to help. Did you get things finalized for *Behind the Sport*?"

I've signed on to host a new series for AST called *Behind the Sport*. It's green-lighted for the first season of ten episodes. Each show will look behind the greatest moments in sports history and see what it took to make them happen.

I say, "Yes, and I got the final production schedule for the next five months. Good news is I don't have any travel for four weeks."

"Starting when?"

"Right now. The not-so-great news is after that, every-thing is sporadic, and I have some big chunks of time I'll be gone."

"Let's sit down with our schedules later this week and see what cities I can meet you in."

"That would be wonderful, thank you. Your dad, how is he?"

At Kathy's insistence, Richard finally found a specialist in their hometown of Seattle. His first appointment was yesterday.

Gavin rolls his eyes. "He insists, never better. Mom, on the other hand, insists his coloring isn't right. So, I don't know. Fine, I guess."

"Men make difficult patients." I lean across the table and kiss him, then stand.

"I'll have you know I am a well-above-average-patient. Nurses love me."

"That's because you're hot."

I pick up our dishes, but Gavin takes them from me.

"You think I'm hot?" he asks.

I wink at him and go to put another load of laundry in. Then I go upstairs and find Gavin naked laid out on my rainbow patterned sheets. I love him, everything about him, especially that he sleeps in the buff. I toss my robe onto the chair and snuggle into his side. He pulls the blanket around us.

"Do you want me to set the alarm for you?" I ask.

"I took the morning off to spend with you."

"Really?"

"I'm all yours until 10:45."

"That's rather precise."

He holds me tight, and says, "I have a doctor appoint-ment at 11:30. Then a packed afternoon."

"Doctor appointment?" I roll onto my belly and click on my bedside light so I can see him. "You hadn't mentioned that."

"I had my regular tests today, and I meet with the doctor tomorrow. I didn't want to bother you with it because you've had so much going on."

I kiss the port and PICC line scars on his chest, and ask, "What tests?"

"I had a PET scan, blood work," he grins and kisses my lips, "and sperm count."

"Sperm test? Some interesting reading or watching with that?"

"None needed, just memories. That and it had been a while."

"Memories?" I lick his nipple, and he flinches.

"Will you tell me how it goes?"

"I expect it to be a healthy checkup like always. I'm healthy as a horse, remember?"

I run my finger over the soft hair of his chest. I say, "We'll have to celebrate tomorrow. We should start a healthy checkup celebration tradition."

"A healthy checkup celebration tradition? I've never done that. Although I can see why I should, or rather why we should."

He pulls me back to him, but I pull away briefly to click off the lamp, then snuggle into the place I feel the most protected.

"Yes. What do you want to do?" I ask.

"Pizza."

"Where would you like to go?"

"I want homemade pizza at the house, just you and me. Is that too selfish to ask for?"

"Gavin, I think it sounds perfect."

•••

The city stretched out below Gavin's house looks like it's sprinkled with powdered sugar. The promised snow arrived in time for the evening commute, creating gridlock according to the news. Luckily, I managed to get all of my laundry done this morning, mail sorted (the Bainbridge bills paid), and repacked. I even had tea with Ms. Marshall. I've brought enough clothes to last me through the weekend, which is more than I've ever brought over. Gavin suggested I pack enough for the month.

A half hour ago I sat down in this comfortable chair with the first fiction book I've been able to crack in months. I haven't made it past the first page. Although Gavin sent me a text message this afternoon to say his checkup was good, I need to feel his body and reassure myself he's still mine.

When Lorenzo was diagnosed with cancer, the only thing that mattered then was beating it. It seemed like such a simple task until we realized the strong man I'd married was no match for the tiny cells multiplying in his body. Then our life wasn't about beating cancer, it was just about getting a few more quality days; just enough medicine to make the existence of life worth the pain until the scales tipped, and spilled into death.

I never wondered what it would be like to love a survivor. Appointments, tests, worry, the what-ifs that stalk us like the Grim Reaper on our coattails. It's a privilege to know I'm in love with a survivor, but it doesn't mean it's easy. I wonder if this worry will subside with time, or if it will always feel like this.

"Hello," Gavin says and snaps me from my trance.

I spring from the chair. The hardcover book lands with a thump on the wood floor. His smile is both gentle and seductive. I pick up the book, then run to him and throw myself into his arms.

"Now this is a treat to come home to," Gavin says.

The sparkle in his vibrant green eyes eases the worry in my heart.

"Welcome to your celebration."

"I feel like every day with you is a celebration." He runs his finger below the spaghetti strap of my top, pale pink silk with matching shorts. "I like this a lot."

I bite my lip, for some reason embarrassed to admit, "I bought it to leave here."

"That alone is something to celebrate. Our closet is jealous of the bathroom and wants to be filled too."

The buzzer beeps.

"Pizza is ready." I run my hands along the armholes of his gray vest. "Do you want to change before we eat?"

"Yes," he says. He turns down the hall. "It smells so good, love."

I spread a blanket out in front of the fireplace. Then I carry out plates, glasses, wine, and finally the pizza. I uncork the bottle and fill our glasses.

"A picnic?" Gavin says.

"There is even dessert."

"Oh, I know there is dessert with you here."

"I meant ice cream. But there are lots of ways you can eat that ice cream."

After dinner we lean back against pillows I piled on the floor. I'm able to see the flames lick up toward the sky in the fireplace, and the snow falling to the earth outside. On one side of my body, I feel the warmth of the fire and on the other the heat from Gavin's body.

"My PET scan and blood work were perfect," Gavin says. "But the sperm counts are still at zero. The doctor said today that because I'm at the four-year mark, and I'm close to forty, that if a family is in my plan, I'll need to consider other ways to make that happen."

"Family in the plan . . . you'd want to use a donor then?"

"God no! I can't stand the thought of putting another man's sperm in you. No, absolutely not."

"You've thought about this?"

"A lot. And I can't do it. Adoption though, maybe? Unless carrying a child is something that is important to you, of course then I'd support the other option."

"We talked about this already. I'm not sure I want kids. With my career, my travel schedule. I just can't see how I could be a mother, not in the way I'd expect of myself."

Gavin lifts one shoulder. "I know." There is disappointment in his voice, though he's trying to sound indifferent. "The most important thing to me is that we are together. Everything else is open for me. But I don't want you to feel like you missed out on something, or had to sacrifice, for me."

Gavin sits up and moves down to my feet. He takes one and begins to work it with his strong hands.

"I want to talk about living together," he says. "Sharing a home would make things a lot easier for you because I can help you out more. I could do your laundry when you get home."

"Oh, you know just how to steal a girl's heart, don't you."

"I know you hate laundry. And we'd have more time together."

"You don't think it's moving too fast?"

"By whose definition?"

"I don't know."

"I definitely don't think it's moving too fast. If any part of me doubted our future together, I wouldn't bring it up."

"When do you want to do this?"

"Since you don't have any travel for the next month, I'd say there is no time like the present."

"Are you serious?"

He nods and slips his hands up my leg and begins to work my calf. My entire body relaxes. Just as my eyes begin to close, he says, "I want you to answer this question without thinking."

"Oh geez. That might be hard."

"If I pull out a ring right now and propose, what would you say?"

My throat goes dry. I sit up on my elbow and drink my wine like water.

"This is a what if, right?"

"It's theoretical." His gaze drops to my leg. "Though the look on your face tells me you might not give me the answer I'd hope for."

"I'd say yes, Gavin. But there are things I still need to do."

"What things?"

"I need to sell that house on Bainbridge, clean it out. I guess I need to finish letting go."

"I'll help you."

"You don't have to."

"I'll help you do anything. We're a team."

My thumb on my left hand instinctively touches the ring finger. Sometimes I feel like I've forgotten to put on my wedding ring and then I remember that I don't wear one anymore. I think I'll always feel the ghostly space left by the absence of my wedding band, even if I fill it with a new one.

CHAPTER 31

"Ah, Little Foot," Pop says as he stands from the table to hug me. "Glad to see you survived Snowpocalypse."

Last week during the snowstorm that shut down the city for three days, Pop called to ask if he could stop by and see me. I had to confess that I was stuck at Gavin's, although I was quite happy about it. The road to the house was nearly impossible to drive, even after the city started to thaw. Gavin and I spent five whole days, only us, hardly clothed. We lay by the fire, read, watched movies, laughed, and made sounds that accompanied sublime experiences.

"I stopped into Gavin's office this morning," Pop says. "I had some documents for him on a new building they're looking at."

Pop doesn't typically do things like this. That's what courier services and email are for.

A waiter sets down a plate.

"Spinach dip," Pop says and pulls back a napkin from the basket of bread. "Gavin is one of the nicest guys I know, happiest too. But you two have lit something in each other's eyes."

"We're talking about moving in together."

He nods with a tiny smile as he scoops dip up with a chunk of bread. "I've heard he's got a great house up there."

"It's a magical place. You'll have to see it."

"I'd hope to get a dinner invitation to my daughter's home. Will you sell yours?"

"I don't know. I want to hold onto it if only to say I have it still. But I don't want to manage renters, or deal with the monthly bills."

"Sell it then."

"I'm also thinking about selling Bainbridge."

"It's about time. What? Don't look so surprised. Since you moved three years ago, you've been back there once, when that tree fell on it. Am I right?"

"You are."

"You could roll that money into a vacation property you'd use," Pop says. "The weather is supposed to be decent this week. You should make a trip up there to tie up any loose ends and get it on the market."

"Do not delay."

His head nods in agreement. "Do not delay, indeed. Haven't you learned by now life is far too short not to enjoy everything we do."

"That is something I've learned, but sometimes it's still hard to do."

"Pat Till, the real estate agent that you purchased your house through, has since retired. I'll send you Gloria Jetter's information. She's a sharp lady and will take good care of you."

Our conversation moves on, mostly to Kevin and Mia. She is due in three months. They've moved into their new house in the suburbs, which is where Pop spent the holidays. For the last month, he's found a reason to fly back each week for work. He's very excited to be a grandpa.

When the bill comes, Pop pulls out his wallet. "Have I told you, Little Foot . . ." For a moment he looks like he might tear up, but his cheeks lift. "How much it means to me to see you happy? You love him, right? Gavin."

"Very much."

He stands, takes my coat off the back of my chair, and holds it up for me. "Your mother would say something like the universe seems to have aligned perfectly for you two. Given everything, what with the experiences, the timing in your lives, the needs of the future."

I turn to face Pop. He pats my shoulder like he always did before a big race.

"I'm happy you love him. He certainly loves you."

I wonder what Gavin and Pop actually met about this morning because he's looking at me like a father that is about to let go of his daughter.

•••

The house on Bainbridge Island is set back on a small piece of property, surrounded by trees and edged by water. There isn't a fence which defines a front yard or backyard. The house still looks the same, painted the color of the sun with blue-gray trim. I don't know why I expect it to look different, to have some evidence of what I've lost here.

Gavin points to the right of the house where the tree had been, and says, "You'd never know there was a hole in the roof."

"No, you wouldn't, would you? The contractor did a good job."

"Whose truck is that?"

Parked on the side of the house is an old white pickup spotted with rust.

"That's Rick's."

At the mention of his name, Rick appears from the back of the house, wiping his hands on a blue rag. He has a sturdy squat frame, weathered skin, and a kind smile.

"Howdy, Nyla," he says. "You must be, Gavin. My paws are a mess, or I'd shake your hand." He twists to look over his shoulder for a brief moment. "Got the windows cleaned today and the screens. The one for the bedroom has a hole it in though. I'll take it back to the shop tonight and fix it. And the windows are open. Figured it'd be a good day to air things out, but it's a little drafty now."

"Thank you, Rick," I say. "The real estate agent will be here shortly."

He nods. "I'll let you know before I head out."

Gavin and I follow the stone path that leads to the front door. My hand shakes as I turn the knob, and I freeze. At my front is the physical remains of my past, and behind me is my future. Gavin touches my shoulder, injecting the strength I need to keep moving.

Inside I'm greeted by the scent of sunshine and ocean, laced with something that reminds me of Lorenzo, the leather of a football mixed with a cologne he always favored. At first, I loved that lingering smell, until I realized I couldn't stop thinking of him. Desperate to get rid of it, I washed everything in the house, had the curtains dry cleaned, and sprayed the fabrics with lavender water. Nothing helped. It's on the walls, the floor, and corners I can't scrub out. This beautiful little house still seems desperate to hold onto him. Sometimes I feel that way too.

Gavin's throat bounces with a difficult swallow.

"Are you sure you want to be here?" I ask.

"Yes." Gavin lifts his baseball cap and leans in to kiss me. He hesitates a moment, looks at my eyes before he closes his, and presses his lips to mine. "Being here doesn't bother me, but seeing you look this nervous does. Are you sure this is what you want to do?"

"Hello!" a chipper voice says, knocking on the front door I'd left open.

I drop Gavin's hand like a woman caught cheating. He looks at me unshaken and reaches for me again. *Sorry*, I mouth.

"Gloria Jetter." She shakes my hand while gently cradling it with the other.

She has jet-black hair, the color of my mother's, and a stiff purse the size of a pillow.

"Gloria, this my boyfriend, Gavin."

She shakes his hand in a much more businesslike way, and says, "You two picked a lovely day for a visit to the island. Where are you staying?"

"Bainbridge Bed and Breakfast," I say.

"That place is charming, what a view."

"I haven't seen it before, but I've heard good things."

"Best crumpets you'll ever have," she says. She looks around the house and waves at Rick passing by the window. "I stopped by a few days ago and looked at the property, but I didn't get inside. Do you mind if I look around?"

"Please do," I say to her.

I feel an overwhelming need to be alone for a moment. "I'm going to go outside for a few minutes," I say to Gavin.

"Do you want me to go with you?"

I shake my head no and begin to pull my hand away from him, but his fingers hold tight. He says, "I love you," then lets me go.

I walk to the edge of my slice of heaven here on the west side of the island. There's a spot at the edge of the water we called our beach, a patch of rocky sand big enough for two beach blankets, depending on the tide. Here we'd sit and look across Squamish Harbor to the Olympic Mountains against the brilliantly clear sky. Lorenzo and I spent many days hiking those peaks, and every day we felt spoiled that they were in our backyard.

Behind me, I hear Gavin's footfalls. I glance over my shoulder and try to smile.

"Gloria has some paperwork to go over."

Gavin and I sit across from Gloria at the dining room table I'd found at a flea market. It is the first and last piece of furniture I tried my hand at restoring. I'm sure it wouldn't pass the scrutiny of an antique specialist, but I sure love it.

"This is a beautiful home," Gloria says. She pulls a folder from her purse with my name written on the tab. "I know it will sell quickly and make for a smooth process. There is one little matter I wanted to make you aware of." She slides a paper across the table. On the top of it is the word "deed."

"It still has," she looks at Gavin and then back to me, "Lorenzo's name on it."

"I'll take care of it," I say.

"It's okay. We can do it at closing. I just wanted you to know I'll need a copy of his—"

"It's fine. Anything you need."

Signing the paperwork to list the property is almost too easy. When we're done, I walk Gloria out. I stop at the end of the stone path and shake her hand. She gets into her car, turns around, and goes back down the driveway.

I linger in the front yard, thinking of all the hopes I had for this property, a life here, that never bloomed. I'd wanted to plant flowers here along the path, like my mother always had. Lorenzo and I imagined two, maybe three, children running around the property. It would have been the coolest place to grow up.

The rumble of Rick's truck snaps me out of the daze. He backs up to where I'm at and rolls his window down.

"There you are," he says. "I'm all done for the day. The windows are still open. Gavin said he'd get them."

"Yes, thank you for everything, Rick."

"Always a pleasure, Nyla."

Back in the house, I meander through. The kitchen cupboards are filled with plates I'd once hosted dinner parties with, and there are the champagne glasses we used at our wedding. In the drawer is the silverware we'd eaten off every day. The walls are bare, bookshelves empty, and surfaces naked.

Down the hall in the master bedroom, it looks like someone woke up just this morning and made the bed. There is the beautiful white four-poster bed with a fluffy navy comforter, and enough pillows for five beds, meticulously arranged. On the wall across from the bed, hangs three large paintings of hummingbirds. Lorenzo purchased them at a street fair here on the island.

"Do you want to tell me what you're thinking?" Gavin asks.

Through the open window a gust of wind pushes in, on its current is a hummingbird with a head the color of an emerald. Its body hangs motionless in the air while its wings move so fast I can hardly see them, but I hear the hum.

"I see you," I whisper to the bird.

A reverse gust of wind pulls from the room, and with it the little bird.

I close the window and tug on the drapes that pool at the floor like a gray waterfall.

"You look like you need to get something off your chest," Gavin says.

"This house has too many memories." I didn't plan to tell Gavin anything else, but words swell up from me. "I woke up early one morning to bright sunshine because I'd forgotten to pull these drapes. I could hear the grinding of a garbage truck, and maybe laughter from someplace.

"I got up to pull the drapes, and I grumbled that I need just a few more minutes of sleep, and just as I was about to close them, a hummingbird stopped in front of the window. It was just like the one that was here, a beautiful emerald head. The strangest thing happened then. All of the other sounds disappeared, and all I could hear was the hum of the hummingbird's wings. The window was closed, how was it possible? But I heard it, an unearthly loud hum.

"Something made me turn away from the bird to look at Lorenzo in our bed. His chest was still, hands crossed over his heart. I looked back at the hummingbird and held my breath hoping it wouldn't leave me because I didn't want to be alone. It watched me. Then my breath rushed out of me with a 'Goodbye,' and it left."

My body begins to shake. "I kept hoping he would get a miracle, but he just . . . left. I was so mad. That's what I felt. I was mad. I should have been happy he wasn't in pain anymore. God knows he was practically gone half the time from everything. And I was selfish because I wanted him to choose us."

I sit on the bed and take a deep breath. Gavin leans against the wall and puts his hands into the pockets of his jeans.

"I always wondered," I say, "why some people make it, and others don't. How some people say with such certainty that they will live as if they already know. Do they live because they are sure?"

Gavin's eyes begin to tear, and he says, "I don't know."

"It's the chicken or the egg question, right? What comes first? Is it hope that allows survival? Or is it that because someone will survive there is hope? That's what wrecked me. I thought if he just hoped harder, if he'd just believed with every cell of his body, he would have lived. But then, I thought perhaps if I was a little better, less worried, less of a mother hen, he would have had more energy to believe.

"As a wife, you want to know that you did everything you could. But when they die, you will never know if you did. I'll never know if I did.

"It was by far the worst day of my life because every day before that, I had some measure of hope, and then it was gone."

CHAPTER 32

$\mathcal{G}$avin and I drive around the perimeter of the island to the east side, where we see the Seattle cityscape. It's filled with skyscrapers, and off in the distance to the left is the Space Needle, which to me has always looked like a UFO balancing on a stick.

At Bainbridge Bed and Breakfast the proprietor, Ms. Davies, checks us in. She is short with a narrow waist and a thick bun at the crown of her head. The key she gives me is attached to a purple tassel.

"Room 2," Ms. Davis says. "Breakfast tomorrow starts at seven. If you're looking for dinner tonight, just down the street is Chinook's. They have the best fish and chips."

Gavin and I walk up the stairs to the second floor and go down to the end of the hall. I unlock the door and hold it open for Gavin, whose hands are full.

"This place is charming," I say.

Gavin sets the bags down on a bench at the end of the bed and looks around the room. "Yes, it is. Flowers and all."

The wallpaper is cream with a periwinkle print of blooming vines.

"It's very English country," I say. "You don't want to redo your bedroom in this then?"

He shakes his head slowly. "No, I don't want to redo our bedroom in this. I like the dramatic gray walls and silk sheets. This place is romantic in a sweet way, but I prefer romance in a," he pauses, then slowly says, "sensual way? I feel like I might have to behave in here."

He walks over to the antique lace drapes and makes a funny face. "How is it possible that I love lace when it's on you, but this," he shakes his head, "reminds me of my grandmother's house?"

"This place turns you off, apparently?"

"Nothing turns me off when you're near me. Just notes for when we decorate the other rooms in the house. None of this, please. Are you hungry?"

I nod yes. "But before we go. I want to say I am sorry about the way I carried on back at the house."

"You never have to apologize for sharing your experiences or feelings with me. No matter what they are."

"Thank you."

Gavin takes my hand and kisses the inside of my wrist. He tucks my hair behind my ear. "You were asking what comes first, hope or survival. The chicken or the egg question. I don't think it's that simple. I think our thoughts do influence, but I don't think we always have the power to change plans bigger than us."

"Did you always know you'd survive?"

His eyes drop to our hands. "It's hard to explain. I was surrounded by people that loved me, but still, I felt alone. As the months wore on, I felt like a burden, especially when I couldn't take care of myself all of the time. There were a lot of nights I prayed that I wouldn't wake up."

There is a glimpse of that darkness in his eyes. Never again do I want him to feel this way. I cup his cheek, and he turns his face and kisses my palm.

He continues, "At my lowest point, I all but begged for the universe to take me. I refused the treatment the doctors wanted me to try. Then I dreamt about you." His cheeks bounce with a smile. "Mystery girl. I didn't wake up that day feeling happy again, but I started to wonder if there was a reason for my living. That day, I signed the waiver for the trial treatment. From that day on, each night that I lay down to sleep, I prayed to wake up tomorrow."

I remember wondering if the universe had made me a widow to prepare me for Gavin. But hearing this, I now believe the universe had been preparing him for me.

For you, all the reasons I survived.

•••

The next day I put on my moving clothes, an old pair of jeans and a black T-shirt with Foo Fighters written on the back. As I braid my hair, I watch Gavin pull his belt through the loops of his jeans.

"Do you realize that you always look sexy?" I say.

He looks at me with loving eyes. "That's funny because I was just thinking the same thing as you pulled your jeans over your—" He grips my backside, and I wiggle it in his hand.

We pack, then Gavin picks up our bags. As I open the door, he says, "Do you know what I realized when I woke up?"

"What's that?"

"We didn't bring any boxes or packing material."

"Those would be important. I know just where we can get everything."

We stop at U-Store and purchase boxes, tape, and packing material. It's across the street from the grocery store I shopped at every week for years. The route we take back to the house is one I've traveled thousands of times.

At the house, Gavin and I carry the packing supplies into the living room. He kneels on the floor and begins to assemble boxes while I go into the kitchen and open the first cupboard. Some of these things, like my bargain dishes, I'll donate. But I'm not sure what to do with the things that have history and importance to them.

"This is nice china," Gavin says as he picks up one of the plates and wraps it in tissue.

"It's my grandparent's china. On my mother's side."

"We can put it in the glass display case in the dining room."

"If my mother heard you say that, she'd have clapped three times and said perfect. She hated that it got stored in the top cupboard to be used once a year."

Gavin grabs a long brown leather box from the next shelf and opens it. Inside is a large set of silverware. He picks up a fork in one hand and a spoon in the other, then sweeps his thumb over the handles that are engraved with G & N.

"What are these from?" he asks.

"Lorenzo's great-grandparents. Their names were Grant, no Gerald, I think, and Nancy. I don't know what to do with some of his family treasures."

"What about his mother? Do you think she wants them back?"

"His mother, Eliana, is a nomad. When her parents died, she passed her things onto us. I don't even know where she is now. After Lorenzo's funeral, we kept in contact via email. But then, one day, about two years after he passed, her email bounced back, and her phone was disconnected."

"Weird."

"Not really, not if you knew her."

He wiggles the utensils in his hand. "Would you want to use them? Rather odd coincidence that it's our initials."

There's a sincere curiosity in his eyes.

"Would you?"

"We don't have anything like this. It's an amazing set. I don't think you could get rid of it, nor should you, and I'd hate to think it's just sitting in a box for eternity."

"What would we tell people?"

He shrugs. "Who cares. Tell them it's a family heirloom. We can tell some people the truth, but not everyone needs an explanation."

I nod in agreement then continue to work my way through the rest of the kitchen. When I'm done, Gavin double checks the cupboards and drawers, and asks, "What's next?"

The only other room with anything left in it is the bedroom.

"I'm not taking anything else. I hope that whoever buys the house will want some of the furniture. Whatever is left Rick said he could arrange to be donated."

"What about the paintings in the bedroom? They're originals, right?"

"Yes."

"They're amazing and would be beautiful in your office."

I walk down the hall to the bedroom and look at three large paintings. Each one is of the same emerald-headed hummingbird at different stages of flight. When

The image

Lorenzo first saw them he was captivated by their fantasy-like quality, and how it seems as if the bird is about fly right off the canvas.

"I do love them," I say.

Gavin carefully removes the first painting from the wall. "I'll wrap them up."

"Thank you. I'm going to go walk the property one last time. I'll be just a few minutes." I look around the room. "I'll be ready to go after that."

"Sounds good. It won't take me too long to wrap and get them in the truck."

I walk the perimeter of the two acres running my fingers along the trees that had been here before us and will still be here after I leave.

For the first time since Lorenzo's death, I let memories pass through me, and I do not feel guilt or sadness, but rather joy in their existence. At the edge of the island, I balance on the rocky edge and reach my hand down into the water. I'd once been worried about what we'd do when we had little ones running around the property, how I'd protect them from this edge, so they wouldn't get swept away. Sometimes worrying is useless, especially when it never comes to pass.

The last night I shared with Lorenzo, we sat on a blanket here, looking at the Olympic Mountains.

•••

Lorenzo lays his head on my lap and grips my thigh as tightly as he can.

"I'm almost done, Nyla," Lorenzo says. "Wow, those are words I never expected to say."

His scalp is smooth, months since he's had his full head of curly black hair, and his skin has a ghostly light to it.

"Thank you for loving me and taking care of me no matter what," he says. "I envy the man who comes next."

"I'll never love anyone else. It's only you."

He rolls his eyes on my thigh, and I feel his tears.

"I pray to God you love someone else, Nyla. The thought of leaving you tears me apart, but I can't bear the thought of you being alone for the rest of your life, because I know it's going to be a long and beautiful one. Be sure he's worthy of you."

I shake my head and look down at his handsome blue eyes which seem to have become lighter since we've left the hospital.

"You have made me the happiest woman in the world. I couldn't ever be with anyone else because I'd always be thinking of you, my one true love." I try to say lightly, but it comes out heavy.

"You'll get a second love."

"I don't want it."

"Keep your eyes open, because when the time is right, I'll send you a sign."

I laugh through my tears at such an insane idea, that the man curled on my lap would reach me beyond the physical world.

"I promise someday you'll recognize it. When you're ready."

•••

My knees sink slowly to the earth. The memory is so real that I can feel the warmth of his head below my hand, the weight of him on my thigh. How has so much time passed?

Silent sobs shake my shoulders.

Gavin kneels down in front of me and puts his hands on my arms. "My love," he says.

I look into his eyes. I've always thought they were the color of moss, just after it rains. But I see them anew, the setting sun bouncing off of them. They are the color of emeralds. The same as the hummingbird's head, the ones that Lorenzo loved.

Some days I feel like I'm in a hot air balloon floating off into dreams of the future, but I've never been able to dream too far because I feel tethered to a past promise, or a past hope. Though now as I close my eyes, I feel something snap, and suddenly I am flooded with a vision of the future: I see the back of Gavin's head, his hair peppered with gray. I hear the laughter of children's voices. A young girl's voice says "Mommy," and I feel a tug on my hand. Gavin turns and smiles. The creases at the corner of his eyes are a little deeper. "There you are, love," he says. "Are you ready?"

The vision disappears.

I open my eyes to Gavin, the water behind him, the towering mountains, the golden sun. One corner of his mouth lifts.

He runs his thumb along my lower lip, and says, "I love your smile."

My breath shutters as I pull in the fresh air. "I see them."

"What?" Gavin asks.

"Your eyes, they are the color of emeralds."

The other corner of his mouth lifts, and he looks over my face like he, too, is seeing something different in me.

"I'm ready," I say.

"For what?" Gavin asks.

"For everything."

CHAPTER 33

The wheels of the plane touch down. I'm back home in Portland after a week at AST's studios in California. It was the first time the crew of *Behind the Sport* came together to begin work on the season. Our days were long, but everything went well.

As the plane taxis to the gate, I pull out my phone and text Gavin, "Just got in. I'm so excited to be home. Love you."

This was my first trip since I moved in with Gavin. I'm not sure what it was exactly, but I missed him more than I ever have before.

My Portland house officially went on the market today. The real estate agent sent me an email earlier which said we'd have three offers by the end of the day. Just like the Bainbridge house, I expect it to be a quick and smooth transaction.

Gavin returns my text message, "I love you. I'm looking forward to your lips. See you very soon."

I get another message, this one from Kevin. "Call me. Mia is in labor, and I'm freaking out."

Luckily I'm in the second row of first class. I grab my bag and walk quickly up the Jetway to the gate. The airport is busy, as expected for a Friday morning. I find a quiet corner and call Kevin.

"Am I an auntie?" I ask.

"It isn't too far away. I don't think anyway. The doctor just told us to head to the hospital."

It's unusual to hear the anxious tone in my brother's voice.

"Is Pop on his way?" I ask.

"He's in a meeting, but I left him a message."

With a spur-of-the-moment decision I say, "I'm coming."

"What? Really?" Kevin asks.

"You sound like you might need a little support too. And how cool would it be to hold my niece on her birthday? Text me the name of the hospital. I'll let you know what I find for flights out of here."

At the ticket counter is a sweet-looking woman. She has grandmotherly eyes and small rectangular glasses set out on the end of her pointy nose. "Good afternoon," she says.

I look at her name badge, and say, "Hello, Alice. I am wondering if you can help me. My sister-in-law is about to have her first baby, and I'm hoping I can catch a flight out to see them."

"Where to and when?"

"Chicago and the first flight I can get out on."

Her fingers move at lightning speed.

"First baby?" She glances up from her screen, and I nod yes. "I have four myself and now two grandbabies. Is anyone else traveling with you?"

I do wish Gavin was traveling with. I grab my phone to call him and see what we can coordinate. Just before I press his name, Alice says, "There is a flight that boards in fifteen minutes out of Gate D. It will be a real push to make it, but if you have running feet, you might just do it."

Gate D is on the opposite end of the airport from where I am, gate C.

I glance down at my pink sneakers and purple leggings. "Good thing I wore running shoes today."

From the bottom of my oversized travel purse, I fish out my wallet and hand Alice my credit card. Then I send Kevin a text, "I'll be on a flight in fifteen minutes. See you soon, brother."

"We won't be able to transfer luggage in time, but we can send it on after," Alice says.

"I don't have any checked bags. Everything is in here." I pat the handle of my carry-on.

Alice hands me my boarding pass and credit card. "Good luck, Ms. Tripple."

"Thank you for your help, Alice."

I stuff everything into my purse, grab the handle of my carry-on, and I take off.

Down the center of the terminal are moving sidewalks. The first one is empty. I hop on it and run. At this speed, I feel superhuman. The moving sidewalks aren't very long, so you have to hop off, walk a little and then get back on. The problem is, the next one is packed. Although people are supposed to stay to the right and let others pass, I decide not to risk it. I run alongside it, picking up my speed.

People turn to watch me. Someone hollers my name, and sets off a chain reaction of yet more people hollering, "Nyla" or "Tripple Threat." It sounds like an echo bouncing around me.

Mid terminal is an open area of shops and restaurants with lines of hungry people. In the center of it is a musician playing the violin. There is a large crowd gathered around her. I dodge them all like I'm on an obstacle course.

I glance at my watch and run faster yet. I'm not at full speed because dragging my suitcase behind me makes it hard. I consider abandoning everything that weighs me down so that I can go, but that makes no sense.

People clap. I keep moving.

I finally make it to the beginning of the terminal, which opens into a large space. It's even more packed here. On my left is security and on my right are more restaurants. There is a large window out of which I see a plane take off in the distance. This amps up my sense of urgency, which already felt maxed out. I turn down the hall that connects the two sides of the airport.

My phone rings. I ignore it and let it go to voicemail.

It rings again. I ignore it.

When it rings a third time I wonder if it's Kevin. I slow my pace, pull the phone from its pocket, and see that it's Gavin. Unable to stop, I send his call to voicemail.

He calls again. Frustrated I answer, and say, "Gavin I can't talk," and hang up.

I'm nearing the end of the hall which will dump me out into terminal C. People are flooding past. I prepare myself for another obstacle course.

My phone rings again. "Gavin! I can't—"

"Stop running," he says. "Where are you going?"

"Kevin said that the baby is on the way, she's early. I'm going to Chicago."

"STOP!" Gavin's voice booms both over the phone and from behind me.

The adrenaline in me keeps my feet churning, while my mind wonders how I just heard what I did.

"I'M BEHIND YOU. NYLA. STOP."

My feet stick to the carpet. I turn. People stare. Immediately my eyes connect with Gavin's. He's hunched over, one hand braced on his knee, the other holding the phone to his ear.

"Mia is in labor. If I don't go, I'll miss the flight."

My thoughts are pulled in opposite directions, but suddenly, like a rubber band, they snap back into a cohesive process, and I say, "What are you doing here?"

I look toward gate D, then back to Gavin. He picks up his guitar case and walks toward me. His breath is heavy.

"Gavin?"

"Please walk this way. Toward me." He laughs. "Fuck, Nyla, how can you run that fast? You always wonder why I don't go running with you. It's because of this. I'm going to have a heart attack from just trying to catch up with you."

I immediately think of his father. "Don't joke about that."

"Sorry, love, a figure of speech."

I look back down the hall. I look at my watch.

"Don't you even think about it." He's getting close enough now I see his eyes have a seductive tilt. "Walk toward me."

"I'll miss my flight."

"No, our flight leaves in an hour. We've got plenty of time."

It isn't just his eyes that are seductive. It's everything about him. Even if I wanted to I can't move, I can't purposefully run away from him. The butterflies in my belly multiply the closer he gets. My phone beeps with another call, I glance at the screen.

Quickly I say to Gavin, "I'm not going to move, but Kevin is on the other line. I need to tell him I'm not going to make the plane to Chicago."

His smile makes my heart swoon.

I take Kevin's call, and say, "Kev, you there?"

"Yes," Kevin says.

"You'll never believe who I just ran into."

"Actually, I have an idea. I was calling you to say don't get on the plane. I, uh, forgot what day it is because I was caught up in the excitement of having a baby."

In the background Mia yells, "Have a good time with your man, NyNy."

Gavin stops in front of me, sets a hand on my hip and kisses the corner of my mouth.

"I will have a good time with my man, wherever we are going," I say to Mia, but I look right at Gavin. "Good luck with having that baby of yours. Call me, please, as soon as she's born. Well, not as soon as, but once you can. Good luck!"

"Thank you," Kevin and Mia say in unison.

I put my phone into my bag. Gavin sets his guitar case down and adjusts the bag on his shoulder. He threads his fingers into my hair and tips my head back, angling my lips just right for him. He kisses me like I crave—passionate, possessive, tender. There are a few whoops and applause. I sink my face into his chest feeling a little embarrassed.

"You are a spectacular sight to see run," Gavin says. "I thought the wheels on your poor suitcase were going to come off."

I lean back in his arms and take a good look at him, head to toe. He's wearing khaki shorts and a green T-shirt. Far too casual for a workday.

"What's going on?" I ask.

"I was waiting by that big window near security. You were supposed to walk by and see me in what would be a super romantic moment. But I looked up, and you were running like the wind and went right past me. You didn't even notice me."

"I always notice you."

"Except this time."

"What did I ruin?"

"Nothing is ruined. I gotcha now."

"Go back."

"Do what?"

"Go back to the open area, by the window. I'll walk by and be shocked to see you."

"Shocked?"

"Completely. We'll have that super romantic moment."

He looks hesitant like maybe he thinks I'm kidding. Then without a word, he picks up his guitar case and walks away without a backward glance.

I move over next to a window and try to catch my breath which is still quick, not from my run, but from they way Gavin just kissed me. His words, *was supposed to be a super romantic moment*, run through my head. I'm excited to walk out there and throw my arms around him, to feel his body against mine, and find out exactly what is going on.

After ten minutes of waiting I walk back down the hallway into the open space. Through the window, I see a plane land just behind Gavin. On his shoulder is his leather bag he uses when he travels and at his feet the guitar case. I have no idea where we are going, but I know he'll be singing for me. He turns his hands up to the sky and nods a little at me as if to say, *come on*. I look down at my still feet. People flow around me like I'm a tiny pebble in a large river. I take one step, another, and Gavin's chest lifts. His tongue slides across his full lower lip, igniting a fire in my body, which turns my walk into a run. I jump into his open arms, and he catches me.

I squeeze my limbs around him. "Please don't tell me you're flying away from me?"

"Ah, no."

"What are you doing here, looking incredibly handsome with your guitar?"

"You know how we keep saying we need to go on vacation together?"

I slip my legs from his body, but he keeps a tight hold on my waist which makes my feet light.

"Yes."

"Since we've been living by the philosophy of no time like the present, I decided to surprise you and whisk you away to paradise."

"You're kidding?"

"Nope. How does Maui sound?"

"I'll go anywhere with you."

Keeping a tight hold on me, Gavin picks up his guitar case, and says, "I'll go anywhere with you too. But if we are ever running, you have to slow way, way down for me. Otherwise, you're impossible."

"Not impossible."

"For us mere mortals, yes."

"You are a superhero to me."

"Well, my superpower isn't speed."

"What would your superpower be?"

He looks as if he is seriously considering the question, but after a few steps, he shakes his head. "I'll have to think about that."

"I didn't pack things for Hawaii."

"I packed for you."

"Is that code for, I'll be naked the whole time we're there?"

He nuzzles his nose into my cheek. "Could you blame me? Have you seen how gorgeous you are?"

I turn my head and whisper into his ear, "As long as you are naked too."

CHAPTER 34

From the Maui airport, Gavin and I take a shuttle to the rental car company where Gavin has reserved a white convertible. He slips into the driver's seat and puts on a pair of mirrored aviator sunglasses. The very sight of him steals my breath.

"You're ready, right?" Gavin says.

"For anything."

Sometimes we don't know how great we can feel, how high we can soar, until we are there. That's what I've realized with Gavin. Before him I was content, I thought I had things figured out. But he's made me realize that I don't, and with him, that's exciting.

We take Highway 380, which cuts through the middle of the island. Then we skirt the edge of the land via Highway 30. In Lahaina, we turn down a small road hardly big enough for two cars. On one side is the beach, on the other are gorgeous houses each at least a quarter mile apart and behind gates. Gavin pulls the car into the last driveway. He reaches into the back where his leather bag is, kisses my cheek, then opens the gate with a small remote.

Getting out of the car, I say, "This place is unbelievable."

The large, sand-toned house is tucked back behind palm trees, some of which barely reach my height while others tower over the roof. Exotic blooming flowers in a rainbow of vivid colors are artfully landscaped all around. I follow the meandering pathway from the driveway toward the front door which is lined by my favorite flower, plumeria. The sweet scent mingles with the ocean air.

"We're staying here?" I ask.

Gavin, who looks like the cat that ate the canary, says, "Looks like a good spot. Don't you think?"

"Well sure, but . . ."

"What?"

"It just seems too good to be true."

We walk up the five steps to a landing where Gavin unlocks the front door and pushes it open for me. I step into a large open area: kitchen, living room, dining room. The creamy white walls are bare. A lovely light blue couch is the only piece of furniture.

"Do the people who rented it to you know we're coming today?" I ask.

He shrugs.

Despite the inadequacy in furnishings, I look around. The materials in the house are high quality: tile floors, marble counters, beautiful light fixtures. Down the hallway are three small bedrooms, two bathrooms; all empty. At the end is a master suite with a new mattress that still has the plastic on it. The bathroom has a shower big enough for two and a jetted tub that sits in front of a window that looks out to the beach.

"What do you think?" Gavin asks.

I look at him suspiciously but refuse to let my thoughts run away with me. "Well, the owners need to get some other furniture in here, but I suppose we have what we need. Aside from sheets." I narrow my eyes at him in question.

He grabs my hand and pulls me down the hall through the open living space to a set of French doors which he opens ceremoniously. The backyard is a private oasis. The thick foliage around the perimeter hides the fence. There is a small pool with a large deck that looks ready for a dining table and barbecue. Up several stairs is another landing with a hot tub. From here we can see the ocean.

I am overwhelmed by the beauty of this place.

"What did you tell me a couple weeks ago?" Gavin asks.

"I told you a lot of things a couple weeks ago," I tease, although I know what he's referring to.

We've been musing over how amazing a vacation home would be, someplace to pick up and go when we need a little sun or to simply get away from it all. Even though Gavin loves Portland, he has a hard time disconnecting from the demands of his work when he drives around and sees his buildings, his responsibilities, everywhere we turn. We'd laid in bed dreaming up the exact requirements of our second dream home. This house, I realize, meets every single requirement, and more.

"This is yours?" I ask.

"Ours, if you like it." He pulls me into his arms, and I feel the hope in his body. "You said you didn't want to have to look for it, that you just wanted to walk right into it. So I started looking for us."

"Was this your business trip last week?"

"Yes, I looked at more than twenty before we came here and I knew right away. Well, I hope, that this is the right one."

"Gavin, you're joking right?"

Back in the house on the kitchen counter my phone rings.

"It might be your brother," Gavin says.

It feels like I'm walking on a soft pillowy cloud as I go back down the stairs and into the house. I answer the phone, put it on speaker, and set it on the counter.

"You're on speaker, Kevin."

There's a tiny cry in the background, then Kevin says, "So are you. Did you hear your niece?"

"She makes a beautiful sound."

"I hope we still feel that way in a few days. She's a healthy six pounds, eleven ounces."

"And mama?" I ask.

"Tired," Mia says. "And attempting to nurse, which is very hard."

"She did great," Kevin says tenderly. "We named her Rania. I hope that's all right with you?"

"It just seemed right the moment we saw her," Mia says.

I press my hand to my cheek, take a moment not to let myself cry, and say, "Mom would be honored."

"She has mom's cute little nose. Just like you," Kevin says.

I laugh and cry a little at the same time. "Yeah?"

Gavin takes both of my hands between his and holds them tight to his chest.

"So where are you?" Mia says in a way that tells me she already knows.

"Maui."

Gavin says quickly, "We just got here."

"Oh, all right," Mia says. "We won't keep you two then. Enjoy paradise."

Gavin ends the call, and says, "Congratulations, Auntie. You do have a cute little nose."

"It isn't little."

"It's cute."

"What is happening, Gavin? I feel like from the moment I got off the plane in Portland I entered into a crazy dream state. How is it possible any of this is real?"

"It isn't just real. It can be permanent if you want to keep the place."

"I want everything about this to be permanent."

Gavin makes a call, and five minutes later there is a knock at the door. A man with a broad jaw and black hair past his ears walks in. He looks like he just stepped out of the ocean across the street.

"Good to see you again," Gavin says. "Nyla, this is Kai, our real estate agent."

"Quite the place isn't it, Ms. Tripple?"

"Nyla, please. It's unbelievable."

Since there isn't a single chair in the house we stand at the kitchen island. Kai opens a folder labeled Boston, Gavin & Nyla. He slides papers in front of Gavin and me.

Gavin opens his leather bag and pulls out the gold pen he uses to sign everything. The notches on the barrel of the pen where he holds it is worn flat from years of use. He pulls out another that looks just like his, only brand new, and hands it to me.

"I've read everything," Gavin says. "But feel free to read anything you want."

"You're putting both our names on it?" I look up to Kai and then to Gavin. "You're sure?"

"I am. Are you?"

On every single paper, I sign right next to Gavin's official-looking signature. I feel a little reckless, but still, it feels right. This might be one of the most spontaneous things I have ever done, although I'm not sure how spontaneous something can be when you know the person standing next to you has taken care of everything.

Gavin sees Kai out. Keeping the door open, he turns back to look at me, and says, "You know, those crazy owners that don't have any furnishing in here need a few basic items for the night."

"Like what?" I ask.

"Sheets for starters."

•••

I grab two beach towels from the dryer and holler down the hallway, "I'm going out to the hot tub." I walk up the steps and sink down into the warm water. The setting sun has painted the sky violet with streaks of pink. This place is exactly what I'd dreamed of. It's a good thing that over the next couple months I have more extended periods when I'm not traveling because I think we'll be here a lot.

Gavin and I spent the afternoon purchasing linens and groceries for the week. There's still a lot to do, but neither of us is in a hurry now that we have the basics.

"For my love." Gavin sets down a can of coconut porter next to my shoulder, takes a sip of his, then gets into the hot tub.

"You read my mind," I say.

"I try."

He puts his arm around me, and I settle into the side of his body.

"I can't believe this is ours. And your house back home, it's unbelievable," I say.

"It's our home in Portland. I'll put your name on that title when we get home."

I think to protest, but he says it so adamantly I don't want to argue.

"And I'm an auntie today. Does it get any better than this? Will it be like this forever? Please tell me it will."

"It does get better."

"How can that be?"

"Think of all the adventures we have yet to take, all the things we have yet to try. And we have each other to do it all with."

"It's true."

Gavin sets his beer on to the deck and sinks his hand into the water. I feel his swim trunks shift against my thigh, and then he wiggles a little.

"You want me to move?" I ask.

Gavin slides his arm back from around me and makes an uncertain laugh as he sinks his other hand below the water too. I can't see what he's doing because the bubbles from the jets on full blast have the water stirred up. He grimaces and then laughs even harder.

"What are you doing?" I begin to laugh with him. "Are you taking your trunks off?"

"I might have to."

"What?"

"Ah, Nyla." He lifts his lime-colored swim trunks out of the water.

"What are you doing?"

"It's our hot tub."

"Someone might see."

"Who?"

I look around. Being the last house on the road there is no one on this side. All I see is open beach which eventually curves and beyond that a vast ocean. This is a public beach but so far I haven't seen anyone on it, and besides where we're at is obscured enough that it's likely no one would ever notice us.

"I need your fingers," Gavin says.

"Oh?"

Gavin shakes his head trying unsuccessfully to stop laughing. "This is embarrassing." He lifts up the drawstring of his shorts at the end of which is a ring; gold inset with a row of emeralds. "I tied it on here when the string was dry so it wouldn't get lost in the water, but now I can't get it untied. You've got nails."

I laugh; my mind races, my heart even faster. I take the string in my hand and work the knot. Even with my nails, it's hard. "Triple knotted? You didn't want to lose it, did you?" My cheeks burn by the time I get it free and hold it flat in my hand.

"I was worried the jets would suck it up," Gavin says taking it from me. "Would you please stand up?" He sinks lower into the water. "You can't tell, but I'm on one knee."

"I wouldn't mind seeing you stand. I like what you're hiding in the water."

Gavin, returning to his fit of laughter, presses the back of my hand to his forehead. "This is not going as smooth as I'd envisioned." He takes a deep breath. "But, it's because of how we laugh through anything, even a wayward proposal, and that smile, the way my body feels near you, in you, all of it and more, is why I want to marry you. I want every day you aren't traveling to wake up next to you. To go on every adventure we can imagine. To fill your whims, longing desires, and dreams. I love you so much, Nyla Tripple. Will you be my wife, my partner in life?"

I feel the purest experience of love as he looks up at me. "Yes. A million times yes."

He slips the ring on my finger and looks at it. "I know it's not traditional, but from everything I gathered, this is something you can always wear."

"Gavin, it is perfect."

He pulls me down into the water and reaches around my ribs.

"What are you doing?"

"I think my fiancée should be in her birthday suit as well." He slips the bottoms from my legs and pulls me onto his lap, not a thing between us, or on us, except for my ring. "You asked earlier if it gets any better. I think we'll keep asking that every day because it does. But right now, it doesn't get any better than this."

CHAPTER 35

Four Months Later
Thursday, August 1

"The bride-to-be!" Linda says when I reach the fourth floor of Boston Smith Company. She rushes over and throws her arms around me, causing coffee to splash from the small holes of the to-go cups in my hands.

"Oh, geez, I'm so sorry about that. Here," she says and pulls a tissue from her pocket. "I'll clean that up." Her expression shifts from excitement to confusion. "Are you here to see Gavin?"

"Yes."

"You've missed him, unfortunately. Trace and I took him out to lunch, and right after we got back, he jetted out."

My excitement deflates like a balloon. "That's what I get for not calling ahead. I missed my flight last night and wanted to surprise him. I'd have been here sooner, but there was a wreck on 405 that shut down the freeway." I lift the coffee I purchased for Gavin, and ask, "Would you be interested in a black coffee?"

"I can't drink coffee like that, but Trace just said he needs one."

"Here you go." I hand her the coffee, happy that it won't go to waste.

I turn to walk back down the stairs but stop when Linda says, "Hang on, I'll walk out with you. Just let me run this to Trace real quick."

While I wait, I call Gavin, but unfortunately, it goes straight to voicemail. "Hey, it's me. I'm sorry I didn't call you when I got in this morning. I wanted to surprise you at work, but I was later than expected because of an accident on 405, and it looks like I missed you. I'm sorry. I look forward to seeing you soon. I love you."

Linda returns, and says, "Ready."

We walk back down the stairs, through the lobby, and into the summer day. It's supposed to be an ideal August afternoon for our wedding this weekend.

"How did your dress alterations turn out?" Linda asks.

My mouth drops open, and I press my hand to my forehead.

Linda's face wrinkles. "You forgot about your dress?"

"Completely." I look at my watch. "It's fine though. I have plenty of time to pick it up."

"Ohh!" Linda claps her hands. "May I go with you?"

Both Linda and I drive our own cars to the Pearl District. A few blocks away from the dress shop we find two parking spots right next to each other. We walk toward Stitched Cloth, a small designer boutique where the owner and her assistant make everything to order. They don't specialize in wedding gowns, but I didn't purchase a traditional dress. Instead, I opted for a sweet summer dress, pale pink, that's snug in the bodice and falls in flowing layers around my legs, like petals of a flower.

"Is that your dad?" Linda asks.

"It is." I pick up my steps. "I'm going to run to catch him."

Pop's office is a few blocks away from here. He often takes a stroll in the afternoon for some fresh air. He has shed his suit jacket, and the sleeves of his dress shirt are rolled up to the elbows.

Just as he lifts his phone to his ear, I tap his shoulder.

He spins. "Little Foot! I was just calling you." He holds up his phone as evidence, then puts it into his pocket and opens his arms to me. "What are you up to?"

"Hello, Mr. Tripple," Linda says.

"Hello, Linda," he says with a kind pat on her shoulder.

"Picking up my wedding dress."

Pop snorts in an amused way. "Cutting it a little close, aren't you?"

"I just got back from a trip."

"I thought you weren't traveling this week."

"It was last minute. I was only supposed to be gone three days, but I missed my flight last night and had to take one this morning."

"I don't know how you do it," he says. "I get exhausted listening to you sometimes."

"I am exhausted despite the coffee I just finished."

He holds up his hand as if he's remembered something. "I was calling to tell you Kevin and the family got in late last night. They haven't seen your house yet. I thought we could meet there, you could give them a little tour, then we could head to the dinner."

Gavin's and my wedding is two days away. Since not all of our family has met, we decided to host a small dinner at Mix tonight before things get busy with the wedding rehearsal tomorrow. Gavin and I planned to pick his family up from the airport this afternoon and head straight to Mix. Even though I want to go with Gavin, I'm sure he'll understand.

"I think that sounds like a great idea," I say.

Pop kisses my forehead and gently moves my shoulder back and forth. "My Little Foot is getting married. All right. We'll be to your house at four."

I give Pop a good-bye hug, then Linda and I head in the opposite direction toward the dress shop. After a few steps, she says, "I think your dad just wants to spend some time with you before the evening kicks off."

"I know. I didn't expect for him to be sad at all."

I understand though because I've noticed that sometimes happy times make us nostalgic for past experiences, and these can invoke memories of happy times that now seem to make us sad. I have missed mom a lot, she would have had fun planning a wedding. It's also reminded me of another happy time in my life, and I find myself missing him.

•••

At Stitched Cloth I try on my dress, which fits perfectly, and am on my way in less than twenty minutes.

Once I get back to my car, I call Gavin again. It rings this time, but still, I get his voicemail. "Hey. There's been a change in plans. Pop, Kevin, and Mia are going to come over to see the house and then take me to dinner. No need to come home and get me. I hope you don't mind. See you at five. Oh, but call me when you get this. I want to hear your voice. I miss you and love you."

All I can think about as I drive home is Gavin. I feel guilty because we've hardly spoken in the last few days with my busy schedule.

When I get home, there is a voicemail from Gavin. I kick myself for accidentally leaving my phone silent. His message says, "Sorry I missed your calls, love." (There is a long pause, almost enough to make me think he'd hung up.) "I can understand why Samuel wants to pick you up and take you. But to be honest, I was looking forward to seeing you too. Ah . . . I love you . . . a lot."

He sounds as if he's forcing an upbeat note, which leaves me feeling unsettled. After a moment of contemplation, I decide I'll call him in a few minutes once I take a quick shower.

I carry my wedding dress in the gray garment bag into the house and hang it in the closet of my office. It took Gavin and me a while to get this room put together, but now it's perfect. The walls are light lavender. I have a beautiful large desk custom made by Gavin's cousin, Stephan. Hung on the wall across from the desk are the hummingbird paintings that we brought back from Bainbridge.

I walk down the hall to our bedroom. I peel my clothes off, toss them into the hamper, and get into the shower. Gavin was right about this shower, it's the best one I've ever been in. The water relaxes my body, and the steam opens my lungs.

I can't stop thinking of Gavin, I love being in this shower with him. I wish I would have asked him to come home before he goes to the airport. I'd like a few minutes with him before everything begins.

CHAPTER 36

*A*s I turn the water off, I hear a loud CRACK, and my senses kick into high alert. I freeze and listen carefully, but I hear nothing else.

Sometimes this house makes funny sounds—crack, pop, snap—as it expands and contracts with the heat of the day. I'm sure that's all it was.

The last few drops of water slip from the showerhead above me. I hear something else . . . the thump, thump, thump of fast-moving footsteps. The skin on my scalp tightens. Goosebumps bloom on my skin. I move slowly, lest I make a sound, and reach for the white towel on the rack. Heavy thudding footsteps are getting louder. Closer. I press the towel to my chest. The knob of the bathroom door turns, it opens just an inch and stops, like someone on the other side has changed their mind. Water slips between my goosebumps like miniature worms.

The door opens, and in a rush of relief, I snap, "You scared the crap out of me, Gavin!"

His eyes rake over me with a red hot lust I rarely see from my perfectly controlled man. I'm ashamed to admit

I crave him like this sometimes; when he completely loses control. Encounters where he owns me in a way that makes him apologize a thousand times, and when I should seek redemption for wanting him to do it again.

I let my towel fall to the floor. I stretch my full height and lift my chest. Gavin moves with inhuman speed, grips my hips and pulls my bare body to his pristine navy blue trousers. I trail my lips along his jaw and feel the tiny pricks of late afternoon stubble.

In Gavin's ear, I whisper, "Miss me?"

A growl rumbles deep in his chest. I feel his growing need, and with it, his grip on me tightens ... tightens ... tightens to that narrow space where pain and pleasure meet. I close my eyes and let my head fall back. I will surrender.

"How much time do we have?" I ask.

The tips of his fingers curl into my flesh, and his nails dig into me.

"Gavin?"

Slowly, he lifts his head. The red-hot lust is gone. There is a saddened vacancy I've never seen before. His lips part and he draws a shuttered breath. I want to shake his shoulders, to wake him up from this possessed state, but my fight or flight instincts ring a bell, and they're telling me to flee.

"Gavin?"

His eyelids flutter, then narrow like he has tears to go with an apology, but nothing comes from him. His grip grows tighter; this is pain.

Fear floods me. I open my mouth to say you're hurting me, but all that comes out is a squeak because the very thought of it feels like a betrayal. I should run. But love overrules all instincts to save myself.

I grab his wrists and try to remove them, but he's like a steel trap. Gently I say, "Gavin, you're hurting me." Tears bloom in my eyes both from the pain caused by his hands and the fear in my heart. "Please let me go."

Gavin's head drops, as if the power plug to his body has been pulled, and hits my collarbone so hard it reverberates through my shoulder, up my neck, and into my teeth. A scream of pain rips from me as my body rears back and slams into the glass wall of the shower, filling the room with a gong-like sound. His body presses me into the glass as if he has no control over his weight.

I put my palms into the indent where his shoulder and chest meet, take a deep breath, and hating the emotions that pump through me, I push him away as if my life depends on it. Gavin's nails rake the skin of my hips as he stumbles back. He looks down at the floor.

I scream, "What is fucking wrong with you!"

His head snaps up, and he steps back toward me. I lift my arm straight out in front of me, and say, "Don't you dare come near me!"

"Tell me you love me," he says, voice strained. He takes three more steps and presses his chest into my hand. "Tell me you love me!"

"I do."

"Tell me! Say it! I love you." He grabs my wrist but doesn't move it. "Say it!"

"Gavin, I do. I love you."

He steps back.

I lower my hand.

Gavin sinks to his knees, palms supine like a man surrendering. I don't know why I didn't notice the moment he walked in, but everything about him is off. His pink shirt is unbuttoned two extra buttons, collar crumpled and tucked in on the right, vest unbuttoned and askew. His hair is mussed like he ran his fingers through it a hundred times.

Gavin stands on his knees and turns pleading eyes up to me. He moves his right knee forward, then the left, the right, and left again. I do not stop him. His vibrating hands lift and set back on my hips.

"What's wrong?" I ask.

Gavin lowers his lips hesitantly the arch of my hip bone. Each kiss warns me, this isn't right. These aren't the kisses of a lover, but rather someone who intends to fuck unapologetically. This isn't my Gavin, even the one that loses control. I put my hands on his shoulders and gently try to nudge him away, but he won't budge.

"You want this," he says. The kisses become firmer, rougher, like a man aching for what he knows he cannot have.

How is it possible that I know I should run, and yet I want him so desperately it feels as if my next breath depends on his kiss, no matter what it feels like? My body betrays me—nipples harden, wetness slicks deep inside readying me for him.

Does this feel good? Do I feel safe?

My mind takes hold. I reach for my white robe and yank it from its hook tearing the fabric loop. I pull it on, and snap, "Let go of me now!"

Gavin's hands fall like autumn leaves as he sinks onto his heels and looks back at me. "I can't marry you," he says so calmly I think I've mistaken his words.

"Excuse me?"

He gets to his feet and leans against the door jamb. His eyes close. "I can't marry you. I'm so sorry, Nyla. I can't."

Again I take in his appearance: unbuttoned shirt, askew collar, mussed hair.

"Are you having an affair?"

His eyes spring open.

Before this moment had anyone accused him of such a thing I'd have called them a liar. But those eyes, his clothes, what else can it be?

"No!" He moves toward me again.

I squeeze my hands into fists at my side. "Don't you dare come any closer to me, Gavin, so help me if you touch me again I will hit you!"

He shuffles his feet side to side.

"Tell me what is going on," I say.

He stops, puts his hands on his hips. "I can't get married right now."

"I heard you. You're off the hook, G—"

"I don't want to be off the hook!" he says as if I've offended him.

"Leave."

"You have to listen."

"I do not have to listen to you!"

"I—"

"Gavin, I know you can't marry me. Frankly, I don't care why right now. But I want to put on some clothes, leave, please."

"I need to talk to you before I go get them."

"Who?"

"My family."

I move around him, out of the bathroom and into the bedroom. He follows me, getting closer. I yank my arm away just as he reaches for me.

"Gavin! I will never talk to you again if you come closer to me. You are never allowed to touch me ever again. Do you hear me? Get out."

Gavin, looking like an injured bear, backs out of the bedroom.

I slam the door shut and huff into the closet. Pulling my robe off I see my hips. Where Gavin held me far too tightly are long angry scratches, and a few of them have pinpricks of blood swelling. I pull tissues from the box on my dresser and dab them until they're clean. A hundred emotions course through my body, many of them opposing. Everything in my body hurts, especially my heart. It wants to explode.

I grab a tank top from a hanger, pull it on, then get a pair of underwear and shorts from a drawer and pull them up.

How do we hurt people we love? How do we fear people we love?

The taps of Gavin's wingtip shoes echo down the hall, pacing like a metronome at an unsustainable pace.

My entire body is shaking. I must calm down and focus so that I can go out there and talk to Gavin.

I close my eyes, then draw a slow and steady breath in. Even inhales and exhales. I slow my heart rate. The shaking tapers off until my body is still. The goosebumps recede. My mind calms and then becomes placid. I'm in race mode, where I can sustain anything, including war.

CHAPTER 37

As I walk out to the living room, I'm mindful of my footfalls so that my bare feet on the cool wood floor makes no sound. Gavin is in the living room, standing in front of the large windows that look out over the spectacular view of Portland. Greedily, I savor the image of this powerful man, his beauty far surpassing that of the view beyond him. Then I notice he's not looking at the city below him. His eyes are turned to a small hummingbird near the fuchsia shaped feeder that Ms. Marshall gave me nearly a year ago. The emerald-headed bird glitters like a faceted jewel in a ray of sunshine. It's watching Gavin.

My race mode threatens to slip, but I refuse to allow the pain in my heart to overtake me. Slow and steady, I can make it on my own.

"Gavin."

He turns quickly as if I've startled him.

"We're all supposed to be at the restaurant in a couple hours," I say, so calmly even I surprise myself. "Do you want to tell them in person, or start making calls?"

"Do you love me?"

"What is it with you? Do I love you? Do you love me?"

He drags both of his hands through his hair and down his face. "I love you more than anything."

"You've got a funny way of showing it."

"Sue called me this afternoon."

"I don't know who Sue is."

"She is a nurse at my oncologist's office. I had an appointment earlier this week, a scan, blood work, fertility testing. Something is off, they need a biopsy." His hand grips his throat.

"You never said anything about an appointment," I say flatly.

"You had this last-minute trip, and the wedding. I didn't want to worry you."

I should care when he says this. That's what a good wife would do. But instead, I stand here. My heart cracks open, spills to my feet, and suddenly I'm heartless.

"I can't do what he did to you," Gavin says.

"Lorenzo?"

"I can't do what he did to you." He grits his teeth, the cords in his neck pop. "I will not be a man that shatters you."

"Fine. We'll tell everyone at dinner that the wedding is off. That you're afraid you have cancer—"

"Don't tell them! I don't want them to know!"

I throw my arms into the air. "What do you want from me? I don't care. You can tell them whatever you want. Tell them you don't love me, that I was just some lapse in judgment and you don't want to marry me. Does that make you happy?" A cold settles over me like I'm alone in the Arctic in the dead of night.

Gavin's eyes drop to my waist, and then they round in horror. "What have I done?"

In the animation of my talking, my shirt has worked its way up. There on my hips are angry lines and bright red blood smeared like a watercolor experiment gone wrong.

Gavin's hands flex. "Heaven help me, what have I done?"

I'm embarrassed that I'd stood in one place and allowed myself to be hurt. I don't just mean my body.

"Are you all right?" he asks.

"I think it's time for you to get going."

"Do you hate me?"

"Do you actually want me to answer that right now?"

Gavin scratches his neck like a madman. "I want to marry you, more than anything. But I need to know when I stand up there and say I do, that I'm able to offer myself to you whole. I don't want you to worry that you're marrying a man that will make you a widow again."

He reaches for me, but I shake my head firmly.

"I am fine on my own," I say.

"I'll fix it."

"You need to go."

"Do you understand that I do want to marry you? I just can't right now, Nyla. I need you to know for sure."

"You'll be late."

"Let's go to this dinner tonight, talk after when we've both had time to think, and we'll go from there."

"Pretend like everything is as it was?"

"Yes."

"I'm not a very good actress."

"Could have fooled me. Or maybe you don't care that I might have cancer again."

An angry shiver rises from my feet.

"You're so damn stubborn!" Gavin says. "Can't you get mad sometimes? I am not the media, that outside world that you have to shield yourself from."

"I think to some degree I need to shield myself from everyone. Clearly."

He paces back and forth. I envy his ability to move right now because my feet stay glued to the floor.

"I'm so sorry I touched you like I did."

In his eyes I see the Gavin I know.

"It was wrong, Nyla. I've never felt fear like this. Never have I had so much to lose and at the same time felt the—"

I turn back toward the bedroom.

"Where are you going?" he asks.

I face him, lift my chin, and say, "I cannot listen to all the reasons you can't marry me. You've had hours to process this, and I'm trying to sort through everything right now. I'm trying to keep myself together, to simply stay upright, because I have family on the way over."

I make a quarter-turn then look back at him. Allowing all of my anger to lace my words, I say, "You might have worried about making me a widow, but do you realize I would have preferred that to you willingly breaking my heart? You didn't do what Lorenzo did to me. What you have done is much, much worse. He didn't have a choice."

Gavin's mouth unhinges and his face crumples. When he looks down at his feet, I turn away and walk back down the hall to the bedroom. Gently, I close the door, not wanting to disturb the air that is as still as death.

CHAPTER 38

$\mathscr{I}$'ve distracted myself with work since Gavin left ten minutes ago. I'm not sure how I'll make it through this night. What will I say when I see him at the restaurant? The idea of him touching me and me touching him like there is nothing wrong seems like an impossibility.

Pop pulls up to the house. He lets himself inside and then comes into my office.

"Hey, Pop," I say. "Where are Kevin and the girls?"

"On the way out of the door, Rania had a diaper explosion that required a bath. They'll meet us at the restaurant."

He walks over to the bookshelf and picks up one of the large shiny wooden boxes. He opens it and shows me the medals inside like I might be surprised to see them.

"I thought maybe you and I could head over there now and have a drink or two before everyone arrives," he says.

"I could use a drink."

"Are you ever going to frame these?"

Pop sets the big box down and then picks up the smaller of the three that's about the size of an envelope. He opens it slowly, like its contents may surprise him.

"I haven't seen these in a long time." He lifts out one of the silver medals Lorenzo won in shot put. "I didn't know you still had them."

"I'd never get rid of them."

"I know. It's just . . ." He shrugs.

"Let's go get that drink."

As we walk out of the house I wonder if I'll ever stay here again.

Pop jingles the keys to his brand new sports car that he purchased a week ago, and asks, "Want to drive?"

"Maybe next time."

I get into the passenger seat that wraps my body like a safety blanket. Everything about this car, inside and out, reminds me of a spaceship that at any time might just lift from the earth and fly.

When we get to where the gravel meets the pavement, where the mailbox looks like the vines around it might swallow it whole, Pop says, "All right, you know I can tell when something has you sad, and I think it's more than Lorenzo."

I try not to look at him, but it's hard. Pop isn't a man I can lie to.

"Gavin and I had a fight."

"Life can get stressful. Do you want to talk about it? Come on. You look like you need to get something off your chest."

"Gavin doesn't want to marry me."

The tears I should have cried when Gavin told me now slip down my cheeks. I brush them away roughly with the back of my hand and then open the glove compartment to find one lone napkin.

Pop says, "Because?"

"It's hard to explain."

"Try, because he's a good man, the—"

"Yes," I snap. "Gavin Boston is such a good man. I get it. So let's just chalk it up to being something wrong with me."

The trees move through my vision in a blur. I take a deep breath, inhale the scent of a new car, leather and maybe plastic. It smells like a new beginning.

"That isn't what I meant," Pop says.

"Seriously, let's just leave it. I do not want to talk about it."

"I'd like to know why on earth two nights before the wedding you're calling it off. Especially since we are on the way to dinner to celebrate you two." Pop looks both ways and turns right onto Burnside. "Just because?"

"No, not just because. Gavin had appointments this week that he didn't bother to tell me about, and they want to scan him Monday, or a biopsy. I can't remember what he said."

"Is he scared?"

"I assume so. I didn't ask a lot of questions."

"Into Nyla focus mode. The task at hand."

"What's that supposed to mean?"

"You have a skill in being able to focus on the one thing you need to and shut out everything else. It's a good skill for a competitor, but it makes it hard to talk through things with you."

"How is it that he's the one that says he doesn't want to marry me, and somehow I'm at fault for shutting down a little? He doesn't deserve my emotions."

Anger begins to boil again and to prevent it from spilling over I stop talking and press my lips together.

We come to a tunnel where green moss hangs down, and the grime of exhaust clings to the curved walls. Every time I go through a tunnel, I wonder what would happen if there were an earthquake. Would it hold? Would it collapse? Would it kill those inside?

Pop switches the music off, and says, "How do you feel about it?"

"It doesn't matter, does it? Whatever the good man Mr. Boston wants, he gets."

"Nyla," he reprimands.

On the other side of the tunnel, the pitch of the hill increases. It's like we're on a roller coaster about to hit the crest where we'll free fall into the ride. No gas needed here where gravity does her job.

"I can appreciate what he's trying to do," I say.

"You are difficult at times."

My phone vibrates in my purse. I pull it out, check it and then turn it back over and set it on my lap.

"Gavin?" Pop asks.

"Yeah."

"Remember his first wife left when he was sick. Maybe in addition to his genuine concern for not wanting to hurt you, he's also kicked into a sort of self-doubt mode. You two have a very unique situation with a heavy past."

"He doesn't want to marry me, Pop."

"Did he actually said he didn't want to?"

I try to think of precisely what he's said, but the memories are jumbled like jigsaw pieces tossed onto the floor.

We come to a red light, the only one on this long stretch before we hit downtown. I wish there were more traffic so that our arrival would be delayed. I'm not ready to see Gavin.

"Remember, it's just a wedding. Being a wife, a husband, or a partner requires us to be a redwood. Solid roots when we feel like life might sweep us away and flexible enough to weather the high winds that whip past."

"I guess I'm not a redwood."

"Is there anything else wrong in your relationship?"

"No."

"You're going to let a few hours of panic ruin everything? He needs you to be willing to hold on when he has a bad day too."

"What if I can't save him?"

Dad gives me his most reassuring smile, the one that he had years ago when he taught me to drive our old brown truck, when I laced up my first running shoes, and the same one that made me give Gavin Boston a chance.

"You can't save anyone," Pop says. "The question is, can you tell him that you love him for better for worse, in sickness and in health? If this was next week, after the wedding, what would you have done?"

I turn my phone over and read Gavin's text message, "I am sorry. I love you more than anything. Meet me outside the restaurant, please."

"I wouldn't have let him push me away," I say.

Dad glances over at me and offers a loving smile. "Vows don't magically start in two days. He needs you, Nyla."

The phone flies from my hand and hangs mid-air in front of my eyes. My hair lifts around my face. The seatbelt squeezes me to the seat, even though a force wants to dismount me. It feels like the earth has lost her gravity, and the spaceship of a car is in full flight. I look through the window and see a blue pickup going below us and then pavement where our tires should be.

CHAPTER 39

The car reshapes like black and tan modeling clay around me. The center console pushes up between us. Airbags wrap around me like a tight hand that means no harm, yet I feel things shatter as they assault me. A large jaw bites down on my left leg. Groans of violence as plastic and metal reorganize in space and time.

I see a hummingbird, squeeze my eyes shut, and I'm sucked back in time.

•••

I put my feet into the starting blocks. This is everything I am, all I've been working toward. My first medal race. I feel the rough track below my fingers. All of my senses are alert. The wind that lifts the tiny hairs on the back of my neck carries the scent of human excitement and fear.

I spring from the blocks, my muscular thighs push me forward for all my worth. I am first, and then, I am nothing. My back is on the track, a cloudless sky above me. I haven't a clue how this happened, how I fell when everything mattered.

I cover my face.

"Are you all right?" Lorenzo asks. "Are you hurt?"

"Just my pride," I say.

"Don't move. I got you."

He swoops me up from the track and carries me off into a quiet place below the bleachers where we think we are alone.

Gently Lorenzo pulls my hands from my face. With a smile, he tips his head to the side, kisses my lips. He's got a full head of curly black hair, short on the sides and long on top, desperately perfect sky blue eyes, and his size is enough to protect me from anything.

"You are okay," he says.

I shake my head, but I don't cry. "No."

"Lucky for you, Nyla, you have more than one chance to win gold." He kisses my lips. "Choose to be brave."

•••

A crack of thunder rips me from Lorenzo's arms.

The spaceship of a car feels like it's been caught by a giant's hand, although I can see nothing. All movement stops, I'm not sure if it's a second or an hour. Something jerks and I feel that earth's gravity is reclaiming us. The car plummets down and crashes on its nose. If it weren't for my belt and the airbags, I'd fall out of the front windshield. I think it's done, but then the car tips, and with a final neck-snapping flip, the ceiling becomes the floor.

I try to take a breath, but something is pressing into my chest. I turn my head with excruciating pain to see Pop. His eyes are open, gazing off someplace, a tiny smile on his face. Blood drips from his nose.

"Papa, I love you," gurgles from me.

I'm not in water, yet I feel like a current has pulled me below, filling my lungs.

When we leave this earth, the bravery it took to do things like putting one's foot into a starting block and pushing off will matter little. The bravery that will echo through time, past our own life, is in the moments we use to lift another to their highest potential because it passes from one to the next like an echo. That is why the story of Lorenzo and I mattered so much to others. He was brave when I was not, which made me believe in my own possibilities, and this, in turn, inspired bravery far beyond me.

The physical pain my body feels is eclipsed by the pain in my soul knowing the last thing Gavin will remember of me, the final touch we shared, is me pushing him away. I'd been brave enough to love him, but not brave enough to hold on.

I try to keep my eyes open, to live on the last bit of air in my lungs, but the water is a force greater than me.

My bones are no longer whole.

My brain is too big for my skull.

The car has become a part of me. Or am I a part of it?

Am I hot, or cold?

The smell of gasoline wafts past.

The repulsive taste of metal fills my mouth.

Does this feel good . . . or does it hurt?

Maybe I am waking from a bad dream . . . or a nightmare.

The confusion clears into exacting reality. I open my mouth to scream—for this pain is too great to bear alive— nothing comes out. The ocean in my lungs has drowned me. My vision begins to narrow, like the ending of those cartoons I watched as a kid, until there is nothing left but darkness, so pure it promises comfort.

To be continued ...

With Endless Gratitude

My dream of writing has been realized only because of the amazing souls that have cheered me along the path. It would take a novel to thank them all, but since I only have one page, here are just a few that helped bring this book to life.

Sean, my editor-in-chief, your unwavering support and love are everything to me. Thank you.

My daughter, Devon, you called me a writer when I wasn't sure I deserved the title, and yet it caused me to think, if you believe in me, I must show you that your belief is well placed. Thank you.

Carla, my mother, you've always believed I was an artist (of some sorts), and that gave me the courage to pursue this art. Thank you.

My dad, Bob, thank you for always instilling in me that I can do, and be, anything I want.

My friend, Kacy, thank you for reading an early draft. Your feedback spurred me to dig deeper.

Cecilia, thank you for editing and cheering me on every step of the way.

Thank you, Karen, for your valuable feedback and editing.

Sarah, my sister, thank you for your help and always being a text message away.

Thank you to the writers who inspire me, wrap me in their stories, and make me want to share the ones that rattle around in my head.

To you, my reader, it's for you that I write. Thank you for sharing your time with me.

About The Author

Nicole is the author of the Bravely trilogy. Read more of her work and learn about her upcoming releases at NicoleDwigans.com.

When not writing, Nicole loves to spend time with family and friends, explore the world, and read.

She resides in Beaverton, Oregon, with her husband, daughter, Brutus Maximus (the Chihuahua), and Minnie (the lab+basset hound).

To stay in touch with Nicole, sign up for her VIP list at NicoleDwigans.com. She welcomes your feedback and book recommendations at Nicole@NicoleDwigans.com.

NicoleDwigans.com
Instagram: NicoleDwigans
Facebook: NicoleDwigansAuthor
Pinterest: NicoleDwigansAuthor